Alexander Grin with Gul-Gul, the young merlin which he tamed in Feodosia, Crimea, 1929.

Alexander Grin

Selected Short Stories

Translated by Nicholas Luker

Ardis, Ann Arbor

Copyright © 1987 by Ardis Publishers
All rights reserved under International and
Pan-American Copyright Conventions.

Printed in the United States of America

Translated from the original Russian

Ardis Publishers
2901 Heatherway
Ann Arbor, Michigan 48104

Library of Congress Cataloging in Publication Data

Grin, A. (Aleksandr), 1880-1932.
Selected short stories.

Translations from the Russian.
1. Grin, A. (Aleksandr), 1880-1932—Translations,
English. I. Luker, Nicholas J. L.   II. Title.
PG3476.G68A25   1985   891.73'4   985-18706
ISBN 0-88233-684-3 (alk. paper)

CONTENTS

Acknowledgments   9

Introduction   11

The Oranges   29

The Arm   37

The Window in the Forest   43

Reno Island   49

He Came and Went   69

The Death of Romelink   73

The Pillory   81

The Long Journey   98

Mystery on a Moonlit Night   101

Fire and Water   103

Ships in Liss   111

The Heart of the Wilderness   131

Voice and Eye   139

Gatt, Witt and Redott   143

Augustus Esborn's Marriage   153

The Snake   159

The Voice of the Siren   163

The Legend of Ferguson   169

The Port Commandant   173

The Green Lamp   181

To my beloved son,

Nathaniel Max,

in whom I am well pleased

Acknowledgments

I wish to express my deep gratitude to the late Max Hayward, Fellow of St. Antony's College, Oxford, England, who first suggested that I undertake postgraduate research into Alexander Grin and then encouraged me to translate his work into English. Without his unfailing enthusiasm and interest this anthology would never have been.

My thanks must also go to Professor Marcus Wheeler of the Queen's University of Belfast, Northern Ireland, who very kindly read my versions of these stories in typescript and corrected inaccuracies and inelegancies in my English. The responsibility for those which remain is wholly mine.

I would also like to record my thanks to Dorothy Honniball of Nottingham University Library, England, who typed my difficult manuscript with the accuracy and care which I have come to expect from her.

Finally, I wish to acknowledge an inestimable debt of gratitude to my young son, Nathaniel, who albeit unwittingly has played a vital part in the production of this anthology. His abiding affection and puckish humour have given me spiritual sustenance on countless occasions when it was sorely needed. This book therefore contains a fragment of his life just as it does of mine.

NICHOLAS LUKER

Grassington,
North Yorkshire,
England

March, 1983

Introduction

I Rara avis

Alexander Grin is one of Russian literature's most fascinating oddities. Succinctly described as "an utter exotic"[1] among his fellow-writers, this self-effacing, solemn man with his rugged face and steady eye was what Russians call a "white raven" (*belaia vorona*), that singular kind of human being beside whom others pale into mediocrity. To this day the mere mention of him conjures up visions of mystery and romance, visions which rise from the bizarre legends that surrounded his name. It was rumoured that he had done forced labour in Siberia for the brutal murder of his first wife; that he had tramped the length and breadth of Russia and sailed the seven seas; that he consorted with stunt-men, wrestlers and sword-swallowers; and that he was a ruthless desperado who systematically plagiarised the writings of an English sea captain whom he had robbed and killed in the Indian Ocean. It was even said that he was an agent of British Intelligence who carefully concealed his excellent knowledge of English.

Such legends were reinforced not only by Grin's chequered youth but also by the curiously foreign flavour of his work, a quality that makes him unique in Russian letters and partly explains the charm he has always held for generations of his countrymen, young and old alike. As Marc Slonim puts it evocatively, Grin wrote of "beautiful isles, foaming oceans, sand dunes covered with heather, and white-walled cities on the shores of warm bays, where lovely women met captains and poets and where strange adventures awaited the traveller."[2] Such was the stuff of which Grin's dreams were made and many are those who have fallen under his spell. One of the most distinguished is Alexander Solzhenitsyn, who in his *Gulag Archipelago*—incongruously perhaps—recalls "the enchanted ports to which Grin enticed us, where rum is drunk in taverns and men pay court to beautiful women."[3]

Perhaps more than is true of many authors, the experiences of Grin's early years were responsible for the substance of his mature fiction. Viatka itself—ultra-conservative, philistine and grey—was much to blame for the frustrations of his youth. His love-hate relationship with his native town was summed up for him by Chekhov's tale *My Life* (*Moia zhizn'*, 1896), aptly subtitled *The Story of a Provincial* (*Rasskaz provintsiala*). "In it," he once said, "I saw my own youth, my longing to break free from the mire of prejudice, falsehood, insincerity and hypocrisy that surrounded me."[4] Compounded by unsympathetic teachers and a dismal home, the suffocating provincial environment drove the sensitive boy to seek excitement in the extraordinarily vivid world of his imagination. The profound spiritual dissatisfaction of his early years became the major stimulus for the creation of his romantic fiction. With the passage of time the naive fantasies of his youth were transposed to his imagined *Grinlandia*, where the adult writer's dreamings acquired the texture and durability of reality.

What obsessed Grin in his youth was the sea—or rather, thoughts of it, for he was fifteen before he first set eyes on it in the Crimea. It intrigued him all the more because he lived so far away from it, in a desperately characterless town lost amid the endless plains of western Russia. As the popular saying had it, one could "gallop for three years" from Viatka and still not reach the coast. Grin's childhood and adolescence were filled with dreams of the sea as a remote but alluring world of seemingly boundless possibilities, a magically exotic environment that contrasted starkly with the drabness of Viatka. Like Grey, the hero of his novella *Alye parusa* (*Scarlet Sails*, 1923), Grin became the devoted slave of his dreams at an early age, avid for impressions of a world so enticingly full of promise. "I tried wherever I could," he wrote in his *Avtobiograficheskaia povest'* (*Autobiographical Tale*, 1931) many years later, "to learn about the sea and shipboard life."[5] Sadly, the reality of life on the waves—like that of life in general—was to fall very short of his naive expectations.

Perhaps the yawning gulf between Grin's youthful aspirations and adult experiences largely explains the alcoholism that bedevilled his career. Perhaps only in drink could he assuage the spiritual pain caused by his realization that neither the world nor his fellow-men were as exciting and splendid as he had believed. His despair drove him to furious drinking bouts either alone—when he sometimes concealed liquor in a teapot—or with his cronies, bouts that would end only when he began to hurl bottles around the room or collapsed insensible into the gutter. So intensely imaginative were his expectations of life that they only made the disenchantment brought by reality harder to bear.

For all its colour and romance, Grin's work won little recognition while he was alive. Looked upon for most of his career as no more than a gifted plagiarist of Western adventure writers, rarely admitted to the pages of prestigious journals during his lifetime, and in the late Stalin period after his death vilified as a "rootless cosmopolitan" hostile to the Soviet regime,[6] Alexander Grin is today one of the most popular writers in the USSR. Many older editions of his work are collector's items, and when a volume of memoirs about him appeared in 1972,[7] scuffles broke out in Moscow and Leningrad bookshops among Grinomaniacs eager to secure the rapidly disappearing copies for themselves. Recent years have seen an extraordinary revival of interest in Grin on the part of biographers and critics, both in Russia and the West,[8] a phenomenon that contrasts with the position in the late 1940's and early 1950's when he was proscribed in the Soviet press and his works were removed from library shelves in his native land. Shortly before his death he spoke of the lack of appreciation which had dogged his career and he declared his belief that his work would not be truly valued until well after he had gone. In his characteristically perceptive way he was right. At long last, a half-century after his death, the visionary is beginning to enjoy the recognition he so richly deserves.

II Childhood and Youth

Alexander Stepanovich Grinevsky was born on August 23, 1880 in the district town of Slobodskoy, thirty kilometres east of Viatka (now Kirov). His father, Stepan Evseevich Grinevsky, was of Polish birth and in 1864 at the age of twenty-one had been exiled from Vitebsk in eastern Poland to Tomsk Province in Siberia for alleged seditious activities. Despite his Polish blood, however, he appears to have quickly become Russified. In 1867 he had been transferred west to Viatka Province and in 1872 had married Anna Stepanovna Liapkova, a native of Viatka who was partly of Swedish descent. While in Slobodskoy, Grinevsky worked as assistant manager of a brewery, but two years after their first son was born the couple moved into Viatka itself, where Grinevsky eventually became an accountant in the town's hospital, a position he held until his death in 1913.

Alexander's childhood was far from happy. His mother suffered from tuberculosis; his father drank in an effort to forget the collapse of his youthful ideals; and as more children came into the family (there were five in all eventually, including a girl, Natalia, adopted before Alexander was born), the debts grew. Rarely mixing with his contemporaries, the boy seems to have grown up without guidance or affection, and to have been left largely to his own devices. Contemplative and solitary, he turned to books as his only consolation in a cheerless home. From the age of five he read voraciously and haphazardly, beginning with Swift's *Gulliver's Travels* and moving on to authors of romantic adventure such as Fenimore Cooper, Gustave Aimard, Mayne Reid and Bret Harte, compensating in impassioned dreams for the inadequacies of his unstimulating environment. "Perpetually in my imagination," he wrote later, "I could see the forests of America, the jungles of Africa, the taiga of Siberia. The words Orinoco, Mississippi and Sumatra rang like music in my ears."[9] It was in these early years filled with dissatisfaction and loneliness that his exotic *Grinlandia*[10] had its beginnings.

The boy was not successful at school. After being taught to read and write at home, in 1889 he was sent to the Viatka high school (*real'noe uchilishche*, non-classical secondary school), a conservative institution that manifestly failed to bring out the best in its gifted pupil. Though his teachers acknowledged his vivid imagination and remarkable memory, they found him over-inquisitive and excessively fond of practical jokes. He annoyed them by refusing to obey rules, quickly earned himself a bad name and was frequently punished. Without doubt it was his incessant reading and the beguiling dreams it engendered that kept the boy's spirit alive in these tedious years. "What I read in books," he wrote later, "even if it were the cheapest fiction, was always an agonisingly longed-for reality to me."[11] In 1891 he was suspended from school for poor conduct and then a year later was expelled altogether for writing a satirical poem critical of the staff. The piece was an imitation of Pushkin's "Sobranie nasekomykh" ("A Collection of Insects," 1829).

The boy was now sent to the local municipal school (*gorodskoe uchilishche*), where he felt happier and where his behaviour improved. He spent the next four years here, a period during which, in 1893, his mother died aged only thirty-seven. It was not long before his father married a local widow, who appears to have had little time and even less affection for her stepson. Feeling more isolated than ever in a home that had never been satisfactory even when his mother was alive, in June, 1896 the fifteen year-old left Viatka for Odessa. In his adolescent naiveté he had resolved to become a seafarer like so many of his beloved heroes in the works of Captain Marryat and Robert Louis Stevenson.

There followed long years of wandering and poverty, privation and despair, years that did much to make Grin as taciturn as he became and that served to bolster the many legends associated with his name. His apprenticeship for life was to be as varied as it was hard.

Reaching Odessa, he ran to catch his first glimpse of the sea that for so long had nourished his dreams. But he was disillusioned. Gazing at the frenzied activity of the harbour and at the astonishing expanse of water stretching away to the horizon beyond it, he felt superfluous and out of place, an uninvited guest in a grandiose world that had a self-sufficient life of its own. It took him much longer to find work than he had expected, for he was ridiculed for his schoolboy's clothes and poor physique. Eventually, after serving as a sailor and cook on Crimean coasters and visiting Sevastopol, Kerch, Batumi and Kherson, he became a warehouseman in Odessa. Then, early in 1897, he made what was to be the only foreign voyage of his life—to Alexandria. Once again, however, his rebellious nature asserted itself: during the return voyage he was relieved of his duties at Smyrna (Izmir) in Turkey for refusing to participate in rowing lessons ordered by the captain, and finished the journey as a passenger. Back in Odessa he worked as a coal-heaver and slept rough in the harbour. "I starved systematically,"[12] he wrote later as he recalled the hardship of this time.

In July, 1897 Grin returned to Viatka, arriving as penniless as when he had left it the year before. He spent the next twelve months at home, taking a variety of tedious jobs that brought him little satisfaction, among them those of office clerk and theater copyist. In July, 1898, oppressed by the stifling conformity of his native town, he set off again, heading for the southern oil town of Baku on the Caspian Sea. Here he spent a grim year in a succession of jobs—pile-driver, ship cleaner, stevedore, painter, porter and fisherman—and was often forced to beg on the streets to avoid starvation. At the beginning of winter, 1898 he suffered his first attack of malaria. All things considered, these months were perhaps the worst of his life. "The winter dragged on for an endless time," he recalled later, "and the gloom and horror of it often drove me to tears."[13]

Early in 1899 Grin found a job in a forge and then in May was employed by fishermen near Baku, where he mended nets and caught sturgeon. Then, together with a fellow-hobo, he tramped the Northern Caucasus before finding work in a bakery. His next job was on a coastal steamer which took him to Astrakhan, but recurrent attacks of malaria soon forced him ashore. In late 1899 he headed for Viatka once more, and arriving home penniless yet again, had to face his father's now familiar reproaches for his shiftlessness. He spent the next few months in Viatka, working as an attorney's clerk.

But the dreamer was indomitable. Just as romantic notions had urged him south to the sea, so now they drove him east to seek adventure on the Urals goldfields. "There I dreamed of hunting for treasure, of finding a nugget that weighed one and a half *poods*," he confessed later, "in a word, I was still under the influence of Rider Haggard and Gustave Aimard."[14] In February, 1900 he left Viatka, making for Slobodskoy where he was born. From there he travelled east to Perm, where a friend of his father's found him work in the railway sheds. But after only two weeks there, Grin moved on—"I was dreaming of camp-fires in the forest... the secret dens of gold-hoarders... bears and Indians..."[15]

Reaching the goldfields, however, he found that his enthusiasm swiftly waned when he did not become rich overnight. Disillusioned, he left and took a job in an iron foundry. Then in April, 1900 he became a lumberjack, sharing a forest cabin with an illiterate giant called Ilia, whom he would entertain at night first by telling him all the fairy tales he knew—Afanasev, Andersen, Perrault and the Brothers Grimm—and then by improvising wherever he could. As far as lumbering was concerned, though, he soon became disenchanted about that too, for the work of felling trees and manoeuvring logs downstream was beyond him. After only a few weeks he left and sailed downriver by raft.

Returning to Viatka in August, 1900, he found work as a railway station attendant and then in April of the following year left for the Kotlas region to the north, full of romantic ideas about living in the forests as a trapper. But after little more than a week he was back in Viatka. He then spent some months working on a barge and sailing the Viatka, Kama and Volga rivers.

Eventually, frustrated by his frequent periods of unemployment and shamed by his father's dismay at his lack of prospects, Grin volunteered for the army. In March, 1902 he was posted south to the 213th Orovaisky infantry battalion in Penza and was enlisted there as a private. Though for once properly clothed and well-fed, he found military life and discipline extremely tiresome—a fact that did not, however, prevent him from distinguishing himself as an excellent shot. He seems to have spent much of his time in the army questioning orders and resisting what he considered unwarranted coercion. In July, 1902 he deserted, but night-blindness hampered his escape and he was captured a week later.

While serving in Penza Grin formed links with the local branch of the Socialist Revolutionary (SR) Party, attending their secret meetings, reading revolutionary propaganda and even scattering SR leaflets near the barracks. In November, 1902, after only nine months' service—a third of it spent in the punishment cell—he successfully deserted from his battalion with the help of the Penza SR's. Little did he realise how momentous the break was to be.

III Literary Apprenticeship

Grin's desertion from the army marked a watershed in his life, for it was while attached to the SR Party that he began to write. After doing propaganda work for the SR's in Simbirsk and Nizhny Novgorod, he was selected to undertake terrorist activity. In the summer of 1903, according to usual practice, he was sent into rural "quarantine" near Tver so that it could be ascertained whether or not he was being watched by the police. His subsequent refusal to carry out the terrorist act—perhaps an assassination—that was apparently planned for him is reflected in the story *Karantin* (*Quarantine*, 1907). Nevertheless, further propaganda activity followed—in Saratov, Tambov, Ekaterinoslav, Kiev and Odessa—rich experience that was to provide him with material for such SR tales as *Marat* (1907) and *Malen'kii komitet* (*The Little Committee*, 1908).

It was not long, however, before his activities attracted the attention of the police, and in November, 1903 he was arrested in Sevastopol for political agitation among the armed forces there. When his real name became known (he had used a false one while working for the SR's), it was discovered that he was a soldier who had deserted. An attempt by fellow-SR's to rescue him from Sevastopol prison failed and he was held in jail until February, 1905, when a military court sentenced him to ten years' exile in Siberia. However, in November of that year—before his sentence had been confirmed—he was released from jail under the amnesty declared for political prisoners after the revolutionary upheaval of 1905. Again, unpleasant though it had been, his prison experience had given him much material on which to draw for such tales as *Apel'siny* (*Oranges*, 1907) and *Prizvanie* (*The Vocation*, 1916), both of which centre on imprisonment.

A month after his release the SR organisation sent Grin to Petersburg, but early in January, 1906 he was arrested during a police raid on SR terrorists in the capital. It was now that he met his future first wife, Vera Pavlovna Abramova, the twenty-four year-old daughter of an important civil servant. She worked for the Political Red Cross and visited Grin in jail in the spring of 1906 as his "fiancée", a method often used at the time to gain access to prisoners. On this occasion, in April, 1906 Grin was sentenced to four years' exile in Tobolsk Province, Siberia. En route to Tobolsk in June, he escaped from his convoy and with the help of fellow-SR's made his way via Samara and Saratov back to Moscow.

It was there, encouraged by his SR regional leader, Naum Bykhovsky, who had recognised his literary ability in revolutionary proclamations he had composed, that Grin wrote his first story, *Zasluga riadovogo Panteleeva* (*Private Panteleev's Service*, 1906). This was a subversive SR propaganda pamphlet (*agitka*) designed for distribution among soldiers. Though both its editor and typesetter were arrested, Grin himself escaped arrest as the pamphlet was unsigned. Returning to the capital, he wrote a second pamphlet, *Slon i Mos'ka* (*The Elephant and the Pug-Dog*, 1906), which was confiscated by the police before it left the printer's. That autumn he wrote a third tale, *V Italiiu* (*To*

Italy, 1906), which was published in the Petersburg paper *Birzhevye vedomosti* (*The Stock-Exchange Gazette*) on December 5, 1906. This was his first "legal" work and was signed with the cryptonym A. A. —v, derived from yet another false name he was using at the time—Alexey Alexeevich Malginov. In March, 1907 he first used the pseudonym that was to become customary for him—A. S. Grin.

After his escape from exile and the publication of his first stories, Grin seems to have lost enthusiasm for the SR cause, and his ties with the party grew steadily weaker. It is doubtful anyway whether he had ever been truly committed to the SR program; he had probably been attracted to the movement by romantic notions of revolutionary struggle rather than by actual political convictions. Now, propaganda activity no longer satisfied him and he became increasingly absorbed in literary work. During these years he began to move in Bohemian circles in the capital, making the acquaintance of many literary figures, notably the writer Alexander Kuprin, the editor Viktor Miroliubov and the critic Arkady Gornfeld, all of whom gave him much encouragement while he was trying to establish himself. Sadly, however, it was also at this time that he began to drink.

The year 1908 was a signal one for him in two ways. It witnessed the publication of his first collection of stories, a volume of ten items written in 1906 and 1907 and entitled *Shapka-Nevidimka* (*The Magic Cap*), with the sub-title *Rasskazy o revoliutsionerakh* (*Tales of Revolutionaries*); and it saw the writing of his exotic tale *Ostrov Reno* (*Reno Island*), which he was always to consider his first work of true artistic merit and the turning-point in his career. The story appeared in the April, 1909 issue of the popular Petersburg monthly *Novyi zhurnal dlia vsekh* (*The New Journal for All*), and later Grin always referred to its editor, Miroliubov, as his literary godfather. The following year brought the publication of a second collection of his work containing not only tales inspired by his SR experiences but also newer ones such as *Reno Island* and *Koloniia Lanfier* (*The Lanfier Colony*, 1910), which heralded his literary maturity.

Fate, however, was not to smile on Grin for long. In July, 1910 he spent some time working in a leper colony in Yamburg west of Petersburg, where a friend of his was a doctor. When he returned to the capital, he was arrested for living on a false passport and the fact that he was an escaped exile came to light. Finding himself in prison yet again, he quickly wrote two petitions, one to the Tsar and the other to the Minister of the Interior, stressing that he was no longer in contact with revolutionaries and asking for clemency. But his pleas went unheard and he was sentenced to two years' exile in Archangel Province, in the extreme north-west of Russia. In October,

1910, before being sent to Pinega, a small town east of Archangel which was his assigned place of residence, he was permitted to marry Vera Pavlovna in the prison chapel. At the end of the month they left the capital by train for Archangel, Grin travelling under guard and his new wife accompanying him voluntarily in a separate carriage.

Unfortunately, their marriage was not to last. For the time being, though, their months together in the north were happy enough, and finding himself able to relax, Grin revelled in the beauty of the forests and lakes around Pinega where he could hunt and fish to his heart's content. In August, 1911 he was permitted by the authorities to move from Pinega to Kegostrov in the Dvina delta, close to Archangel, and in March of the following year was allowed to move into Archangel itself, where he remained until his term of exile ended two months later.

Soon after their return to Petersburg in May, 1912, relations between Grin and his wife became extremely strained, largely because of Grin's heavy drinking. By the spring of 1913 Vera Pavlovna found that she could no longer bear his prolonged absences from home and decided to leave him. When an attempt at reconciliation during the summer failed, they separated for good and eventually became divorced. Distressed by his wife's departure and overwhelmed by loneliness, Grin turned to drink for solace.

Though there can be no doubt that Grin's alcoholism was the major reason for the breakdown of his marriage, it must be said that his relationship with Vera Pavlovna was not helped by the enormous differences in their backgrounds. While she was a well-educated but relatively inexperienced girl from the Petersburg intelligentsia, he was a self-reliant, provincial vagabond who had come to value the independence learnt in his difficult youth. More important still, Vera Pavlovna lacked confidence in her husband as a writer, something that he found increasingly hard to bear as the years went by. While liking his early revolutionary tales, which eventually dissatisfied Grin himself, she disapproved of later works such as *Reno Island* which were far more representative both of his artistic inclinations and his ability.

Exempted as unfit from service in the Tsarist Army when World War I broke out in 1914, Grin continued his disorderly way of life in the capital. Amazingly, though, his literary work did not suffer unduly, and during the next four years he contributed scores of stories, fables and poems to various cheaper periodicals, notably *Novyi Satirikon* (*The New Satyricon*), *Sinii zhurnal* (*The Blue Journal*) and the popular *Dvadtsatyi vek* (*The Twentieth Century*). The war prompted him to write many short stories on military themes, among them *Mystery on a Moonlit Night*, included in this anthology. Though as might be expected, the majority of them are highly chauvinistic in tone, several are talented pieces that display great sensitivity to the feelings of ordinary people about war.

It was not long, however, before Grin fell foul of the authorities once more. In late 1916 he was banished from Petrograd to Finland for making derogatory remarks about Nicholas II in a restaurant. He stayed in a Finnish village forty miles from Petrograd and did not return to the capital until after the February Revolution in 1917. The story of his journey back to the city—most of it on foot—is told in his autobiographical sketch *Peshkom na revoliutsiiu* (*On Foot to the Revolution*, 1917). "The uncertainty of what was happening in Petrograd," he recalled, "drew me to the capital with irresistible force."[16] As far as is known, however, he wrote very little that directly reflects the political and social crises suffered by Russia in 1917. Only the tales *Krasnye bryzgi* (*Red Splashes of Blood*) and *Trupy* (*The Corpses*), probably written shortly before the Bolshevik *coup d'état* in October, 1917, give some impression of the upheavals of that time.[17]

In the summer of 1919, when he was almost forty, Grin was called up for service in the Red Army. In September of that year he was transferred from Petrograd to Ostrov, 200 miles south-west of the capital, where his unit was detailed to lay telephone lines over deep snow. His physical condition was poor enough as it was, but as the weeks passed he became exhausted. Eventually, in March, 1920 tuberculosis was suspected and he was sent back to Petrograd. There he was found to have typhus, and but for the timely help of the writer Maxim Gorky, who miraculously found him a hospital bed in the overcrowded capital, Grin may never have survived. After a month in hospital, he roamed the starving city for weeks on end, spending the night with friends whenever possible and living from hand to mouth.

In mid-1920 Gorky came to Grin's aid once more, when he assigned him an official food ration and arranged accommodation for him in the House of Arts (*Dom iskusstv*), a hostel for writers, artists and scholars opened in Petrograd in 1919. Established through the efforts of Gorky, who was concerned to ensure the survival of Russian culture after the Revolution, the House rapidly became a focus of artistic life in the city. Among the writers who occupied rooms there were Mikhail Slonimsky, Viktor Shklovsky, Konstantin Fedin, Lev Lunts, Nikolay Tikhonov and Mikhail Zoshchenko. (Almost all of them, with others, were to become members of the Serapion Brotherhood, a group of independent, non-political writers formed in the House early in 1921.) Grin, however, kept very much to himself and played almost no part in the cultural activities organised by the institution. Another inmate, the poet Vladislav Khodasevich, remembers him as "a gloomy, tubercular man, who... struck up acquaintance with practically nobody and... spent his time training cockroaches."[18]

Whatever else Grin may have done in the House of Arts, he set out to complete his first novella, *Scarlet Sails*, the work now traditionally associated with his name. He had been working intermittently on it since 1916, after being struck by the sight of a beautiful yacht with scarlet sails in a Petrograd toyshop. His fondness for the project is demonstrated by the fact that he carried the manuscript in his kit-bag throughout his months of war service. As far as is known, he published nothing in 1920 and presumably worked on the novella for most of that year. On December 4, 1920 he read the first completed draft to Slonimsky and four days later read it again to a gathering of members of the House. Finally finished in April of the following year, the novella was eventually published in 1923.

In late 1918 Grin had met Nina Nikolaevna Koroshkova (*née* Mironova), who at the time was working for the newspaper *Petrogradskoe ekho* (*The Petrograd Echo*) in the capital. Her friends had warned her to beware of this strange character who was fourteen years her senior: "He's a dangerous man... his past is very shady, and they say... that when he was a sailor, he killed an English captain somewhere in Africa and stole his trunk containing manuscripts. He knows English but carefully conceals it, and is gradually publishing the manuscripts as his own."[19] But the alarming rumours were of no avail: Nina Nikolaevna married Grin in May, 1921.

This second marriage marked the beginning of the most productive and settled years of Grin's career, years which were to see the publication of five more novels and dozens of tales. Encouraged by his understanding wife, he not only worked more steadily but also drank less, perhaps sensing how close to destruction he had come during the bleak years after his separation from Vera Pavlovna in 1913. Nina Nikolaevna was to bring him both stability in his domestic life and a renewed sense of purpose in his work, and it is largely to her that the literary success he now enjoys is due.

IV The Mature Years

During the summer of 1921 Grin and his wife rented part of a *dacha* at Toksovo, forty kilometres from Petrograd near the Finnish border. Here Grin embarked on his second novel, *Blistaiushchii mir* (*The Shining World*), experiencing considerable difficulty since it was his longest work so far. Indeed, the writing of it took up most of 1921 and another eighteen months were to elapse before it was published.

1922 witnessed the appearance of a collection of three stories which included the moving *Korabli v Lisse* (*Ships in Liss*), one of Grin's finest tales. The following year saw the publication of both *Scarlet Sails* and *The Shining World*, but perhaps more important still, brought welcome royalties which improved the couple's financial position and enabled them to take a holiday in the Crimea. They visited Sevastopol, Balaklava and Yalta, and then stayed briefly in Moscow on the way home.

Their visit to the Crimea convinced Grin and his wife that they should leave the north. For her part, Nina Nikolaevna felt that if her husband escaped the company of his boon companions in Petrograd, his need for drink would diminish. Unfortunately, her hopes were to be only partly fulfilled. Though Grin certainly drank less after their move to the south, he never broke the habit completely, and occasionally even hid liquor in his room so that he could drink secretly at night.

Early in May, 1924 Grin and his wife left Petrograd by train for the Crimea. Arriving inFeodosia on the Black Sea, they took a hotel room until they could find permanent accommodation. Soon, however, what little money they possessed ran out and they were forced to resort to the pawnbroker. This was only the beginning of a painful association with local money-lenders that was to last for the next six years.

When they had found a small apartment, Grin began work on his third novel, *Zolotaia tsep'* (*The Golden Chain*). After his difficulties with *The Shining World*, the writing of this far less complex piece seemed effortless. It was finished within a few months in 1924 and serialised in the journal *Novyi mir (New World)* the following year.

The writing of his next major work, *Begushchaia po volnam* (*She Who Runs on the Waves*), proved infinitely more laborious. Finding the beginning of it especially troublesome, Grin made over forty drafts before he was satisfied with the result. Altogether, the novel took him more than eighteen months to write—from early 1925 until late 1926—and at the end of it he was exhausted. So drained of creativity did he feel that for a while he feared his literary career was at an end. Nor were his low spirits lifted by the fact that he found it impossible to arrange the work's publication, since journals considered it insufficiently up-to-date. Not until 1928 did it appear in book form.

After the completion of *She Who Runs on the Waves* there followed an interval of some ten months, during which Grin wrote a handful of successful short stories, among them *Brak Avgusta Esborna* (*Augustus Esborn's Marriage*) and *Zmeia* (*The Snake*). In addition, 1925 and 1926 brought the publication of no fewer than six collections of his tales, while 1927 saw the appearance of two volumes of a projected fifteen-volume edition of his works. In May and June, 1927 Grin and his wife used some of the royalties they had received to take a holiday in the spa town of Kislovodsk in the Caucasus.

Early in the winter of 1927, relieved that his creativity had not deserted him after all, Grin embarked on his next novel, *Dzhessi i Morgiana* (*Jessy and Morgiana*), a work which was to prove the least successful of his major pieces. Once again, though, he wrote with ease and by late April, 1928 the novel was finished. That enabled him to continue work on what was to be his last novel, *Doroga nikuda* (*The Road to Nowhere*), which had occupied him intermittently during the writing of its predecessor. Initially called *Na tenevoi storone* (*On the Shady Side*), it was not given its final title until the summer of 1928, when Grin happened to see an unusual engraving by the English artist John Greenwood in a Moscow exhibition. Completed in March, 1929, the novel was published in Moscow a year later.

Early in 1930 Grin reluctantly began work on his *Autobiographical Tale*, a partly fictional and elsewhere rather inaccurate account of his life. He wrote it purely for financial reasons, so profound was his aversion for disclosing details of his biography. Forced as he was to relive the misfortunes of his youth as he wrote, he found it so painful an exercise that he could not finish it. Consequently, the *Tale* breaks off in October, 1905, leaving Grin in Sevastopol just after his release from prison. Well aware of the legends surrounding his name, he expected that readers of his autobiography would not believe it was true, and so decided to call it *Legenda o sebe* (*Legend about Myself*). (The work was given its uninspired present title by the Leningrad publisher who issued it in 1932 shortly before Grin's death). For all its failings, however, the *Tale* remains one of the extremely few available sources of information about the author's life.

It was *The Road to Nowhere* that gave Grin the idea for *Nedotroga* (*Touch-Me-Not*), a novel left unfinished at his death. Having conceived it in 1930, he had begun it towards the end of that year, even before the *Autobiographical Tale* was finished. But while his thoughts on the new work were clear enough, its plot did not form readily in his mind and seemed disjointed. Assuring his wife that *Touch-Me-Not* would be even finer than the splendid *She Who Runs on the Waves*, he was to go on wrestling with it until he died.

The last three years of Grin's life, from 1929 to 1932, saw the dictatorship of the Russian Association of Proletarian Writers, or RAPP. That period coincided with the early years of the first Five-Year Plan of industrialisation and collectivisation, a colossal national scheme to which everything else in the USSR—including literature—

was subordinated. Soviet writers were expected to deal with contemporary topics and put their talents to the service of the Five-Year Plan. They were exhorted to reject pure fiction and turn instead to factual writing about construction projects, industrial complexes and collective farms. In addition, they were urged to form "artistic brigades," engage in collective writing schemes and participate in the "socialist emulation" becoming popular among workers in industry. Needless to say, such activities held little attraction for an inveterate individualist like Grin. All the same, though, RAPP effectively soured the last few years of his life. By the time the organisation was disbanded by Party decree in April, 1932, he was too ill to benefit from the change in literary climate.

Under the exigencies of the policies implemented by RAPP, Grin soon found it virtually impossible to have his work accepted by publishers. Filled as it was with personal themes and imaginative motifs, his writing was considered insufficiently contemporary, too far removed from the literature of "social command" (*sotsial'nyi zakaz*) prescribed by the critic Leopold Averbakh and the poet Alexander Bezymensky, the militant leaders of RAPP. 1930 showed the growing effects of RAPP's literary domination: Grin had fewer than ten items published, among them the tale *Zelenaia lampa* (*The Green Lamp*) and a collection of stories entitled *Ogon' i voda* (*Fire and Water*). 1931 was to prove far worse, however, for it would see only five publications—chapters of his *Autobiographical Tale* printed in the journal *Zvezda* (*The Star*), and that due only to the generosity of the poet Nikolai Tikhonov and other friends on the editorial board. But Grin could find no journal which would publish three new tales—among them *Komendant porta* (*The Port Commandant*)—and they appeared only posthumously, in 1933, when the dictatorship of RAPP was over.

The rigid policies of the RAPP organisation not only severely affected Grin's work and stifled his creativity; they also made him extremely poor because they effectively barred him from appearing in print. But he absolutely refused to bow to literary demands that ran totally counter to his personal inclinations. Consequently, 1930 found Grin and his wife in dire material straits and they were forced to borrow in order to survive. In November of that year, worried by their grave financial position, they decided to move to the quiet little town of Stary Krim, twenty-five kilometres inland, where accommodation and the cost of living were much cheaper than in the busier Feodosia. Unfortunately, however, the move brought no significant financial improvement, and the autumn of 1931—by which time famine had struck the Crimea—found them practically starving.

By late 1931 they were so desperate for money that Grin had to travel to Moscow in order to claim the royalties due for his *Autobiographical Tale* published earlier that year. He returned to Stary Krim not only completely exhausted but also profoundly depressed, for while in Moscow he had heard that his works were being removed from libraries because RAPP considered them undesirable. Yet for all the sadness it brought him, the news stiffened his resolve to resist the tyranny of Russia's literary masters. Though it would undoubtedly have alleviated his financial difficulties, he still refused to produce the topical literature that RAPP required. Never, he declared, could he become a writer of factual industrial sketches (*ocherkist*) in the way that so many of his fellow-authors had obediently done. Not only was such work completely uninteresting to him; he also found it utterly detestable. He preferred instead to go on writing in his own peculiar way, whether his work was published or not. But by now his days were numbered. Very soon, to the pain of literary ostracism and the humiliation of poverty was to be added the crushing burden of mortal illness.

By the winter of 1931 Grin's health showed a marked deterioration. Already ill when he returned from Moscow, he was first thought to be suffering from malaria, but then further investigations suggested tuberculosis. Growing weaker and finding himself unable to work, he wrote to the Union of Writers asking for a pension on grounds of ill-health, but there was no response and the couple were forced to pawn their possessions to buy food. Though Grin's condition grew steadily worse as the months passed—so much so that by late March, 1932 he was too feeble to get out of bed—it was not until the end of June that cancer of the stomach was finally diagnosed. There was no hope. He died a week later, on July 8, 1932, and was buried the following day in the little cemetery of Stary Krim, within distant sight of the sea that he had loved so much. The small house in which he died is now a museum devoted to his memory, and until her own death in September, 1970 his widow, Nina Nikolaevna, was its ever-attentive curator.[20]

NOTES

[1] B. G. Guerney, *An Anthology of Russian Literature in the Soviet Period,* New York, Vintage, 1960, p. 387.

[2] Marc Slonim, *Soviet Russian Literature*, New York, Oxford University Press, 1967, p. 113.

[3] Alexander Solzhenitsyn, *The Gulag Archipelago I-II*, London, Collins/Fontana, 1974, p. 533.

[4] Vl. Sandler (ed.), *Vospominaniia ob Aleksandre Grine*, Leningrad, "Lenizdat," 1972, p. 397.

[5] A. S. Grin, *Sobranie sochinenii v shesti tomakh,* Biblioteka "Ogonek," Izd-vo "Pravda," Moscow, 1965, Vol. 6, p. 247. This is the most comprehensive collection of Grin's work available. Three useful single-volume editions are *Fandango*, Simferopol', Izd-vo "Krym," 1966; *Dzhessi i Morgiana*, Leningrad, "Lenizdat," 1966; and *Belyi shar*, Moscow, "Molodaia gvardiia," 1966.

[6] See, for example, the articles by V. Vazhdaev, "Propovednik kosmopolitizma. Nechistyi smysl 'chistogo iskusstva' A. Grina," *Novyi mir*, No. 1, 1950, pp. 257-72; and A. Tarasenkov, "O natsional'nykh traditsiiakh i burzhuaznom kosmopolitizme," *Znamia*, No. 1, 1950, pp. 152-64.

[7] See note 4.

[8] See, for example, the following books: V. Kovskii, *Romanticheskii mir Aleksandra Grina,* Moscow, "Nauka," 1969; E. Prokhorov, *Aleksandr Grin,* Moscow, "Prosveshchenie," 1970; L. Mikhailova, *Aleksandr Grin*, Moscow, "Khudozhestvennaia literatura," 1972; N. J. L. Luker, *Alexander Grin,* Letchworth, England, Bradda Books, 1973. And the following articles: Vl. Rossel's, "Dorevoliutsionnaia proza Grina," in A. S. Grin, *Sobranie sochinenii v shesti tomakh,* Moscow, "Pravda," 1965, Vol. 1, pp. 445-53; Vl. Rossel's, "A. Grin. Iz neizdannogo i zabytogo," *Literaturnoe nasledstvo,* Vol. 74, Moscow, "Nauka," 1965, pp. 628-48; Vl. Rossel's, "A. S. Grin," *Istoriia russkoi sovetskoi literatury,* Tom I, 1917-29, Moscow, "Nauka," 1967, pp. 370-91; Vl. Sandler, "Shel po zemle mechtatel'," foreword to A. S. Grin, *Dzhessi i Morgiana,* Leningrad, "Lenizdat," 1966, pp. 3-20; Vl. Sandler, "O cheloveke i pisatele," foreword to A. S. Grin, *Belyi shar*, Moscow, "Molodaia gvardiia," 1966, pp. 3-25; Vl. Sandler, "Chetyre goda za Grinom," Al'manakh *Prometei*, Vol. V, Moscow, "Molodaia gvardiia," 1968, pp. 190-207; V. Vikhrov, "Rytsar mechty," foreword to A. S. Grin, *Sobranie sochinenii v shesti tomakh,* 1965, Vol. 1, pp. 3-36; P. Castaing, "Le thème du conflit chez Aleksandr Grin," *Cahiers du Monde Russe et Soviétique*, Vol. XII-3, July-September, 1971, pp. 217-46; J. Croisé, "Alexandre Grine et l'Irréel," *La Revue des Deux Mondes,* December, 1959, pp. 707-11; C. Frioux, "Alexandre Grin," *Revue des Etudes Slaves,* Vol. 38, 1961, pp. 81-7; C. Frioux, "Sur deux romans d'Aleksandr Grin," *Cahiers du Monde Russe et Soviétique*, Vol. III-4, October-December, 1962, pp. 546-63; Nicholas Luker, "Alexander Grin: A Survey," *Russian Literature Triquarterly*, No. 8, Winter, 1974, pp. 341-61; Barry Scherr, "Aleksandr Grin's *Scarlet Sails* and the Fairy Tale," *Slavic and East European Journal,* Vol. 20, No. 4, Winter, 1976, pp. 387-99.

[9] A. S. Grin, *Sobranie sochinenii, op. cit.*, Vol. 6, p. 231.

[10] See R. Freeborn (ed.), *Russian and Slavic Literature,* Cambridge, Mass., Slavica Publishers, 1976, pp. 190-209.

[11] A. S. Grin, *op. cit.*, p. 231.

[12] *Ibid.*, p. 280.

[13] *Ibid.*, p. 304.

[14] *Ibid.*, p. 321.

[15] *Ibid.*, p. 327.

[16] A. S. Grin, *Fandango, op. cit.*, p. 523.

[17] See *Russian Literature Triquarterly*, No. 11, Winter, 1975, pp. 88-94.

[18] Vl. Khodasevich, *Literaturnye stat'i i vospominaniia*, New York, Chekhov Publishing House, 1954, p. 406.

[19] Nicholas Luker, *Alexander Grin: The Forgotten Visionary*, Newtonville, Mass., Oriental Research Partners, 1980, p. 35.

[20] Nina Nikolaevna has left a detailed and revealing account of her years with Grin. See N. N. Grin, "Iz zapisok ob A. S. Grine," in Vl. Sandler (ed.), *Vospominaniia ob Aleksandre Grine,* Leningrad, "Lenizdat," 1972, pp. 322-404.

The Oranges

I

Bron walked away from the window and began to think. Yes, it was wonderfully beautiful out there! Golden sunlight and the blue river! And the river was wide and free...

The cool spring air blew so strongly into his sunlit cell that his eyes filled with tears and his heart leapt with irrepressible joy. Everything was not dead yet. There was still hope. All would pass, like a dream, and one day, close before him, he would see the cold, blue sweep of the river with its myriad quivering ripples. He would see everything... Like a young eagle he would soar into the sky, free in the empty expanse of air, and—cry out!... What did it matter? He would cry out—and his cry would ring with the sheer joy of being alive.

So he thought, and his glance fell on the little tarnished mirror hanging on the wall. From the glass there peered back at him a pale, tired face framed by thin, dishevelled hair. A wiry neck protruded sadly from the crumpled collar of a dirty cotton shirt. Mechanically he passed his hand over his shining eyes and began to think once more.

He sat and smoked, but a feeling of irritation and restlessness ran through him like an agonising electric current, making his legs itch. He began to pace his cage-like cell. Each time he turned by the window, its large, barred rectangle glittered before him full of sunlight, azure sky and greenery. His thoughts took wing like the restless birds by the river that kept fluttering up over the velvet reeds and wheeling with their harsh, sobbing cry.

II

It is doubly unpleasant to be in prison, feeling lonely, and to know that nobody cares about you except those in charge of this vast hotel with its iron curtains.

So he thought, and bitter anger welled up in his heart against those who knew him and had once called him "comrade", but who now would not even bother to write him a couple of lines or send him the few roubles that he needed so desperately. At times when he had not been in prison, solitude had been a necessary condition of his existence. But to be in solitary confinement and to feel forgotten was sometimes very unpleasant and painful.

He walked up and down his cell, while spring looked in at the window with her innumerable, tender eyes, exciting and soothing him with her melodious, languorous sounds. Spangled with golden sequins, the blue river flashed, while down below, far beneath his window, the little green birches prattled like frolicsome children.

"It's hard being in prison in spring," he thought, and heaved a sigh. "My third spring inside. . ."

Another thought occurred to him too, a thought he would never have revealed to anyone, ever. Profoundly disturbing, it took shape in his mind's eye as a familiar likeness, with big, dark eyes and a slender, gentle face. . .

"And that's gone too. . . What for? Yes, what for?" he repeated. "This wretched, servile country. . ."

Bron looked up once more to where the golden torrent of sunlight came streaming in, hot and dusty; suppressing a momentary feeling of pain, he sat down and opened *Das Kapital*. The mathematically lucid, arid lines whirled before his eyes, plunging into a bizarre void to be lost like snowflakes in the darkness. And those pitiless lines that were as malicious as the laugh of Mephistopheles and as assured as the swinging of a pendulum, made him feel bored and cold.

III

A key rattled in the lock and with a clang the peep-hole opened in the blank, yellow door. A row of buttons and a bristly moustache appeared in the rectangular opening, and a hoarse voice said impassively:

"Parcel!"

At first Bron did not realise the word was addressed to him. Then he got up, went over to the door and took a heavy packet from the warder's hands. The peep-hole immediately slammed shut again, and filled with excitement and joy, Bron hurried to put the parcel on his bed and see what it contained. Someone's solicitous hands had included everything he needed—tea, sugar, tobacco, various things to eat, stamps and oranges. Bron stood in the middle of his cell and smiled broadly as he looked at these treasures that had come through his peep-hole so unexpectedly. And because the day was fine and warm, and because this unexpected trouble taken by a stranger had caressed his soul, he felt very cheerful and gay.

"Now who on earth could have sent it?", he wondered. For a moment the face with dark eyes rose before him, but it was immediately blotted out by a picture of the frozen north. "N-no. . .

Anyway, I'll see in a minute. If there's a note, that means it's from one of ours. . ."

He began to rummage quickly among the provisions. But there was no note to be found. Feeling rather tired and disappointed after his fruitless search, he began to peel a bright red orange. Suddenly, deep in the heart of the fruit, he glimpsed a speck of silver. Quickly sinking his fingers into the juicy pulp, he pulled out a slender little scroll of paper that was tightly rolled up inside the head of a bullet.

"Here it is. How small! But what a clever idea!. . ."

The scroll turned out to be a ribbon of white paper that bore the delicate scent of perfume mingled with the sharp smell of the orange. A woman's minute handwriting covered the paper and riveted Bron's quick eyes.

"Comrade!" ran the note. "I found out by chance that you're in prison and very much in need. So don't be angry with me for sending you something. My address is N.B., 8, 11L., V.O.* It must be awfully hard for you being in prison—after all it's spring now. Anyway, I won't annoy you with that. Good-bye, and if you need anything, write. N.B."

Then Bron remembered how a week ago, knocking on the wall to his neighbour, he had asked him to tell those "outside" that he urgently needed a few basic necessities. Now it was clear that the parcel and note had been sent by someone from. . . After reading the scrap of paper twice, Bron felt like talking to his unknown correspondent, and began to do so by means of paper and ink. His letter proved long and detailed, and he did not miss the opportunity of displaying his wit in it. Towards the end he had a gentle knock at the Cadets, calling them "politically immature Falstaffs." Only after he had finished did he remember he was writing to a stranger.

"But I'll send it all the same," he decided, reassuring himself with the thought that his reply was merely a polite duty. "After all, it's so boring being in prison. . ."

So he thought as he stood in the middle of his cell with an orange in his hand. And hidden somewhere deep inside him, his second self said:

"How nice it is when people care about you. I want this woman to write to me again. And what's more I want to feel the kindness and warmth of someone's attentive, friendly concern every day. . ."

The excitement caused by the parcel subsided. Bron put the letter aside and began to eat. After feeling hungry for so long, everything seemed unusually appetising to him. Having eaten his fill

---

* i.e. The 11th *Liniya* (Line or Street) on Vasilyevsky Ostrov (Vasilyevsky Island), a district of St. Petersburg where Grin lived in the early 1900's (translator's note).

he began to read *Das Kapital* again, and as his eyes followed the great economist's lines, he smiled at the thought of his letter.

IV

Thursday was the day for visits and parcels again, and once more Bron received a paper packet containing oranges and food. In one of the oranges he again found a little scroll of paper rolled up inside a bullet. N.B. wrote that she had received his letter and that she was very grateful for it. The next part of the note left him in no doubt that it was written by someone who was young, ingenuous and sincere:

". . .I read your letter and thought about you all day long imprisoned in that awful place. If only you knew how much I want to suffer for the same cause that they are tormenting you for! It seems to me that I have no right, that I cannot, must not, remain free while so many fine people are languishing in prison. Write again. Why am I saying this to you? I don't know. N.B."

After reading the note, Bron immediately sat down and wrote a long letter, in which he explained that their "sufferings" were nothing in comparison with those that the people had borne for centuries. "Thank you very much for the oranges and pies," he added. "Please write again. Bron."

Opening a copy of Hertz before he went to sleep and drowsily following the neat little statistical tables with his eyes, Bron came to the conclusion that N.B. must be a tall, slim brunette in a wide-brimmed hat with a dark blue veil. That helped him to finish the chapter and inwardly to laugh at the "opportunist" Hertz.

V

A week later the correspondence had assumed extensive, firm proportions, and it was always with impatience but without examining his feelings very deeply that Bron waited for the notes, sending in reply long, detailed letters which in an eloquent, melancholy way contained his thoughts and aspirations. The quiet, tender sadness of this strange friendship comforted his soul like the sound of distant music. Sensing this but scarcely realising it, with every passing day he became more and more aware of the terrible contrast in his life, its two faces separated by the bars on his window—a contrast between the blue river, the invigorating expanse of distance, and bordering closely on it, the solitary little cell with a pale, hunched man inside it. . .

So the days passed, days that were monotonous when there were no parcels, but radiantly bright when Bron's cell was filled with the thoughts—brilliant as a shower of crystals—jotted down on the ribbon of paper in a hurried, almost child-like hand. The girl said that she too found life cramped and that, feeling imprisoned in a world full of sordid complacency, she longed to struggle against the dark forces which prevented the fresh, green shoots of the new life from bathing in the warm spring air and sunlight. As he read these melodious, plaintive lines where laughter, sorrow and tears mingled together and sparkled like expensive wine, Bron recalled the past with its rosy dreams and the unfeigned courage of youth that had demanded so much both of oneself and of others.

VI

One Thursday, as the voices and steps of the warders echoed somewhere far below, Bron received his parcel and found only one orange in it. But it was blood-red and huge. Pulling out a note, he sat down and read:

"Dear Bron! You really must be awfully bored. So don't be angry with me for calling at the police department yesterday and getting permission to visit you as your 'legal wife'. It was rather difficult, but anyway I arranged it. My name's Nina Borisova. This is only a very short note—after all we'll be seeing each other today and we can have a long talk.

I'm in high spirits, and it's so warm and gay outside. N.B."

"And it's so warm and gay outside," thought Bron. He read the note again and then with a pounding heart went to his little old suitcase and began to take out a clean blue shirt. But just then four whistles rang out down below and a shrill voice cried:

"Number 56! Visiting time!"

Suddenly Bron was filled with apathy and fatigue. He felt like saying he did not want to see his visitor. But when the warder flung open his door, swept the cell with a practised eye, and said: "This way!", Bron began to hurry. Hastily smoothing his hair and drawing himself up, he walked out of the cell.

Downstairs, the long, cleanly-swept corridor rang with the shouts of warders and the jangling of keys, and as always at visiting time people were scurrying about in every direction. Catching sight of Bron, the visiting room warder—a fat man with a big moustache and a row of medals—asked quickly:

"You've got a visitor, have you? Go to the end then, into the cell on the right!"

Bron set off down the long corridor, walking with the swift, easy gait of people who have been sitting for a long time without moving. Another warder, a mournful-looking man with his hair brushed smooth, led him into an empty cell that had been freshly painted grey, and then came out again, closing the door behind him. A few agonising minutes followed, minutes that Bron tried to ignore by smoking, unable as he was to overcome his feelings of tense expectation, awkwardness and unease. At last the door was flung open and the same warder said in an indifferent tone:

"This way, please!"

Bron's heart began to pound and with two steps he was led into another cell with a small table in it covered with newspaper. At it sat a police captain, a young man with a complacent, pale face and prominent lower jaw. Bron went in and stopped awkwardly in the middle of the cell. The captain's little eyes slid vacantly over him and it seemed to Bron that he was suppressing a smile. Bron blushed and turned towards the door.

VII

Into the cell, waddling slightly, came a modestly dressed, plain-looking, rather plump girl with pink cheeks and bright, embarrassed little eyes that widened a little as they came to rest on Bron. He stepped towards her and shook her outstreched hand unnaturally hard.

"Well... hello!" he said with a cough. "How are you then?" he added hastily, feeling a tell-tale blush spreading across his face.

"Sit down, please!" came the captain's rasping voice, and Bron moved obediently, sinking on to his chair without taking his eyes off the girl's face. She sat down too, but the captain's podgy white hands lay on the table between them. A few moments passed, during which Bron tried desperately but in vain to think of something to say. His thoughts went whirling by with horrifying speed and one of them kept hammering at his brain:

"I'm sitting here so stupidly, like a fool! A fool! A fool!"

"Well, say something then," said the girl quietly and smiled apologetically. Her voice was soft and husky. "It's awful how little time they give you for visiting. Only five minutes... Over in the remand prison they give you longer, they say..."

"Yes, they give you longer there," agreed Bron in a meaningful tone. "They give you ten minutes there..."

Again he fell silent, listening to the echo of his own voice and wishing that the five minutes were already over.

"I was in such a hurry to get here," the girl went on. "And I've got somewhere else to go to next. . . I had to wait an hour. . . or was it more? Yes, an hour and a half. . ."

"Thanks for coming," said Bron in a wooden voice. "It's very boring in here. . ." 'Why on earth am I complaining?' he wondered, frowning inwardly. "And you. . . how are you?"

"Me?" asked the girl absently. "Oh, just the same. . ."

They were silent for a little longer, glancing at each other from time to time, and for some reason they both felt sad. The captain stifled a yawn, drummed his fingers on the table for a moment, and then snapping open an enormous watch, said as he got to his feet:

"Time's up. . . Finish now please!. . ."

Bron and Borisova stood up and smiled pitifully in their embarrassment, tormented by their feeling of awkwardness and the alien, hostile atmosphere around them. The girl walked to the door but turned as she reached it and said quickly:

"I'll come next Thursday. . . So keep your spirits up!"

Perhaps she had been expecting to meet someone quite different, a man who was tempered by experience, as strong and proud as his letters were, with quick movements and gentle eyes. . . Anything is possible. Perhaps too, coming out on to the street, she cast a long glance at the gloomy façade of the prison that concealed so many fine souls behind its iron bars. . . Perhaps too. . . But then anything is possible.

Bron slowly climbed the stairs back to his cell. He felt pained and uncomfortable, like a wrong-doer caught in the act, though he did not know why he felt as he did. . . He thought about the strange things in life, about the secret recesses of the soul where desires are born and die—desires that have two sides to them, like everything else in the world, desires that are both clear and obscure, strong and weak. And he pitied them, those beautiful but fleeting blossoms, those poor stepchildren of life wafted by poetic fancies, those longings that live and die like butterflies, no one knows why. . .

Entering his cell, he went up to the window, sighed and gazed out at the brilliant colours of spring enfolding the expanse of distance in their motley cloak. The river shone blue and, filling the air with sound, the exciting echo of the busy streets rang out and brimmed over like a cascade. And a new wrinkle appeared on Bron's soul. . .

1907

The Arm

I

Outside the window of the third-class carriage a dull, grey drizzle was falling, and through the rattling, misted panes the green birch woods floating by in the uncertain light of early dawn looked sullen and grey. The telegraph wires streamed past, slowly rising and falling in rhythmic waves. Gazing drowsily at them, Kostrov watched their black lines flowing by, closing his eyes from time to time and trying to guess from the rhythm of the wheels when he should open them again so that the little white insulators were exactly opposite his window. After an uncomfortable, sleepless night this distracted him a little.

He had been trying to drop off ever since Tver, but without success. Doors kept slamming and then currents of cold night air would creep down his neck, irritating him like the touch of chilly fingers. Or just as he was about to nod off, one of the guards would appear, brushing against his legs as he passed down the carriage, his boots clumping noisily. Chased away, Kostrov's drowsiness would follow after him.

Apart from this, Kostrov's sleeplessness was sustained and intensified by the vaguely disquieting fear of *not falling asleep*, a fear that steadily increases with every sound and with every movement of the body. This fear is alarming because it demonstrates the powerlessness of the human will and makes us annoyingly aware of our dependence upon external factors. For a long time he tossed and turned, then smoked and counted to a hundred, noticing with irritation that this agitated him even more. Eventually he decided that to fall asleep that night was a sheer impossibility. Once he had acknowledged this, the inevitability of it helped to soothe his frayed nerves. Getting up from his seat, he sat down by the window, and staring out into the cold darkness, began to smoke one cigarette after another, carefully waving the smoke away from the young woman lying opposite.

II

Kostrov had not noticed when she had got into the carriage. It must have been when capricious, faltering sleep had settled close beside his head for a moment, only to melt away once more amid the rhythmic rattling of the wheels. Wrapped tightly in a shawl, she lay peacefully and deeply asleep, as sweet and graceful as a kitten. Her figure and face breathed the gentle, child-like trustfulness of a living creature youthful in body and spirit. She had moved in her sleep and her dark, fluffy hair had become rather tousled, its snake-like strands covering her little flushed ear and her temple with its transparent, bluish veins. She breathed deeply and evenly, lying with her hands folded under her cheek and resting her head on the white lace cover of a magnificent high pillow.

For a while Kostrov looked with respect and envy at this person who had managed to fall asleep so serenely amid all the commotion and discomfort of a third-class carriage. Holding his cigarette in his right hand, with his left he kept waving away the wisps of smoke that drifted towards the delicate, fine profile of the young girl in front of him. She was young all right—Kostrov decided that straightaway and then thought no more about it.

She was asleep, sound asleep, but the smoke from his cigarette might disturb and wake her. And so, not wishing either to deprive himself of the pleasure of looking at her or to cause her any unpleasantness, he inhaled quickly and deeply so as to finish his cigarette, then put it out and threw it on the floor.

Swaying in its headlong flight, the carriage hurtled on. The window-panes rattled and the rain drummed on the iron roof, but all around him in the reddish twilight of the grubby compartment everyone was fast asleep. The fat merchant in the English waistcoat and bottle-green boots was asleep; lying curled up, the railway official was asleep—something which made the green piping on his double-breasted jacket seem completely unnecessary and useless; the woman in the cotton kerchief with a basket under her head was asleep; and the girl was asleep too.

III

How involved and strange it would seem if in the city, amid all the rigidity and triteness of human relations, a man were to find himself sitting awake only two steps from a sleeping woman he did not know, and gazing intently into her face! But here, on the train, Kostrov's rather sentimental affection for this sleeping girl-child seemed so natural despite their artificial proximity, that he felt it was only fine and tender. A strong young man is sure to prevent anything from disturbing the peaceful sleep of a woman, if only because she is asleep and he is not. Kostrov's awareness of this, logical as it seemed in the present situation, was gratifying to him—all the more so as the girl was attractive.

He smiled fondly and crossed his legs, trying not to bang the seat with his boot; his half-closed, heavy eyes rested pleasurably on the soft outlines of the sleeping form opposite, a form that seemed so dear to him in this train rushing headlong through the night. Solitary and half-asleep, he began to imagine he was married and travelling with his young wife on a long journey. His wife was the girl in front of him; she was sleeping peacefully, happy in the closeness of her beloved. A minute went by, then another. She moved in her sleep and her shoulders became uncovered. Her shawl slipped lower and lower until it fell to the floor, exposing her shoulders and breast to the night's chill. But he went up to her and trying not to wake her, gently lifted the shawl and wrapped the dear creature up once more, feeling warm inside because of his concern for her and the affectionate, tender stirrings of his soul. When she woke, blinking sleepily, the sunlight would laugh and flash in her eyes—eyes that were so good and true to him and knew him so well.

The girl was asleep, occasionally moving her full lips that were as moist as buds laden with dew. Kostrov's gaze rested upon them and something child-like smiled within him, stirring like a string touched by a gay hand.

Pulling up her legs and heaving a sigh, the girl freed a hand from under her cheek. Slipping over the edge of the seat, her arm hung down heavily. Involuntarily trying to correct its uncomfortable position, the arm bent at the elbow, but its effort was too feeble, and overcome by its own weight, it hung in the air once more. This was repeated several times, but the girl was evidently too soundly asleep to wake up straightaway and move it.

IV

Kostrov watched his neighbour's feeble movements with a feeling of pity. One or two more minutes, he thought, and she'll be so uncomfortable that she'll wake up. Then she might not be able to drop off again and will sit here like me, her head heavy with lack of sleep, feeling irritable and sullen.

Snatching at the carriages, the autumn night went flying by, its black face quivering at the window and its mysterious lights flickering in the darkness. Hesitantly, Kostrov leant forward and carefully, gently, lifted the girl's arm in his palm. It was heavy and warm. But when he tried to bend it and lay it on the seat, he was filled with a feeling of incomprehensible shyness and let the arm go. She might wake up, he thought, interpret his gesture wrongly and perhaps even take offence. Her warmth was someone else's warmth, and he had no right to worry about her.

"What's wrong then?" he wondered, lighting a fresh cigarette and trying hard to understand the barrier that clearly existed between them and prevented him from rendering her a friendly service. "I can see she's uncomfortable like that and I want to help her—that's fine. But why's it wrong? Why might it cause a misunderstanding and even make her call the chief guard? One thing's clear, though: I've got no right to help her and in all probability she doesn't think so either. But why?"

The answer was on the tip of his tongue, an answer that included the words: "it would be an odd thing to do". . ., followed by something about the stupid, mean logic of life. Although he banished the idea so as to concentrate on the given situation, his thoughts found themselves in an impasse and went round and round like a mill-wheel, forever turning on one and the same spot.

"When she wakes up, I swear I'll ask her. . . It would be interesting to know. . . I'll say: would you like it if a stranger helped to make you more comfortable while you were asleep?"

V

Kostrov looked at the girl's arm hanging down with its little veins swollen at the wrist, and felt the familiar desire stirring in his soul. Once again he wanted to put the arm into a more comfortable position. After hesitating a little longer, he suddenly blushed, and with a pounding heart gently but decisively took the girl's warm, sleepy fingers in his big, strong hand, laid them on the pillow and carefully covered them with the shawl. Having done so, he looked round in alarm, but everyone was still fast asleep.

Now, though, he wanted his neighbour to wake up, and he waited, feeling sure that she would. She did so that very minute. Dark-brown eyes, wide-open and still uncomprehending, looked up into Kostrov's face. Leaning forward and calmly meeting her gaze, he said:

"Ma'am, I. . ."

"Eh? What is it? What's the matter. . .?" she asked sleepily, sitting up anxiously and trying to understand what this big, grave man wanted from her.

Without hurrying, speaking in a steady voice and trying to sound as sincere as he could, Kostrov began again:

"Ma'am, I noticed that while you were asleep, your arm got itself into an uncomfortable position, and so I moved it. . . If you are angry with me for doing this, I shall be very sad, because I only wanted to make you more comfortable, that's all..."

He took a breath.

"Oh, it's all right," said the girl, feeling reassured and putting her head down on the pillow again. "You needn't have worried... Thank you."

After a few moments she fell asleep again. Kostrov sat and smoked, feeling rather ashamed of something as if he were just a silly little boy.

The grey rain of dawn scratched at the window, while the telegraph wires rose and fell as they streamed silently by. All that day, as a result of this chance encounter, the big, sleepless man was filled with joyous faith—faith in the power of sincerity.

1908

The Window in the Forest

I

Realising he was lost, the hunter climbed a hillock and looked around anxiously. On every side, stretching right to the forest that showed dark and low on the horizon, lay an unfamiliar, sinister plain, covered with yellowish-white, gloomy-looking moss and sparse clusters of aspens. Furiously the autumn wind bent the slender saplings, soughing dolefully through their tossing foliage. Incessantly, bending almost to the earth, they paid homage to the darkening, cloudy sky, while the icy wind blew on and on towards the chill, crimson sunset.

Terns wheeled above the hunter's head with the piercing shrieks of creatures being put to death. The animals living in the marshes scattered over the plain had hidden in the reeds, the hares had vanished, and weakened by the storm, the ponderous ravens had settled on the ground. The whistling lament of the wind united sky and earth as everything tossed and bent low. Taking on fantastic shapes, the dark clouds raced into the stormy distance, wreathing like smoke from an invisible fire before drifting apart and breaking up.

The hunter stood quite still, holding on to his hat with his hand. The damp, raw wind chapped the skin on his reddened face while his chilled legs shivered impatiently. Ravaged by the storm, the earth's emptiness filled him with unaccountable fear. Numb with fatigue, his limbs cried out for rest. Imperceptibly, his hunger had increased, and from a faint, almost unconscious desire for food, had turned into a soundless cry uttered by his avid body. He felt confused by the uncertainty of his whereabouts and frightened by the closeness of nightfall, while his consciousness grew more and more feeble, giving way to the instinctive need to walk on for the sake of it, in the blind hope of finding his bearings and feeling reassured.

He set off once more, keeping to the direction he had taken earlier. With long, hurried strides he made for the forest. Countless voices accompanied him, and it was as if countless accursed creatures, transformed into the vegetation of the swamps, were sobbing shrilly all around him, choking with impotent terror and crying out in supplication. Streaking the misty air with their frenzied, darting flight, the terns swooped to right and left, and in the man's disturbed imagination they became mysterious creatures endowed with secret powers. Unceasingly, like spirits of despair, they flung out their repulsively shrill cry, and terror itself came creeping from the seething, dusky void.

Shivering with cold, the hunter stopped. Like great black coals, storm-clouds were spilling over the dimming hearth of the west, and the sun made haste to set so as not to behold the earth in the grip of madness. Against a pale strip of sky branches tossed in fury. There was a buzzing in the man's ears and his muscles ached with the dampness. Straining his lungs, he gave a shout, but his plaintive cry was lost amid the uproar around him. Blindly, he trudged on once more, stumbling over tree-stumps as he went.

Gradually, an irrepressible feeling of despair filled the hunter's soul. Everything around him came alive and assumed immense, terrifying proportions. The plain seemed endless and its confines were lost in his imagination, while the earth itself became an accursed place of inexpressible sorrow and desolation. The grown man became a child. Staring into the night, he walked on and on, famished and lost, weak and defenceless. His mind began to resurrect the legends of old, summoning up the images of shaggy forest spirits, and he smiled wryly in the darkness as he tried to banish the thoughts that possessed him. On he went, listening with fearful apprehension to the slightest sound of a twig snapping underfoot.

Night was raging like the soul of a felon. The hunter's breathing was laboured and his thoughts were lost in space. His loneliness sharpened his sense of awareness and his feet did not seem to feel the ground. Invisible, living branches tore at his clothes, beating him silently in the face and lashing frenziedly at his terror-stricken back. He did not stop again. Quickening his pace, he headed instinctively towards the forest, longing to shelter in its damp depths from the triumphant ravages of the storm.

The first rough tree-trunk that his outstretched hand touched in the darkness seemed like a living creature, a friend who had come out to meet an exhausted comrade. As he made his way deeper into the forest, he noticed with a growing feeling of calm how the howling of the wind gradually died away to become a distant rustling in the tops of the pines. Thundering like an invisible waterfall, the storm roared far above his head, and the wild orchestra of creaking tree-trunks plucked achingly at his heart. The half-rotted pine-needles felt soft and slippery underfoot, and, steeped in the smell of the forest, the damp blackness strained his unseeing eyes, stinging them with sparks that leapt from his benumbed brain.

And then, like a little red ember glimmering on a dark cloth, a light flared in the pitch-black darkness. The man could not believe it, and rubbing his eyes with his fist, continued on his way. Screened by the trees, the ember vanished, flashed again, went out, and gleamed once more like a solitary little eye.

Then the hunter was filled with irrepressible gladness. It was as if his body had suddenly been regenerated, losing all its heaviness and fatigue. Involuntarily his face broke into a blissful smile. Longing outstripped his steady stride and, breaking loose like a spirited horse, raced ahead to the place where it sensed human habitation.

His hunger stirred with sharpened force, but now he no longer tried to suppress it. Instead he roused it, rejoicing that gratification was so close at hand. Full of alluring comfort, all the windows he had ever seen at night arose in his mind's eye. But that light—was it not just a camp-fire?

II

Filled with curiosity and impatience, the hunter went nearer and made out a frame silhouetted against panes reddish with fire. It was the window of a house and the work of human hands. It was a godsend that promised infinite reassurance.

In the obscure depths of the light-filled room moved blurred shapes with soundlessly stirring lips and arms, and yellow profiles. Leaping up in the twinkling of an eye, shadows danced across the ceiling to the walls and vanished. The life glimpsed through this window in the night—a life that was foreign and ghostly to the man peering in from the darkness—was focused in the small, bright square of glass.

According to man's peculiar habit of approaching his fellow-creature even more warily than wild animals do, the hunter crept slowly forward, trying to see who was inside. Enticing visions of hot food and welcome rest in the company of a hard-working, peaceful family urged him on more quickly than he was accustomed to go. A sound sleep under a friendly roof with the hundred voices of the wind howling outside and the kindly smiles of hospitable hosts around him—surely he had a right to expect this?

His heart beating nervously, the hunter pressed his face to the window. Wearied by the gloom, his eyes could not make out what was inside straightaway, but soon, concentrating hard, he was able to see the whole interior of the dwelling, together with the people who lived beyond the misted glass. He had apparently stumbled on a forester's hut. In the wall opposite the window was a door, and above it hung several rifles, a net for catching quail, an ammunition-pouch, a horn full of gunpowder, and some yellowed fishing-rods. To the right of the door, beside a small, poorly-whitewashed stove, could be seen a red bed-curtain. The shelves of the hut were piled with earthenware crockery and various other household articles, while the soot-blackened walls were hung with pictures of a religious and fairytale kind. To the left of the window, in the corner, stood a big table that was covered with a dark blue cloth and had a cheap tin lamp burning on it.

There were three people in the room. They had evidently just had supper, as an unfinished slice of bread and a yellow earthenware pot with spoons scattered round it were lying on a wooden bench. Sitting on a low stool by the stove was a bent old woman busy with her knitting, while at the table, absorbed in something that at first sight seemed incomprehensible, sat a boy of about eleven and a middle-aged, thickset peasant. The boy was leaning forward with his elbows on the table, and his thoughtful face—unusually delicate for a peasant's—shone with a gay smile. From time to time he tossed his close-cropped, dark head and showed his white teeth in a soundless laugh. The man's dirty, coloured shirt was undone at the neck, and his weather-beaten face with its thick, tangled beard looked sullen but not unkind. Pursing his lips in a painstaking way, he blinked and was completely absorbed in what he was doing. Without hurrying, he kept catching something running over the table, held it for a short while in his broad, calloused palm, and then let it go.

The hunter looked more intently for a moment and then shuddered with revulsion. Across the table, its wings smashed by shot, fluttered a little marsh snipe. Its delicate beak kept opening and closing and its glittering black eyes leapt from their sockets in terror. Matted with dried blood, its dishevelled feathers stuck up like bristles. Hopping along on its slender, brown legs, it kept running to the edge of the table, where, squeezing the bird's bloody head in his fingers, the peasant would catch it and then methodically, taking careful aim, would pierce its skull with a thick needle. The snipe stood stock-still. Slowly, crippling its brain, the needle emerged on the other side of its head. Then, released by the man's fingers, the bird would dash away, unable to cry out, crazed by pain and the agony of imminent death, until the same fingers seized it once more and pierced its defenceless little head in a new place.

The hunter held his breath. The peasant turned and screwing up his eyes, peered at the window, where a motionless, weary face watched him from the darkness. The peasant could not see the hunter and turning away, continued his game. The little snipe was moving more and more slowly now, falling again and again and quivering all over. Trying to take to the air, it kept leaping up and, demented by pain, battered itself against the glass of the lamp.

The forest was filled with a muffled roaring and the cold darkness was wet with rain. Seized with boundless fury, the lost man raised his arm. Suddenly enveloped in a torrid haze, he shouldered his gun, took aim and fired. Both barrels spoke, shattering the window-panes with a thundering echo that rolled away into the distance.

He was answered by a cry from the injured man and a crash as the bench fell over. Instantly the forest came to life, resounding with a thousand voices. Suddenly accessible to the hunter through the jagged tracery of splintered glass, the interior of the hut became a reality. He only had to stretch out his hand to touch the table and the dishevelled head that had crashed down on the crumpled cloth. Beside himself with terror, the boy was shaking and shouting something.

Reeling like a drunk, the hunter walked quickly away. The tree-trunks pressed ever closer as the impassive, dense forest swallowed him up, yet on and on he went, further and further into the ravenous, sleepless darkness full of wild beasts.

1909

Reno Island

> Hearken only unto the voice that speaks without a sound.
> (Ancient Hindu scripture)

I

One Man is Missing

The lieutenant stood at the clipper's starboard rail and gazed at the sunset. The mighty ocean lay still. The blurred horizon smoked in the fiery glow of the setting sun, and like a huge drop of molten metal, the blazing orb sank quickly into the sea, throwing towards the clipper a wide stream of light that glittered like golden scales.

The sun's rays grew fewer and fewer, dimming as they touched the water, and the flaming disc swiftly became no more than a dying ember. Behind the lieutenant the shadows climbed into the sky and silently lengthened. There came a breath of chill air. The mast lights gleamed in the pitch-black water, while overhead the Southern Cross lay strewn on the dark velvet sky like a cluster of big, bright diamonds. The fading expanse of distance drew in closer and closer around the ship, and the lieutenant felt as if he were looking out through a chink in a dark box. The last ray of light flickered hesitantly on the horizon, flared up with a final effort, and then died.

The lieutenant lit a cigarette, buttoned his jacket, and turned to look at the island. The night masked the distance and made the black bulk of the shore seem quite near. It was as if the clipper were moored alongside rocks that were invisible in the darkness, though in reality she lay over a cable's length from the beach. The shore wind brought with it the damp, stifling heat of the dense forest along the coast. All was quiet, and one could easily imagine that the island was inhabited by thousands of cunning foes who were watching the vessel from the darkness and waiting their chance to fall upon it, slaughter the crew to a man, and set the stillness echoing with howls of delight.

The lieutenant imagined a sizeable mob of savages—perhaps two hundred of them—and mentally treated them to a double charge of grape-shot. Then he remembered with regret that the island was inhabited only by monkeys, though it was true there were enough of them to supply all the zoos of Europe. So guns were quite out of place here. Moreover, there was not even a miserable pirate on the island to attack any of the five men sent ashore three hours ago for water. Thinking of that, the lieutenant reflected that the boat really was a long time coming back. After all, there were no ale-houses here, and there was a river mouth quite close by where there was fresh water.

"Come to think of it," the lieutenant muttered, "the fellows certainly don't seem to be in much of a hurry."

The ocean sighed softly. Heavy steps approached along the deck and the stooping figure of the bosun appeared out of the gloom. The flickering lantern lit up his thin-lipped, wrinkled face. He gave a hollow cough and said:

"The men haven't come back yet."

"No, they haven't—and you should know more about that than me," replied the officer drily. "They've been gone four hours now. What do you think about that, bosun?"

The bosun moved his lips in an absent-minded way and spat out the tobacco he was chewing. He believed one should never start worrying too soon.

"So what do you think?" asked the lieutenant impatiently.

"They'll come," said the bosun, "they'll not spend the night ashore—there aren't any women there."

"No, that's true, but they might have drowned."

"Five of them, sir?"

"Yes, perhaps. Don't forget there are wild animals on shore too."

"Five men with a gun each..." muttered the bosun, "no animal would stand a chance..."

Then he turned his head and began to listen. His expression seemed to say: "Might it be? Yes... perhaps..."

The shrouds and stays cast their criss-crossing shadows on the deck, while the water alongside shone black. The expanse around the clipper was hidden in impenetrable darkness, and she was lost in it, small and silent.

"What can you hear out there?" asked the officer. "You'd better make sure you send good men ashore in future, not idlers. What is it?"

"Oars," replied the bosun briefly, knitting his brows. "Just listen," he added after a silence, "that's Bull rowing. And that's Rantay splashing about, the devil. He'll never learn to row, sir, you can be sure of that."

The lieutenant listened, but for a while all he could hear was the gentle lapping of water in the hawse-holes, the creaking of the gaff, and the bosun's hoarse breathing. Suddenly, suspecting it rather than hearing it, he detected a distant stirring in the air that resembled the sound of a stone falling into water. Then everything grew quiet once more. The bosun stood there for a little longer, then blinked confidently and straightened up.

"They're coming!" he said through his teeth, spitting out his tobacco with relish. "Rantay's always after the girls, damn him! Put him on a barren reef and he'll fall in love in a flash. He can find a woman anywhere... even here! I bet he could turn the devil into a girl if he wanted to..."

"Bosun," said the lieutenant, interrupting him, "can you really hear something?"

"Me?" The sailor gave a leisurely sigh and smiled craftily. "You see, sir, I've suffered from this ever since I was a child. I can often tell who's coming a mile away. There always seems to be an orchestra playing in my ears, you know, even if there's a dead calm."

"Yes," said the lieutenant, "you're right—I think I can hear something myself now."

From the pitch darkness came the rhythmic splashing of oars together with muffled shouts and the squeak of rowlocks. Then the boat swung into the half-light cast by the ship. Walking over to the ladder, the lieutenant bent down and said in a loud voice:

"You lazy devils!"

The boat bumped against the clipper's side with a hollow thud. One after another the sailors climbed the ladder and lined up on the quarter-deck facing the rail.

The lieutenant began to count:

"One, two, three... But wait... How many of them did you say there were, Matthew?"

"Five, sir... That's funny!"

"Well," asked the officer impatiently, "where's the fifth then?"

"The fifth?" said the sailor who had come up last. "That was Tart, sir."

Then after a pause he explained hesitantly:

"He's lost... Sorry, sir, I mean we don't know where he is."

There was an expressive silence. The sailor waited a moment as though unable to find the right words, then spread his hands in a gesture of helplessness and added:

"I mean he's vanished completely, sir, just as if the earth had swallowed him up. We couldn't find him anywhere and that's why we're late. Rantay said: 'We must go,' but I said: 'How can we? Tart hasn't got a boat... That's right,' I said, 'he hasn't got a boat...'"

The sailor grinned and scratched his head, while the lieutenant shrugged nervously and glanced at the bosun. The old salt seemed preoccupied and moved his wrinkled lips slowly.

"Wait," said the lieutenant incredulously, "how could he just disappear like that? And where to? I expect you took a bottle of rum with you and Tart's lying about under a tree somewhere!"

Filled with the desire to supply details of the affair, the sailor was becoming agitated and would have gone on shifting from one foot to the other for longer still had the sharp-eyed Rantay not come to his aid. Waving his arm in a categorical gesture, he told all.

As he described it, this is what had happened: no one had noticed Tart walking off and leaving the others. When it was time to go back to the ship, they had begun to get worried and had fired a few warning shots. It grew dark. One of the sailors said he'd had enough, so they had decided to wait another half-hour and then leave.

The lieutenant looked worried and was unsure what to do. The sailors said nothing. The bosun kept spitting out the tobacco he was chewing and frowned.

Calling in to give the captain the evening report, the lieutenant found him absorbed in a game of patience. Sitting in his braces with his collar undone and his face covered in sweat, he looked for all the world like a farmer flushed by his beer. Before him stood a fat little glass and a squat jug of wine. From time to time he filled the glass and sipped from it carefully, licking his black moustache that was streaked with grey. Turning to the lieutenant occasionally, he gazed at him with motionless, red eyes, then flicked his cards once more, saying over and over again:

"The ace to the left, the queen to the right, and now I need the seven. Where on earth's it got to, damn it?"

The game would not come out. Heaving a sigh, the captain shuffled the cards, drained his glass, and asked:

"So you say this idler's disappeared, do you? Tell me what happened then."

The lieutenant told the story again. This time the captain listened much more carefully and did not miss a single word. Then, without letting the officer finish, he banged the table with his palm and said:

"Tomorrow, at first light, send six men ashore and have them search every corner of the island. He's probably got sunstroke. He's a northerner, isn't he?"

"I don't know, sir," replied the lieutenant, "but. . ."

"Of course," said the captain, interrupting him again and narrowing his gimlet eyes, "the whole thing's quite clear. They're weak in the head, these northerners, you know. That's the tenth this voyage. But there's no point worrying about him. If he's dead, then to hell with him, and if he's still alive, then give him a hundred lashes!"

The captain's cabin was becoming rather crowded now. The surgeon had arrived, followed by the chief lieutenant and the quartermaster. After losing three months' pay at faro, the lieutenant remembered that he really ought to send some money to his old mother, so he went off to his cabin. But the close heat there made sleep impossible. The blood roared in his head and he was soon filled with a painful feeling of tension.

He went up on deck and with his mind blank and his body heavy with drowsiness, gazed out for a long time at the dark line of the shore that was as mysterious as the human soul itself. Somewhere there Tart was roaming about or perhaps already lying dead, his face pinched and yellow and his rotting corpse giving off its stench into the night air.

"We'll all die one day," he thought, but then heaved a cheerful sigh as he remembered that he was still alive and that in six months' time he would be going home, back to his old, low-ceilinged house where the sunlit sand glittered and the chestnuts rustled outside.

II

What the Forest Says

When the five sailors came ashore, they decided to stretch their legs before filling the water-barrels, and fired off a couple of rounds at the feathered inhabitants of the island. Tart left his comrades and walked off, making his way through the luxuriant undergrowth and rejoicing like a child at the unprecedented magnificence of the forest. He was surrounded by strange, fantastic thickets. Blue-grey, russet and brown, the tree-trunks shone with their iridescent tracery of light and shadow and lifted their tangled crowns to the sky, their leaves gleaming with every shade of green, from pale to dark. There was no name for this world and Tart gazed at it in silence, scanning its wild beauty with wide-open eyes. It was as if a pair of whimsical scissors had cut a countless multitude of luxuriant patterns from a vast length of green cloth. The sun's rays broke through the trees like golden swords gleaming on emerald velvet. Scores of gaily-coloured birds fluttered and called all around him. Brown with crimson crests, yellow with light blue wings, green flecked with scarlet, black with long purple tails—plumage of every hue flitted about the forest as the birds rose into the air or fussed on their branches. Flying from the mossy shade into a shaft of light, the smallest of them flashed by like brilliant gems whose radiance was suddenly extinguished as they hid behind the leaves. Grass so tall that it resembled low bushes or giant moss swayed in every direction, concealing a life that was full of mystery. The mingled fragrance of the bright flowers made his head spin. There were more of them on the creepers than anywhere else, intertwined in the light like seaweed in sunlit water. White, soft pink, dark blue, and brown with translucent veins, their gorgeous colours wearied the eye, delighting and exciting him at the same time.

Tart walked on like a drunk, intoxicated by the heady air and the unprecedented bounteousness of the earth. Compared with the island, the beech woods of home seemed like a man's bald pate beside a woman's black curls. Filled with curiosity and joyous bewilderment, he flung back his head and watched a troop of monkeys streaking by. Hanging upside down from the trees and swinging their tails as they went, they raced past with a chattering and crashing that frightened the birds. Then the little creatures disappeared and the melodious stillness of the forest rang in his ears once more as he stood motionless, his finger on the trigger of his gun. Then slowly, feeling that someone was watching him, he took a deep breath and instinctively looked round.

But there was no one there. Just as it had a moment ago, the living fabric of greenery still towered above his head, shutting out the sky. The birds still flitted to and fro, and great ripe fruits covered with spines still gleamed yellow in the gloom. Shifting his gaze to the nearest tangle of leaves, he noticed something small and green hanging there like an unripe plum. Suddenly he became aware of the presence of intensely concentrated power just three paces away. The plum swayed very slightly on its invisible stalk, and the sailor stirred uneasily, unable to explain the alarm he felt as he looked at this almost imperceptible fruit. He stretched out his hand but then, suddenly filled with a loathsome quivering, jerked it back. Glittering like molten metal, the flattened head of a small snake sliced through the air and slid away among the leaves. Frowning, he hit it with the barrel of his carbine, and with a faint hiss the creature fell into the grass. He leapt aside and hurried on his way.

From somewhere in the distance came the sound of a shot, and then another: his comrades seemed to be hunting in earnest now. Deep in thought, Tart stopped. Then a third shot echoed through the stillness, and he suddenly realised he had gone further than he should. His legs were tired and he felt thirsty, but his ecstatic feeling of intoxication urged him on, making him walk without realising what he was doing. First he felt as if he were spinning on the spot in a fantastic dance and that everything was living and breathing around him while he remained fast asleep with his eyes wide-open. Then he felt that neither the clipper nor the ocean existed any more, and that he had never lived among his fellow-men at all. Instead, he had always wandered here, listening to the music of quietness, to the sound of his own breathing, and to the voice of distant forebodings that were as indistinct as the dreams of a child.

The forest grew darker as the tree-trunks crowded closer together and the green canopy above his head became more tightly interwoven. His feet sank into the lush carpet beneath them and the calls of the birds gradually died away. Obscure visions went drifting by in the forest twilight and lived their ephemeral lives. Invisible, their countless eyes seemed to throng all around him, glittering like brilliant green insects and shedding dewdrops on his hands before they vanished, as full of reverie as a sad memory. On and on he went, lost in torpor and melancholy.

Finally he could go no further. He was surrounded by a dense wilderness whose darkness breathed the heady smell of rotting vegetation. Stretching out his hands, he touched the delicate tissue of leaves, the moist stems of parasites, and the fine tips of pliant spines. Gasping with the heat, oppressed by unaccountable agitation and anxiety, he lit a wax taper and illumined the green vault that surrounded him. It was as if he were shut in a box. Masses of greenery towered all around him, and gleaming with moisture, the tree-trunks showed dimly through them.

He flung the taper down and, overwhelmed by the darkness, rushed headlong at the green wall. It was the desperate struggle of a man with the forest, of a living body with a well-nigh insuperable obstacle. He took every step by storm. Thousands of flailing branches lashed his face and chest, tearing his flesh and bruising his limbs as the frenzied arms of the forest flung him back again and again. Instinctively, gasping for breath, he tore blindly onwards. Then he halted to fill his lungs before plunging on through the dark wilderness once more.

The light came suddenly, just when he was least expecting it. Exhausted but immensely relieved, wiping his lacerated, sweating face on his shirt-sleeve, he straightened up and opened his eyes. But then with a shudder he closed them again. For a moment, quivering with delight, he could not bring himself to open them, fearing that the unexpected splendour of his surroundings might have been an illusion. But the fiery light penetrated his closed eyes and, filled with glad impatience, he opened them once more.

Before him lay an oval forest clearing that was covered with lush green grass. It was the height of a man's waist, and its brilliant emerald colour was extraordinarily fresh and soft. Some thirty yards away, hiding the nearest trees from view, were rocks of dark pink granite. Forming an irregular arc, they looked like a crooked horseshoe with its ends pointing towards him. There was nothing vast or bulky about them. Instead, pointed and light, as though moulded by slender fingers from reddish wax, they lay sparkling around the edge of the glade like a coral necklace flung down on emerald silk. The iridescent spray of waterfalls rose above them, and dozens of gossamer-fine streams cascaded down in perfect harmony, as though frozen in the air.

There were very many of them. Now side by side, clustering together, they traced an irrepressible pattern of flowing silver against the light, and now in groups of two and three they plunged from their rocky channels into the invisible pool below. Here a solitary cascade leapt from a high crest and hurtled down, scattering its transparent silver in the air. There a glass-smooth stretch of water roared as it burst against the rocks and flung up a glittering shower of spray. Flashing yellow and gold, the tropical sun exulted in the play of sparkling water, while the delicate cascades went on quietly falling, falling, like an endless string of glass beads.

Heaving a sigh, Tart laughed, and a gentle smile played on his face. The trees around the clearing amazed him too, with their dark, spreading roots that rose above the ground. Their broad, green leaves grew lighter as they neared the trunk, growing pale and gleaming translucent the deeper they went, while in the very heart of the tree where they were rose-coloured and slender, they glowed with the pink fire of early dawn.

Again Tart shifted his gaze to the meadow that was so joyously fresh and velvet-green. The bright distance shimmered as the waterfalls played their incessant melody, while the fiery pink leaves deep in the trees revealed all their primordial beauty to the torrential sunlight.

Trembling with instinctive love for this world, Tart stretched out his hand and in his mind's eye touched the crests of the rocks. An unaccountable delight rooted his soul in the deserted forest, and an invisible, tender hand seemed to touch his throat, cramping his breathing with suppressed tears. Then, filling the stillness around him with living sound, he gave a cry, shouting aloud as the tears sparkled in his eyes. The sound of his voice flew to the waterfalls, beat against their jagged rocks, and repeated by the echo, became a song that was impassioned yet simple, a song evoked by his poignant amazement at everything around him:

> Who slumbers at the helm,
> Without opening his eyes?
> Gloomily the stunsails slap,
> The compass swings,
> And the sleeping shore awaits
> Us who are her cheerful guests.
> The drowsy hand grows feeble,

> The helm is silent and still;
> While night—the sailor's menace—
> Conceals an ominous squall;
> It whirls towards us from afar,
> Rages awhile, then vanishes in the gloom.
> The deep is full of terrors,
> But we gaze on ahead,
> To where a sunlit land
> Blossoms with beauties fair.
> Sleep not, sailor! Take a glass of wine,
> Then grasp the wet sail in your hand!
> Into harbour with a chorus of song
> We'll come racing like fearful foes,
> Like a drum on the roadway
> Our merry steps will sound!
> So awake, you gloomy helmsman,
> It's dark, and black as pitch!

Tart was carried away by the melody, and for a long time he went on singing the vigorous yet sad sailor's song. Devoid of desire and almost devoid of thought, deeply moved by the realisation of how little there had been in his life that was as beautiful as the wild paradise of this island—he stood at the edge of the meadow, suddenly and delightfully oblivious of life's burdens and toils, of the grim periods in man's existence when, like a caterpillar, the soul prepares to cast its skin and sleeps for a while before fluttering its brilliant new wings. Festive, joyous days clustered round him and the hands of women he had loved caressed his cheeks like silken hair. Hunting expeditions in his native woods and nights spent under a starry sky rose once more in his memory, full of freedom and solitude, danger and luck. And now, with a heart that was suddenly great and new, he saw himself as he used to be in those hours of reverie, sitting on the slope of deserted hills gazing at the setting sun.

Unslinging his gun, he lay down on the grass and thought with horror of the inevitable day tomorrow—a part of his life given up to others...

The scent of flowers made him dizzy. His arms and legs were trembling with fatigue, his face was burning hot, and there was a pink mist floating before his eyes.

He did not resist. A profound, caressing torpor slowly immersed him in the quiet ocean of sleep, where the untroubled gladness of fulfilled desires holds sway. He slept, and when he woke it was night—starlit, dark and still.

III

Blemer Finds Tart

Tart sat cross-legged by the fire he had lit, listening and thinking. He had not slept that night. A pensive anxiety puckered up his face, and his fingers moved awkwardly as they gathered the shreds of tobacco springing from under his knife. His certainty that no one was watching him lent his face that peculiarly relaxed expressiveness where a man's every muscle and glance reveal his mood just as clearly as the fair copy of a letter. The fire crackled feebly and sputtered, flickering on the smooth steel of his gun and casting its pale light into his eyes. Around him, motionless in the close heat of noon, the forest dozed, but invisible life still quivered in it, stirring the soul with the strange fascination of boundless strength and solitude.

The sailor got to his feet and poured the shredded tobacco into a little tin. Then he picked up his rifle and stood for a long time in silence, listening to the cries of the birds. Occasionally the elusive silhouette of an animal flitted through the foliage before him, and he gave a start. Light alternated with shade in the depths of the forest, and his eyes probed the greenery around him, searching for the horned, graceful creature with its moist black eyes that he had glimpsed in the gloom.

The forest surrounded him with its melodious drowsiness, its smell of swamps and rotting vegetation, and its fabulous, wild beauty. First close by, then further away, the undergrowth rustled as mysterious creatures stirred in it, and in his imagination they either took on monstrous proportions or paled and shrank when the rustling fell silent.

The shrill cry of a bird fluttering up in alarm roused him from his torpor. Instinctively he raised his head but immediately looked down again, cocking his gun as he scanned the bright, rippling leaves.

At first it was hard to say what it was—a small, still shadow or a patch of animal hair. An inquisitive yet cautious presence made itself felt no more than ten yards away, confusing him so much that he was left with nothing but a burning desire to look the creature in the eye. He moved forward softly and was about to give a shout so as to make the animal leap from cover, when suddenly, deep in the green foliage, he glimpsed a glittering black eye. He gave a start and drew himself up. The gun began to shake in his hands but for two or three seconds he could not bring himself to fire—such infinite curiosity and amazement sparkled in the brilliant little eye.

It continued to examine him, drew closer, and then was joined by another. Their searching gaze began to annoy him. It was as if someone were asking: who are you? Raising his gun, he took aim, but then quickly dropped his arm again as he heard the breathless cry:

"Well I'll be damned! It's you, Tart!"

With a sinking feeling he turned towards the shout. There was a furious crashing in the undergrowth as a little pair of twisted horns flashed by and vanished. Blemer's face was streaming with sweat. Bloodshot with fatigue, his eyes searched Tart's face, while his full lips puckered as he did his best to suppress a laugh. Taking off his cap, he wiped his brow with his shirt-sleeve, then yelled again at the top of his powerful voice: "And you managed to get lost, you fool! Three miles long and three across! It's like the bottom of a tea cup, not an island! Of course, some islands have plenty of room for a fellow to walk about on—Ceylon, for instance, or Zeeland—but not this miserable apology! We all thought you'd got eaten by an orang-outang or gone and hanged yourself, but I'm damned glad you haven't!"

He seized Tart's hand and began to shake it, making the fingers crack. Tart looked at him carefully. He knew Blemer would give him away—it would be terribly naive to think otherwise. He was a simple, rather stupid man, kind enough but inclined to be brutal too. Besides, he was indiscreet and not averse to currying favour with his superiors. He was already looking at Tart with a proprietary air, mentally rubbing his hands and smacking his lips in anticipation of the praise that the captain would bestow on him.

He unslung his rifle and with a sigh of relief, began talking again in an effort to reassure himself. Tart's silence disturbed him. Unable to bring himself to say straight out: "Let's go!", he chattered loudly, became confused, and then for the umpteenth time set about describing the general alarm caused by Tart's disappearance. His voice sounded increasingly unsure as the minutes passed, and Tart listened to him more and more absent-mindedly, smiling at first then frowning. He felt as if he were both there and not there, completely himself yet at the same time curiously withdrawn and strange.

"I feel done in," gasped Blemer, "and I'm soaked to the skin. We couldn't leave without you, of course, so they told us to track you down dead or alive... The cook's gone and knocked back a glass of vinegar essence that he mistook for whisky, so he's lying there sick as a dog... and tomorrow they're giving us four months' pay in gold! Silvester's got his eye on my money because I've owed him fourteen crowns ever since Hong Kong, but he can win them back from me first, damn him! Didn't I let him have two brand-new shirts over a game of macao? But d'you know, Tart... they're all saying that

... please don't get angry though... is it true?"

"What?" asked Tart, turning the ramrod in the barrel of his gun.

"Well, you see... now you needn't pretend... But if it isn't true, then it doesn't matter..."

Blemer lowered his voice and his face expressed timid respect. But Tart was busy with his gun. Taking out the wad, he slowly turned the carbine butt upwards, and a shining stream of shot rolled on to the ground.

Blemer was waiting impatiently, and when Tart began to ram in a bullet, tapping loudly against it with the rod, he said:

"That's a live charge you've ruined! Anyway, how can you go hunting now? It's time for dinner."

Tart pulled the ramrod out and looked up. His eyes were tired and sunken, but Blemer failed to see the glint of steadfast resolve in them. He thought Tart wanted to say something, and heaving a sigh, waited for him to answer. But Tart was evidently in no hurry.

"So... is it true, then?" Blemer asked.

"Is what true?" cried Tart, and his eyes blazed with such anger that the sailor instinctively stepped back. "What are all those silly fools saying about me, eh?"

"Tart, what's wrong with you? They're not saying anything, honestly!" replied the sailor hurriedly, "they're just... saying that you..."

"Well, go on then," muttered Tart, taking a deep breath and trying hard to control himself. "What's it all about?"

"Well, you see..." said Blemer, spreading his hands and finding it hard to speak, "... they say that you know all about magic spells and that... you've seen the devil... D'you understand? They say that's why you're always so quiet and... But I don't think it's true because I've seen you with my own eyes reading a prayer-book."

Deeply disturbed, Blemer fell silent. He now believed what everybody said. The living stillness of the forest was agonisingly tense, and he suddenly felt unaccountably afraid, as though the green wilderness were whispering all around him and watching him with its myriad eyes.

Tart made a wry face, then gave a vexed but gentle smile.

"Blemer," he said, "off you go now, and get your dinner. I'm not hungry, and besides, I'm not feeling quite myself."

"What d'you mean?" asked Blemer in amazement, "they're all waiting for you, don't you understand?"

"I'll come later."

"Later?"

"Yes, I don't feel like coming right now."

The sailor gave a hesitant laugh—he simply could not understand it.

"Blemer," said Tart suddenly in a decisive voice and looked away, "go and tell them I'm not coming back. Do you understand? Just say that Tart's staying behind on the island. He doesn't want to serve his country any longer, he doesn't want to grovel or go to places he doesn't like any more. Say you tried to persuade me, you begged and threatened me, but it was no good. Just tell them I said I'd shoot you if you didn't leave me in peace."

Tart took a breath, adjusted his belt and glanced at Blemer's face. He saw how the veins on his temples were throbbing and how he fingered his collar nervously with his right hand, while his eyes darted here and there, round with amazement. There was a silence.

"You're joking," said Blemer, forcing out the words in a stiff voice. "Why the hell are you talking such nonsense? Look, if we set off now we might catch up with the others. It's hard rowing with only two, you know."

"Blemer," said Tart, stamping his foot in annoyance, "I'm not coming, so go back by yourself. This isn't a joke—you know me well enough by now. So go back and say that as far as Tart's concerned, other people no longer exist. He sends his apologies, but he's made up his mind to live by himself. Do you understand?"

Blemer stopped breathing and his frightened eyes searched for the shadow of a smile on Tart's grave face. "He's gone mad!" he thought. "They say there are flowers in these swamps that you shouldn't touch... He's probably gone and picked some of them—that's the kind of fellow he is...!"

"Good-bye," said Tart. "When you get back to the ship, give them all my regards."

He gave a brief sigh, and holding his carbine level, began to walk away. Blemer watched his swaying figure and still could not believe what was happening, but when Tart bent down and plunged into the dazzling green forest, he could not contain himself any longer. Choking with sudden anger and afraid that Tart might escape, he ran across the clearing, cocking his gun as he went, and shouted to where the undergrowth swayed and crashed:

"Hey! Stop, or I'll kill you!"

The sound of his voice was lost without trace in the green wilderness. He waited a moment then suddenly, with angry haste, fired. With a drawling whine the bullet whistled through the air, snorting as it smashed through the leaves in its path. The birds fell silent and the forest was filled with an oppressive stillness.

"Stop!" he yelled again, dashing off in pursuit. "You deserter! You swine!"

Brandishing his rifle and stumbling in his agitation, he took a dozen more steps, but then caught sight of Tart again and suddenly felt his excitement subside. Tart had his finger on the trigger and was aiming at his chest.

Instinctively, trying to shield himself, Blemer stepped back and began to take aim too. But because of his confusion, he did not find the foresight straightaway. He swore angrily and stood stock-still, expecting Tart to fire. Tart looked up. Sweating with fear, Blemer drew back and pulled the trigger. At that very moment Tart's bullet pierced him through as easily as a needle passes through canvas.

What had once been Blemer sank to the ground, then stretched out, spread its legs and lay still. The air wheezed in its lungs and the bared head quivered as the body struggled to rise and ward off a second shot. With a pained smile Tart squatted down beside the wounded man and pulled from his clenched fists the grass he had torn up as he writhed on the ground. Unable to do anything more for him, he knelt there, filled with silent alarm.

Gulping back the blood welling in his throat, Blemer turned his head and swore. Tart seemed like a monster to him, almost a cannibal. He looked up, and seeing the hot, blue sky, remembered about death.

"You're a swine, a swine!" he groaned. "Why did you do it?"

"Stop asking stupid questions," answered Tart, tearing a length of material off the bottom of his shirt. "You were hunting me down just like an animal, but you'd forgotten that this animal knows how to shoot. If it weren't you, then it'd be me lying here now—the whole thing was unavoidable."

He made an improvised bandage and unbuttoning Blemer's jacket, tried to staunch the blood. But the warm, sticky liquid seeped through his fingers and he could feel the heart beating feebly under his hand. He pressed harder on the bandage, making Blemer wince and frown.

"The pain's hellish," he said through clenched teeth, his breathing loud and raucous. "Stop it, you'll not do any good. The bullet's gone right through and I'm done for. You're laughing, you bastard!. . ."

"No I'm not," replied Tart with a grave smile. "Forgive me, I didn't mean to do it."

Without looking away for a moment, he gazed into the sailor's pinched face. There were bluish shadows around the eyes now, and the broad, unshaven chin jutted sharply upwards.

"The grass is damp," groaned Blemer, shifting his body a little. "I'm going to die, d'you know that? But what for?"

Indifferently serene and distant, the sky shone blue, while here on the ground, bathed in the cold sweat of his agony, a man was dying—a sacrifice to free will.

"Blemer," said Tart, "you were walking through this forest looking for me and you found me. But if I didn't want to come with you, what made you think you could try to force me without getting hurt?"

"Go to hell!" groaned Blemer, spitting out pink saliva. "You're just a bastard and a traitor!" He was silent for a while but soon began to moan again, so loudly now that Tart shuddered. The wounded man made a last desperate effort to lift his head. His eyes were covered with the film of death and he began to seem like little more than a red ant that has been crushed underfoot.

"Are you in much pain?" asked Tart.

"Pain? Ha!" cried Blemer, "I know you're a deserter and a swine, Tart, but just remember, I beg you, that there's a sick bay on the *Aurora*!... Run back and tell them I'm dying!..."

Tart shook his head. Blemer kept stretching out, first resting his head on the ground and moving his arms, then pressing his back to the damp grass once more. A spasm ran swiftly over his pale, drawn face, and he began to curse. Softly at first then more and more loudly, he muttered a complex stream of foul abuse. Tart watched and waited, and when Blemer's eyes became glazed, started to load his gun.

"Just bear it a little longer, Blemer," he said, "it'll all be over soon."

Blemer did not reply, but through his lips that were bitten till the blood came, Tart sensed a host of cries suppressed by fury and suffering. He walked away to one side so that Blemer would not guess what he was about to do, then aimed at the back of his head and fired.

Blemer quivered, sighed and lay still.

Now he was dead. The green throng of forest grass clustered round his strong body and, swaying in the breeze, peered into his face.

IV

"Rooster Street, Garnash"

On the beach, almost at the water's edge, in the shade of an enormous waringin tree, stood a stout oak barrel tightly covered with a tarpaulin. There was no lock on it because it was an international post-box. Letters addressed to all corners of the earth were dropped into it from passing ships. A vessel bound for Australia picked up the mail for Australia, while one bound for Europe did the same.

The clipper made ready to sail. With slow persistence the heavy windlass creaked as it turned on its iron mountings. The cable crept from the water, dragging with it the anchor that was thickly covered with seaweed, shells and slime. Listless with the heat, the men wandered over the deck making fast the rigging, or sat on the yards unfurling the bone-dry sails. Just then a boat with six men in it came ashore, and jumping out on to the sand, the clipper's second lieutenant went up to the barrel. Folding back the tarpaulin, he took out several packages and dropped in a bundle of letters.

Then they all rowed away and soon were only a black speck moving on the water. Slowly the clipper was transformed, as from yard to yard, hiding the masts, her voluminous sails bellied with the wind. She was like a bird hanging motionless in the air—the embodiment of tense expectation and swift flight, of power held firmly in check and impatience to be away.

Slowly her bowsprit described a semicircle from west to southeast. She came heavily about, her rudder stirring the dark blue water of the anchorage to foam. Now she looked like a man turning his back on a night's resting place that he is about to leave forever. The trail of foam stretched out in an even line at her stern and the ship was under way.

Moving like a low-flying albatross, she grew smaller and paler, her graceful white shape heeling slightly as she went. And from the shore of the luxuriant island a man watched her go. It was Tart.

He waited with indifference for the clipper to disappear. She carried away with her a few dozen fellow-countrymen, monotonous discipline, paltry pay and nothing more. Everything he needed was here, close at hand. He could walk about as he pleased, eat and drink when he liked, and do just as he wished. Thankfully, he cast from his shoulders the burden which people describe with that terrible, brief word "homeland", without realising it should mean the country where a person is born and nothing more.

He watched the clipper sail away, knowing full well that it was he whom they considered responsible for Blemer's death. But why had they given up the search for him? Why was it that only six days after his disappearance the ship had set sail for Australia? Did they think he was dead? But everybody knew the island was just not big enough for them to give up hope of finding a man or at least his remains on it. The *Aurora*'s behaviour irritated Tart and he felt offended. Extremely headstrong and proud by nature, he was used to his enemies treating him as they would a foe in war. But wasn't the clipper running away from him now?

He remembered his hiding-place—a rocky ravine with a roof of flowering bushes and a floor as smooth as parquet. There was nothing surprising about the fact that the ship had left without finding him. As far as her crew was concerned, Tart must have drowned. Besides, who was particularly worried about Blemer? There were a hundred sailors on board, so two fewer could hardly make any difference. Moreover, it was a busy time, with Chinese pirates weaving in and out of the archipelago like wasps, so a patrolling man-of-war couldn't remain idle for long.

Tart walked slowly along the shore, his head sunk on his chest. His position seemed very clear: if he felt like leaving the island, he would keep a look-out for a passing merchantman, and then light a bonfire in the dark. That signal would bring him a brief refuge on an unfamiliar deck. But where would he go, what for, why?

He did not think about that, though. Terrifying in all its boundlessness, freedom breathed in his face, carried by the moist wind stirring the damp foliage that was limp in the heat. His was the desperate ecstasy of a gambler who has put everything he possesses on a single card and won more than his stake. But having triumphed, he does not ask himself what he will do with the money or think of making any plans, for the music of gold sets his heart pounding and fills him with a whirlwind of tantalising desires that are breathtakingly splendid yet utterly impracticable. Tomorrow, perhaps, fate may take from him all that he has won today, but tomorrow is still a long way off, is it not?

How magnificent is the unknown!

Slowly, obeying a feeling of curiosity that was mingled with foreboding, Tart folded back the tarpaulin, and standing on the stones laid at the base of the barrel, opened it. Down at the bottom a heap of packets showed grey. There were about twenty of them, and he looked at them all carefully.

It was strangely pleasurable to hold in his hands the material traces left by people who had gone away, and to talk to them, as it were, without their knowing anything about it. He was particularly interested in the sailors' letters, and examined their awkward handwriting with care, dimly suspecting that they might have said something about him. Disturbed by the idea, he set aside a few envelopes that were addressed to places near where he had been born. He began to search for the very closest fellow-countryman, rummaging in the barrel with fingers that quivered with impatience and spreading the grey envelopes out on the sand. Then suddenly he read:

"Rooster Street, Garnash."

Garnash! He had been born only ten miles from that little town! He could still remember its carts laden with vegetables and its dusty street that he used to run down as a boy! He laid a bet with himself that the person who had written the letter was none other than fat Rill.

Yes, here was his name, printed in block capitals! Tart took out his knife and slit the thick envelope. Rill had written a lot. He had completely covered four sheets with scrawl, giving details of the voyage, telling of things he had seen, and sending awkwardly affectionate greetings to his wife. Tart scanned the lines hurriedly. Then suddenly his fingers began to tremble and his face turned pale with alarm. His eyes flashed as he threw the letter down and instinctively seized his rifle.

But all around him everything was as deserted as before. The gentle surf still rustled the dry sea-weed and stirred the round pebbles at his feet. As though imprinted on his memory were the lines of the letter he had crumpled up and flung aside: "...if he's dead, then it serves him right. But we think he's still alive, so we'll come back in four days' time, and should catch him without any trouble, because he'll be walking about quite freely by then. Six men against one is easy enough. They say, God forgive me, that he's taken up with the devil, but I don't know if it's true."

"I must get away!" muttered Tart, struggling to regain his composure. What he had just read seemed utterly fantastic. Everything around him suddenly looked different, cowering stock-still like a frightened crowd. The sun seemed to have lost its fiery heat while his legs had become heavy and his movements immensely slow, as though his body had been turned to stone by a paroxysm of blind rage. His thoughts had lost their fluency too, as he concentrated only on the painful feeling that there were invisible enemies around him. All of a sudden a silent loathing for this hidden danger welled up from the depths of his soul, together with an unbearable yearning to put an end to it all.

"Six?" asked Tart, coming to a halt. "So there are six of you, are there?"

The blood rushed to his head and blinded him for a moment. Almost unaware of what he was doing, he raised his gun with a defiant gesture and pulled the trigger. The shot echoed through the stillness, and then immediately, without the slightest unnecessary movement, he quickly reloaded.

As before, silence reigned—the uncanny silence of a desert island at noon. He listened, and the silence exasperated him, and shaking his fist, he burst into a torrent of abuse. Then, weakened by his fit of anger, he walked on, smashing through the undergrowth and knocking off the succulent leaves with his gun as he went. Realising that escape was impossible now and that someone must have heard his shot, he felt both immense audacity and gay indifference. His confidence was restored as the minutes passed and the forest's green embrace folded closer around him, enveloping him in fragrant gloom. On he walked, while behind him and catching up with him ran his six pursuers, stopping now and then to listen to the rustling sounds made by their quarry.

"Tart!" shouted a tall, black-haired sailor who was breathless with running. "Hey, Tart, wait a minute!"

And after him all the rest cried urgently:

"Tart!"

"Hey, Tart!"

"Tart! Tart!"

He turned almost with relief, with the gladness of a warrior parrying the first blow. And immediately the six all stopped.

"We're looking for you," said the black-haired man. "It is you, isn't it? Hello, old fellow! Your leave's over now, so perhaps you'll come with us!"

"Tomorrow," said Tart, turning the butt of his gun over and over in his hands. "I don't want to see you. And what d'you want me for? Leave me alone. What good will it do you if I go back to that clipper? None at all. I want to stay here, and that's all there is to it. I've nothing more to say.

"Tart!" shouted another of the six, a thin little peasant who was very frightened now, "you're finished. I know it's all the same to you because you're done for, but we're serving our country and we've been ordered to find you!"

"I don't give a damn for your country!" said Tart scornfully. "You bloody fool! I expect you're going to say it's my country too, aren't you? Well I've spent three years on that lousy ship of yours, and now I want to live, not serve my country! Do I have to waste the best years of my life just because there are a few million fools like you? Every man for himself, my friend!"

"Tart," said a third sailor who had a round, stupid-looking face, "it's all over now, so don't try to resist. We'll kill you, you know, if..."

But he did not have time to finish. The moment the wisp of smoke rose from Tart's gun his body slumped into the bushes and began to sway to and fro on the pliant branches with its legs spread wide. Using his pistol now, Tart took aim again, and because of the momentary confusion among the sailors, he managed to hit another of them... With his mouth wide open, the black-haired man went down on all fours, gasping for air.

Then everything went dark before Tart's eyes.

Calmly he faced the shots fired in reply, then a bullet passed through his hand, and he dropped his gun. But he quickly picked it up again with the other hand and fired at someone's white face that was distorted with fear.

Then he fell, and for an agonisingly long time could not understand why shots kept flashing around him and why a dull pain smashed again and again into his body as he lay on the ground. And then everything became a dream. Delicate waterfalls sparkled in the sunlight and shimmered on rosy granite glistening with spray, while a velvet-green glade spread away to the dark roots of trees whose leaves glowed fiery pink like little furnaces. Then, as swift as an arrow, silence fell, closing the eyes of what had once been Tart.

1909

He Came and Went

I

When Battle threw his kit-bag on his bed and looked up, he saw three men standing in front of him. The trio were examining the newcomer with the intent stare of an inquisitive parrot. Long-haired, sleepy and half-naked because of the intolerable heat, they shifted idly from one foot to the other. Battle's new uniform reminded them dimly of what life had been like back in the regiment.

"You've got yourself into a real hole," said one of them, a former clerk. "Did they put you on a serious charge, then?"

"Not at all," Battle replied. "I was transferred here at my own request."

The soldiers exchanged glances and grinned.

Battle frowned.

"What's wrong?" he asked uneasily. "You should've lived in Poket for a bit like I did—it was so depressing and boring there. Serving here's probably more dangerous and it might be a harder life, but square-bashing's a thousand times worse."

"So you reckon life's harder here then?" asked another of the three, a giant of a man with a straw-coloured beard.

"Yes, I do."

"The worst thing of all," declared the third soldier, "is the lousy water. It gives you terrible stomach-ache. There's a lot of lime and sand round here, you see, and the water's so bad it makes you feel as if someone's scraping your guts out all the time."

Battle examined the speaker's face carefully, but could find no trace of mockery in it. A few moments later he was left alone, as his new comrades went off—to cart water.

After standing for a while amid the dusty heat that rose from the baked clay walls, he went out into the yard.

Scurrying about under his feet, an enormous number of hens filled the fort with their clucking. He counted no fewer than two hundred of them. A herd of fat pigs blocked his path by the steps leading up to the commandant's quarters. As if that was not enough, movement across the yard was hindered by linen sheets and women's chemises hung out to dry on lines that stretched in every direction.

There were no human voices to be heard. Not far away, though, someone was strumming a crude native instrument whose harsh twanging jarred on the ear. Battle walked towards the sound, and turning a corner of the rampart, came upon a little garden overgrown with something that looked like enormous dusty lettuces. There, at a large wooden table, sat five people—three men and two women.

Hanging his head, the commandant had his legs stretched out and was smoking gloomily. The two junior officers, their heads cropped almost bare, were drinking from grimy glasses, sucking a cloudy liquid through reed straws. Very sunburnt, the younger of the two women was yawning all the time, while the other, who had an air of extreme lassitude, kept running her fingers over the strings of an instrument that looked rather like a pair of tongs. All five of them were drinking whisky. Dishevelled and half-naked, stultified by heat, liquor and idleness, they hardly even bothered to move—except perhaps to pick up their glass or drive away a fly.

Battle stood there for about five minutes but did not hear them say a single word. They seemed to be vying with each other in the art of keeping silent. Then he climbed the rampart that was overgrown with coarse, prickly grass. The boundless desert surrounding the fort shimmered like burnished metal in the heat. The place was forgotten both by the enemy and by life itself. And where was the enemy anyway? The truth stirred dimly somewhere at the back of Battle's mind. Perhaps about thirty years ago these crude earthworks really had held the natives along the border in check... but now... He gave an enormous yawn.

From on top of the rampart he examined the interior of the fort. In corners, among the outbuildings and in the cool shade of roofs and walls, several soldiers were asleep. He looked at them until he saw the giant with the straw-coloured beard whom he had met earlier. The big fellow was lying on his side with his knees pulled up under his chin like an infant in its mother's womb, and was snoring loudly. There was something pathetic about the way he lay there.

II

Ten tedious, empty days drove Battle into a cold fury. At night, in an effort to amuse himself, he would eat the fruit-drops he had brought from Poket, and muse on all the adventures that had failed to materialise.

When he stood guard, he talked to his shadow. Radiant with pleasure at being so full, the moon followed his movements with her chill, harsh light, and his rifle gleamed like mother-of-pearl. Slowly he walked from the powder magazine to the cookhouse and back again. Canopied with its thousands of white and blue stars, the desert came striding over the ramparts into the fort. The silence of despair kept senseless watch over the solitary man. His steps became more and more measured and slow, as though he were gradually falling prey to profound depression.

Finally, on one of these nights, Battle turned his weary face to the moon. He was *afraid*. Fear had first stirred in him the moment he imagined the vast expanse of distance separating the fort from all the railways and cities so far away. But the silent, moonlit night affected him much more deeply than his sense of geographical isolation. Tears of resentment welled up in his breast, for he was active, restless, and above all, still young.

After walking about the yard for two hours, Battle became a criminal, and for thirty minutes behaved irresponsibly.

But no one ever found out. Smashed by the point of his bayonet, the padlock on the powder magazine door broke from its fastenings and fell to the ground. He struck a match and went through the low, square doorway. The close air and the squeaking of mice that he encountered inside were highly suspicious. Then there rang out the most terrible oaths ever uttered by man, for apart from a few empty powder kegs that had long since rotted away, the magazine was completely empty.

A lump of clay fell from the ceiling and hit Battle on the back of the head. He came outside again to find himself bathed in mocking moonlight. Then, without hurrying, he hung the lock back in its place. There had been an explosion—though only in his imagination. But there had been an explosion of a different kind too: the man who had failed to blow the fort to smithereens was suddenly only a ruin of his former self.

"The firework display didn't come off," he muttered, covering up the traces of what he had done, "but it wasn't my fault."

III

The next morning witnessed a rare occurrence. Dressed in full kit, a man walked out of the fort. It was Battle.

He came out of the barracks to the bewilderment and disapproval of his silent fellow-soldiers, crossed the yard squashing a chick on the way, and passed through the gates. Just then the commandant climbed to the top of the rampart, accompanied by his wife and a lieutenant.

"Who's that, Sils?" he asked, seeing the erect figure walking steadily away.

"It looks like one of our men, sir," replied the officer languidly. "He's walking. . . yes. . . walking. . . somewhere. . ."

"Why?"

"Difficult to say, sir," replied the lieutenant after a long pause.

"At least, I don't think I can answer that question."

"He's quite small now," exclaimed the commandant's wife.

No one replied. The three people watched Battle walk mysteriously away. Across the plain shimmering with brilliant light he walked, no bigger than a toy soldier. On and on he went, without turning round or stopping, moving with steady strides towards the grey strip of forest that looked like a delicate, pensive eyebrow on the distant horizon.

"Why's he going further and further away?" asked the commandant thoughtfully, watching Battle growing smaller still.

"Is he. . . running away?"

"Running?. . . No, he's walking," the lieutenant replied.

A silence fell. The sun rose higher in the sky and several soldiers who had climbed the rampart shaded their eyes with their hand.

But Battle had disappeared amid the glitter of sun and sand.

Then the commandant said:

"Sils, send someone to ask that man what he's looking for out there, would you?"

"We're just seeing things," the woman remarked. "It's only a speck of dust."

"Possibly," said the commandant.

"It's just a trick of the light," said Sils.

And with a sigh, they went down to the table in the garden.

1910

The Death of Romelink

I

Romelink was not content with life. However, an abundant supply of money and constant travelling enabled him occasionally to suppress the chill melancholy of spirit that was the real reason for the restless life he had led for several years now, moving from one place to another with almost no curiosity whatsoever. His intent, steady gaze paused on all things and registered every detail, even the intonation of a voice, but the world passed before him with an existence of its own that was forever strange to him, like a forest glimpsed from a speeding train.

Now that he was over forty it was perhaps rather late to believe in a happy accident, an extraordinary and delightful change in his existence, and the idea of it lay buried somewhere deep in the storehouse of other thoughts that in their time had been full of life and vigour too. Romelink lived with his eyes but he looked upon the world with neither surprise nor envy, full of unconscious benevolence towards everything, absolutely everything, that did not disturb the peace he had gradually acquired over the years. He drew on this small acquisition extremely sparingly, taking care to avoid any kind of disturbance, psychological or otherwise, where he might leave behind a part of himself without receiving any return for it.

After visiting America and Africa, his thoughts had turned to Australia. Now he was sailing there on a splendid English liner, filled with boredom amid her boundless comforts and surrounded by faces that rapidly became familiar at the table d'hôte. There, interminable arguments went on about colonial policy and stock-exchange prices, while the names of cities scattered over the globe were constantly to be heard. On board this ship the world resembled a gigantic hotel from whose rooms dozens of people had emerged and gathered by chance in the same corridor. Most of the passengers were travelling with their families. They were newly-appointed civil servants and officers, two or three tourists with effete European faces, and a handful of women.

Usually Romelink would stay in his cabin until evening. Then—when the ocean and sky began to cool and the velvet expanse of sea glowed red against clouds that resembled distant, snow-capped peaks—he would come up on deck, sit down by the rail and smoke. As he gazed out over the ocean, the stars were born before his eyes and the mysterious silence of night gradually filled the expanse around him. Lingeringly, like nocturnal birds on the wing, his silent thoughts would carry his soul to the shores of distant continents where images of the past faded and died.

II

One Friday the ship left Bombay, and on the following Monday a group of small islands appeared to the south.

"Coral reefs," said the captain to Romelink when the passenger brought his wandering gaze to bear on them. "We're sailing through an archipelago, so there are many more of them to come."

He began to tell of the strange flora found on atolls, the peace of their lagoons, and the sharp teeth of coral lying deep in the limpid water. But after thanking him, Romelink walked away to the quarter-deck. He always liked to learn about things for himself.

When evening came he was filled with melancholy once more. The feeling brought with it a strange yearning that always accompanied him in open spaces everywhere, be it desert or ocean, wide river or plain. A light mist hung low over the horizon as the ship rolled on the gentle swell, and the dimming sun sank into the distant ocean like a crimson sphere. The heads of the passengers sitting by the rail were outlined against the evening sea like pale sketches for a watercolour.

It grew dark and the swell became heavier. There were fewer stars than usual, and only the brightest of them could be seen through the mist, gleaming like dull gold. Romelink got up from his seat and just then the officer of the watch and the first lieutenant went by. They bade him good evening and then were lost in the gloom. They were talking about something. Romelink only caught one word of what they were saying, and he repeated it mechanically:

"Barometer."

As he stood in the doorway of his cabin with his face turned to the wind gusting through the open porthole, he felt a momentary urge to acknowledge something that had recently filled him with growing disquiet. Though his soul was not profoundly stirred by it, a series of words flashed through his mind that resembled numbers in their stark simplicity:

"My name's Romelink. I'm in my forties. I used to be a tobacco manufacturer. I worked hard. Now I'm rich. I travel a lot. It's boring."

He switched on the light, undressed, and before falling sound asleep as he always did, read a chapter of Lubbock* that talked about the joy of being alive, of feeling and seeing.

III

All of a sudden Romelink's sleep was disturbed by a series of jolts, but his body overcame them immediately without releasing him from his state of drowsy torpor. Dimly, and physically rather than consciously, he kept sensing a shift in his centre of gravity, as one minute his legs came to rest against the cabin wall and the next slowly pulled his body down after them. His arms kept slipping towards his knees, and sometimes it seemed as if the whole of him were full of heavy weights that were rolling about inside him, pressing his chest down on the bed and then releasing it before beginning their slow, silent movement once more. At one point he was shaken very violently and woke up completely, but realising that the ship was rolling heavily, took refuge in sleep as before.

He came to once and for all when he felt himself falling to the floor. He flailed his arms convulsively but his hands met nothing but air, and then a heavy blow on the head stunned him for a moment. Leaping up, he spread his legs like a sailor on a pitching deck, but could not keep his feet and was flung into a corner of the cabin. Suitcases, chairs and other things crashed around him, while the concepts of floor and ceiling kept disappearing as the cabin first seemed to topple over on top of him and then briefly regained its former position. Dazed and afraid, he made incredible efforts to stay in one place, trying to get up and keep his limbs steady. But the raging ocean robbed his movements of all co-ordination, depriving him of weight and the ability to control his body. He was like a little toy—a cardboard clown flinging out its arms and legs and tossing its head, yet remaining inexorably on the spot.

Stumbling and sprawling, he crawled to the rail where his clothes were hanging. It was as hard for him to dress as it is for a chimney-sweep to stay clean. Frightened now by the storm, he was in a hurry to get up on deck. Bewildered and exhausted, he held on to the edge of his bunk with his left hand, while with his right he straightened the parts of his clothing that required particular attention. From the deck above came a muffled rumbling and the

---

*Sir John Lubbock (1834-1913), author of scientific works on anthropology, archaeology and botany, as well as of popular philosophical studies, eg. *The Pleasures of Life* (1887) and *Peace and Happiness* (1909) (translator's note).

drumming and stamping of feet, while ragged waves lashed through the open porthole, flinging spray across the cabin and sending pools of foam washing from wall to wall. Whipped to a frenzy by the storm, the night sea was waking in all its cruel fury. Bumping into the sides of the panelled corridor where the cabin doors kept swinging open then slamming shut again, Romelink lurched towards the companionway, clutching at the hand-rail as he went. A minute later he was on deck, clinging to the lever of a derrick.

To begin with he could not breathe because the wind lashing the deck was so strong. The salt spume of wave-crests beat him in the face as the ship plunged and reared, lurching wildly from side to side. In the flickering, murky light of the lanterns dark shapes ran by, clutching at rails, shrouds and hatches before being lost in the gloom. They kept shouting indistinct orders, questions and oaths, cries that sounded like the hoarse trumpeting of bugles or the agonised groans of wounded. It was quite impossible to walk. Romelink gave a cry but nobody paid him the slightest attention.

Over the deck rushed a frightened crowd that kept clutching at each other, falling down and crawling on hands and knees. All the sensations that Romelink had ever experienced were gone now, and a new, totally unfamiliar agitation filled his breast together with his heart which was hammering so dangerously that it seemed made of metal. Soaked to the skin, barefoot and hatless, he felt as if he had become one with the derrick. His arms ached with the constant exertion, and it seemed as though the darkness were trying with all its might to tear the lever from his clenched fingers and in an instant fling him to the deck.

He remembered everything else later. It was a sickeningly chill nightmare of water, jolting, wind and panic. Suddenly the ship leapt up, his knees gave way with the shock, and the vessel was filled with a muffled groaning that seemed to come from the bowels of the earth. Echoing from her masts to her keel, a prolonged rending sound rumbled through her holds then died away. All of a sudden the deck tilted until it was almost vertical, so that Romelink struck his chin against the derrick and clung there for a time, hanging out over the void with the wind shrieking in the rigging high above. Suddenly he was seized by an insuperable feeling of weakness. He felt ready to let go, give himself up to the frenzied horror of the elements, and be engulfed—but the cries ringing out nearby roused his instinct for self-preservation.

"Put out the boats! Cut the tackle with axes! Women and children first!"

Slowly, like a wild beast rising to its feet after being seriously wounded, the ship righted herself. Letting go of the derrick,

Romelink dropped to the deck and crawled forward. A huddle of half-naked men and women were crowding by the rail in front of him, while slung out over the side, a lifeboat swung to and fro. Romelink got up, grabbed hold of a girder, and quickly found himself in the middle of the crowd, but as he did so he noticed that the boat was already full. Just then it suddenly became light as day as a clap of thunder made sea and sky one, and he caught sight of a towering, streaming wall just a few yards from the ship's side. "It's a rock!" he thought, and only in the darkness that followed the flash of lightning was he frozen motionless with terror, filled with the agonising chill felt by a man hurtling into the abyss. It was a wave.

He had no time either to prepare himself or lose his head. Rooted to the spot, in a single instant he experienced in his imagination the blow of the mountain of water before it hit the ship, and the experience was like death itself. Then the furious wave knocked him off his feet and almost choked him. Ringing in his ears and lifting him up as if he were as light as a feather, it flung him over the side.

IV

At first Romelink spun round and round in the deep whirlpool of water flooding off the ship, then he began to kick out with his feet and struggled to the surface. The waves rolled by with a muffled roar, rearing beneath him, sweeping him along on their foaming backs, and then flinging him down into their watery troughs. Keeping as calm as he could, he turned on his back, trying to move as little as possible to avoid becoming tired too quickly, and remained like that for several minutes. But it soon became unthinkable to stay in this position any longer—the water kept filling his nose and mouth, and the occasional deep breaths that he did manage to take were at the expense of strength-sapping periods when he had to stop breathing altogether. Exhausted, he turned over and began to swim, trying to shield his face as much as he could from the lashing waves and driving spray flung up by the wind. His sodden clothes weighed him down and made swimming very difficult, but it was quite impossible to throw them off: devoid of all rhythm, the haphazard movement of the waves sent the water first this way then that, threatening to turn him over at the slightest careless movement—something that could cost him several mouthfuls of salt water. From time to time a brief roll of thunder shook the gloom and a deathly pale flash of lightning revealed the raging, greenish sea.

These moments of desperate yet absurdly careful struggle to

save a life that was already surely lost, were not moments of fear for Romelink. Fear would have been too insignificant a thing to cause him suffering now. Instead, he was experiencing something very much greater than that—he was looking into the eyes of Death. Those eyes had robbed him of all awareness, all will. He himself, his soul, were gone now, and only his body was left, submitting blindly to Death and yet fighting for one more breath, one more movement of a finger. It was the hopeless haggling of a man with oblivion, of blood with water, of instinct with the storm, of failing strength with the yawning abyss. He felt neither despair nor faith in salvation. He was merely a writhing automaton with a heart full of agony and darkness.

At the very moment when his strength was ebbing away—as intolerable cramp gripped his legs, thousands of needles coursed through his body, and he felt as heavy as lead—just then there came another clap of thunder and a few slivers of light fell upon the sea. He caught a brief glimpse of a plank and the keel of a lifeboat overturned by the storm. With the terrible swiftness lent by a sudden surge of despair, his hands lunged from the water to grip the wet wood and his chest struck something hard. For a few more anguished moments he prolonged the insanity of his superhuman efforts to breathe, holding on till his fingers ached with the unbearable pain. And yet this pain seemed like the bliss of paradise.

V

Coming to with a dull ache filling his body, Romelink got to his feet and, dazzled by the light, closed his eyes. He was standing on the beach of a small coral island, right at the water's edge. Not far away lay a lifeboat, its keel uppermost. Near the stern, lying on her back with her face towards him, was a young woman who was half-naked.

He should have been amazed and immensely glad to see someone white-skinned who was perhaps still alive, but at first a sense of physical joy at his own survival blinded him to everything else. Then, mechanically and still reeling with weakness, he went up to her, lifted her by the shoulders and listened. She was breathing, but only faintly, and her compressed lips and deep pallor showed that she was in a dead faint.

Tired by this slight exertion, Romelink sat down on the sand. With his head spinning and his body quivering with fatigue, he gazed intently into the woman's face. He remembered her: she had been travelling with her brother and had probably survived as he himself had by clinging to the keel of the lifeboat. Perhaps their fingers had intertwined as, battered senseless by the storm, they were swept along in the water.

As the voice of his saved life began to speak within him, Romelink looked up, and his face broke into an irrepressible smile. He started to laugh with a convulsive little chuckle that grew louder and louder, filled as he was with half-crazed ecstasy at the light blue sky, the palms and the boundless expanse of sea. He felt like a man who has been reborn. He looked at the sand, feeling extraordinarily good as he watched the play of the breakers, and rocked to and fro as the happy laughter rose in his throat. He was alive. It was as if the ocean had washed him clean inside and out, rousing all his dulled instincts with the horror of death. At this moment the earth seemed like paradise and his wretchedly inert existence as splendid as the gaze of a deity or the flight of fancy. Now he was no longer Romelink, a melancholic, or a former tobacco manufacturer, but a man who felt miraculously new.

The woman groaned. He went up to her and bending down, did all he could to bring her round. His efforts met with some success, for she opened her eyes and closed them again. Then he saw that she was strikingly beautiful, and a strange feeling of infinite love, swift as thought itself, filled his soul with warmth. He stretched out his arms...

Suddenly something heavy and cold rent his chest, spasms gripped his throat, and a strange roaring echoed through his body. Then came pain, darkness and death.

*　　　*　　　*　　　*

The storm went on. Rolling over and over like an empty bottle, Romelink's twisted body floated in the water, and after a while sank gently to the bottom.

1910

The Pillory

I

While the settlers of Canterville colony were roaming the swamps uprooting tree-stumps so enormous that half a dozen men could sit on them dangling their feet with ease, while they were busy with the rude tasks of satisfying their hunger, struggling against nomadic elements in the country, and sinking piles for the foundations of their homes—the strictest devotee of morality could have accused them of nothing more than a liking for forceful expressions.

But when the houses were built, the fields ploughed, a few signs put up bearing inscriptions such as "school", "hotel" and "prison", and when life had started to take its tediously functional course, like water flowing down a drain-pipe—events began to occur. The first of them was when the inveterate miser Glasin lost everything he had to the spendthrift Petagr, who was fond of living it up: he lost his house, horses, clothes and farm machinery, and was left only in his underwear.

Then came thefts, a forged will, and a barricade at the crossroads when three madmen armed with revolvers defended their right to own a plot of land. One of them got killed and was found later with a cigar clenched firmly between his teeth. One settler's wife ran away, while another, who had two small children and a delightful spouse, was visited by a beautifully dressed, tearful woman from the far west who had somehow found out his address. She had magnificent, brand-new luggage and ginger hair. But what most annoyed the big-boned women and bearded men of Canterville—people who, let it be said, had tasted all the delights of crude flirtation during the eight months they had spent in their immigrants' tents—was the infamous abduction of the charming Daisy Krok, a deed unworthy of any respectable man. She was very pretty and quiet, and whoever looked at her for a while began to feel as if his body were wrapped in bright, quivering gossamer. Daisy had many admirers but it was Goan Gnor who abducted her one evening, when looking down the dusty street lit up by the setting sun, it was hard to make out whether the oxen were fighting on their way back from the watering-place or whether someone on horseback had his hand over a girl's mouth and was hoisting her into the saddle. Goan had always been courteous, even though he did live by himself—something which, as everyone knows, tends to make a man rather coarse. So no-one would ever have expected such an act of folly from him.

One thing is certain, though: at a dance a week earlier Goan had talked quietly to the girl for a long time. Those watching saw him standing there looking very pale and sad and not at all himself. "I don't love anyone, Goan, believe me," said the girl. A woman who overheard these words was in the seventh heaven for three days and kept repeating them to her friends with various intonations and comments. After the abduction Goan's horse stumbled in a gully as it raced along the edge of the forest, and broke a leg, with the result that the offender was caught exactly an hour after committing his crime.

The crowd of riders who gathered where the horse had fallen was so dense that it was impossible to make anything out at all in the mass of furiously whirling arms and legs. Finally, the ring of people broke up and the girl was dragged away into the bushes in a faint. Despite the fact that Goan had already been crushed by his horse, Daisy's brothers, father and uncle beat him for a long time in silence, and then, sweating and exhausted, walked away, their eyes flashing with anger. Then the battered semblance of a man rose from the ground, spitting thick blood. Goan's face was covered with enormous bruises, and he was pitiful to behold as he staggered away, making wheezing noises that sounded like words.

Though in this instance there were no clear reasons to deprive Goan of his life, the imperfect laws of those remote parts nevertheless called him to account for his grave affront to the Krok family and the girl. After a great deal of wrangling and uproar, a wooden post was driven into the ground in front of the hotel and Goan was tied to it with his arms fastened behind his back. He was to stand there without food or water for twenty-four hours and then clear off wherever he liked while the going was good.

Fluttering weakly like an injured fly, Goan allowed the whole ceremony to be performed on him. He said nothing. The leading men of Canterville and other settlers who were curious stepped back a suitable distance to admire their handiwork and then slowly went their separate ways.

It grew dark. Licking his smashed lips that were stuck to his teeth with dried blood, Goan did his best to work out a plan of revenge. His soul was burnt out and he felt neither fury nor shame. Devastated, he tried to remember exactly who had beaten him the hardest, shouted at him the loudest, and cursed him the most. This kind of thing costs a great deal of effort and he soon felt tired. Then he began to think of how he would never see Daisy again. He remembered the sweet heaviness of her trembling body and the swift thudding of her heart that for those few happy minutes had beat against his chest. And he remembered the way she had lain with her head flung back and how he had planted a kiss—the only one—in the place where a button had come undone on her breast. Straining his arms, he began to moan with insatiable yearning, while the ropes burnt the skin on his wrists. There was still a night ahead of him and then another day!

He stood there shifting from one foot to the other. Now and again he tried to convince himself that it was all a dream, and then flinging back his head and banging it against the post, he shattered the illusion. Close by he kept hearing the sound of stealthy footsteps that stopped in front of him and then slowly died away at the crossroads. The lights had gone out in the windows now. Suddenly a dim silhouette drew near, halting frequently as it did so. Then the man at the post blazed up with emotion and blushed to the roots of his hair in the darkness. The veins on his temples swelled with blood and began to throb rapidly. A flood of overwhelming shame drowned his reason, and with a groan, he closed his eyes, only to open them again straightaway. Daisy's sorrowful face was right in front of him and staring at him, but he could not stretch out a hand to ask for forgiveness.

"So you've come . . . to have a look too," he said softly, "go away, and please forgive me!"

"I'll go in a minute," said the girl in a hurried whisper. "But why did you let them do this to you, why didn't you defend yourself?"

"Oh!" said Goan. "Don't pity me, Daisy, it's too late for that! You're tormenting me, but I love you all the same. Go away, no, don't. . . . yes, do. . . . perhaps you'd better."

"I feel awfully sorry for you," she said, stretching out her hand and stroking his dishevelled hair with a quick, motherly gesture. "There then, don't cry! You. . . no, I'd better go or people might see us."

She stepped back into the darkness and he could hear her no more. Trembling and smiling, he gulped down the big, salty tears streaming from his unblinking eyes, and they warmed his cheeks and heart.

Whistling through the air, a stone hit the post, struck Goan on the ear as it bounced away, and then fell at his feet with a thud.

"For you, Daisy," he said, "just for you."

II

The next morning, when people began to gather on the streets—many of them had gone without sleep so as to be sure of seeing the prisoner at first light—Goan was untied. Grinning awkwardly, a group of young fellows came up to the post from the rear, behind Goan's back. Daisy's brother, a lanky giant of a man with teeth like fangs, cut the rope with a knife.

"We've been told to let you go," he muttered, hawking as he spoke, "so mind you. . . don't hang around here any more."

Goan fell to the ground. Then, pressing his hands against the earth, he got to his feet and, swaying from side to side as though on the deck of a ship in a storm, he set off home. Stepping back to let him pass, the crowd watched him intently.

An hour later there was a padlock hanging on the door of Goan's little house. The boarded-up windows, the hoofprints by the fence, the silent walls—everything indicated that the colony's will had been done. People saw Goan riding his second horse—a white animal with a chestnut crupper and tail—and making his way along the track behind the houses towards the Kroks' hay field. Beyond it there was a path running into the forest that was often taken by animals and hunters.

Goan rode at a walking pace, filled with painful longing to turn back and have one last look at Daisy's familiar window. Pulling on the reins, he struggled to hold up his swollen arms. Reaching the stream, he stopped his horse and gazed down into the sparkling water. A dark, distended face stared up at him. To choose a place to live seemed like child's play to him—after all, the earth is not small.

Where the track turned towards the mountains and where, beyond the forest showing dark blue in the distance, a road wound its way to a large port, Goan caught the faint sound of galloping behind him. Turning his head, he rode on and continued to think gloomily about the future. But the drumming of hooves became more and more audible and so he stopped. Gasping for breath, Daisy caught up with him.

The look of staggering bewilderment on Goan's face helped to loosen her tongue. Filled with embarrassment, she listened to all his exclamations of surprise. He thought he understood what was happening but hardly dared believe it. Coming closer, she said:

"Goan, take me with you. I can't live at home any more. Everybody's finding fault with me and spreading rumours that I was in league with you. They're even saying we've got a child hidden away somewhere."

Goan was silent. The horse on which she sat seemed as if it were cast out of the brilliant morning light.

"My father's insulted me," Daisy went on. "He says it was all nothing but a farce and that I'm to blame. But you know that's not true. And you won't have to kidnap me again either. I've heard enough insults to last me a lifetime."

"Darling," said Goan, smiling all over his battered face, "the men would have victimised you now because they hadn't taken you for themselves. . . and the women would have tormented you because someone had preferred you to them. People hate love. Don't come near me, Daisy, or I swear I shan't be able to stop myself kissing you. Forgive me!"

But soon their heads drew close together, and two loves—one new-born, the other long ablaze with passion—flowed together as a forest stream joins a mighty river.

They both lived a long time and died on the same day.

1911

The Long Journey

I

Shelter

While travelling once in the mountains, I grew tired of slipping on quartz that was as smooth as glass, and feeling very weary, stopped at a small inn—one of those remote establishments that are generally both agreeable and useful. My guide, José Chusito, had long been complaining of his cough and looking meaningfully at me, making sucking noises with his lips all the time. As this way of dropping a hint had become a habit with him and was starting to annoy me, I shot him a gracious glance and said:

"José, we must find a place for the night and have some supper."

He stopped coughing. After negotiating a few more spiralling paths that sometimes fell sheer to rocks outlined in the grey abyss below, we came out on to an area of level ground. In the gathering dusk there glimmered before our weary eyes a cluster of dim lights that were just as welcome as the festive illuminations for a royal coronation. Unslinging our rifles, we walked towards a rough stone building, and as we drew near its open door, the smell of human habitation began to tickle our glad nostrils, finely attuned as they already were by the fragrant aromas of mountain grass and snow.

Round the crudely-fashioned, enormous hearth sat a large number of people. As far as I could tell, they were hunters, shepherds, workers from nearby estates, and chance visitors like ourselves. Their bright, multi-coloured clothes consisted of striped woollen blankets worn over the shoulder or round the waist, cotton shirts, wide belts, and trousers trimmed down the seams with horsehair or feathers. Their wide-brimmed hats made all their faces look alike, lending them an indefinable similarity of expression under this strange headgear. Some of them carried heavy revolvers in leather holsters at their hip, but others wore old-fashioned pistols instead. (As I have ascertained on more than one occasion, the owners of these weapons are excellent shots). Altogether there were fourteen people in the hut apart from us. Three of them were lying on their bellies in front of the fire, bending their heads occasionally to sip from the glasses standing before them, while two more were chatting by the counter. The rest were sitting on stumps of wood maintaining an assiduous silence. They had their arms folded on their chests and were smoking steadily.

The fire blazed fiercely, casting a ghostly light on all the half-wild faces and intent eyes around us. Flung down in a corner, a pile of picks and spades glittered and flashed as the flames leapt high. Behind the counter above the landlord's head—he was an unprepossessing man with thick lips and a ring in his ear—there were various weapons hanging on the wall. Immersed in his bookkeeping, he sucked his pencil studiously and scratched his head. José had stayed outside with the mules and I could hear their bells jingling impatiently. The poor beasts were probably just as hungry as we were by then. Attracting general attention because of the way I was dressed, I went up to the counter and asked whether we could stay the night.

The price turned out to be high, something that was evidently wholly dependent upon the landlord's whim. Nodding my acceptance but glancing condescendingly at his thick lips at the same time, I went outside, accompanied by a stable-boy. After installing and feeding the mules, we returned to the shelter of the inn.

However critical the attention I had attracted ten minutes earlier, nobody seemed to notice me now, and I might just as well not have been there. My wanderings had taught me to be reserved. Taking a bottle of wine, José and I spread out our cloaks and sat down by the wall. The roast pork, coarse bread and wine soon cheered us up, and with his mouth full of food, José embarked on a long story about Mount Seniar, assuring me that it was the highest mountain in the world, and explaining that its spirit, a certain Pedro di Santuaro, the relative of a rich cattle-dealer, had stolen all the gold from the mountain so as to ransom his wife's soul that had been condemned to languish in Gehenna for selling a crucifix to a heathen rogue.

Half-asleep, I listened to this legend, mollified by the food and drink, and wondering at the fervid imagination of this man who could tell tall stories all night long for the sake of a bottle of wine. "Pedro di Santuaro," he kept saying, without forgetting his glass for a single moment, "sent a hundred ships to hell laden with gold, but Satan demanded as many times more as Seniar is bigger than a vanilla seed. Then Pedro..."

He was about to go on, but just then a man who had come in as José said "Pedro", turned round as if someone had called his name and examined us attentively. Without realising it, I scrutinised him more carefully than I had the other customers, feeling that I had seen him before. This is often the impression produced by a national type with which one is very familiar but which one unexpectedly encounters amid people who are alien to it.

I will describe the man's appearance in advance, though he does not yet play a part in this story. His pock-marked face was just as manly and strong as any of those in the room. His eyes were small, set wide apart and almost devoid of eyebrows—something that made them seem weak-sighted at first. But a moment later I saw they were bright and clear. A light brown beard covered his chin, while his small, fair moustache stood out strangely against the tanned skin of his face. He was wearing gaily-coloured, coarse clothing, carried a short-barrelled carbine, and moved in a gentle, easy way.

I had pins and needles in my leg so I got up and took a few steps towards the fire. As if lifeless, the aching limb slipped away from under me, and rubbing my knee, I swore in Russian. At this the stranger smiled in amazement, banged his gun on the floor, and looking meaningfully at me, repeated what I had just said. Then he asked: "Who are you?", saying this in Russian too without the slightest trace of an accent.

"I'm Russian," I replied, staring at him in astonishment, and gave my name.

He continued to look me intently in the face, then frowned and said loudly:

"I belong to these parts, so I don't understand you."

With this, he moved away and went out. The curious bystanders who had been attracted by the sound of an unfamiliar tongue, began to move away too.

"He's Russian," I said to myself, more interested at this moment in my fellow-countryman than in the new species of parrot I had discovered a fortnight earlier.

José tugged at my cloak.

"Shall we have another bottle and then get some sleep?" he asked in a voice as soft as a flute.

I gave him permission to do whatever he liked. Then, on my way out of the inn, I looked round and saw the Russian sitting on a ledge of rock by the door.

He seemed to be deep in thought, but at the sound of my footsteps, turned with the haste of a man who is accustomed to being on his guard in places as dangerous as these.

"This is hardly like meeting on the corner of Dvoryanskaya and Spasskaya Streets, is it?" I said. "Can we talk? It would certainly be very interesting!"

"I wouldn't speak to you at all," he replied after a pause, (and it was odder to hear real Russian spoken by a native of this region—someone whose profession was so obscure—than to see grey hair on a young man's head), "if I weren't sitting here thinking about something."

"Are you an émigré?"

"No."

I said nothing for a while, expecting the familiar questions from him. But he said nothing either, and engulfed by the stillness of the mountains around us, our silence became rather awkward. Then, wishing to continue the conversation, I made a frivolous forecast of stormy weather and rain for the following day. Referring to his knowledge of the area, he replied to the contrary. I agreed and added that I thought the local wine was poor. He passed over this remark in silence and praised the region's horses. I moved on to the morals and women of those parts. He expressed the hope that they were better than perhaps they seemed. I touched on politics, while he remarked in passing that people were naive. I began to talk about Europe and he about Russia. At this point I struck cunningly at his evasiveness by saying that he did not look like a Russian at all.

Only when all this conversation—one that was so completely Russian in both spirit and style—had brought us by a roundabout way to the stranger's identity, was I able to hear the profoundly human tale of one of those few triumphs that are as brilliantly heroic as the victory of mind over body. My brief notes were subsequently transformed into this story which I now tell in a fragmentary and inadequate way, but which possesses in it the kind of moments that listeners have ears for.

II

The Official

"My name was Peter Shilderov and I worked as Head Clerk in the Treasury Office. The town where I lived with my family was as terrible and silent as the grave. It consisted of a long row of houses with a dismal, deathly appearance—official buildings that stretched along the bank of the river from the white monastery with its golden domes as far as the provincial prison. There were two churches in the middle of the market square which was surrounded by old stalls with padlocks that weighed as much as twenty pounds. Watchdogs howled constantly in the yards. The deserted streets had grass growing on them here and there, while the wooden houses were painted yellow and grey and looked like the buildings of a lunatic asylum. Autumn saw us up to our necks in mud, winter in snowdrifts, and summer in dust. Around the town was an area of common pasture—dried-up marshland.

I worked here for five years and in the sixth I began to drink. Sometimes—when I was in what we provincials used to call 'attendance,' that is to say when I was at work—I noticed that the monotonous rustling of papers and the scratching of pens gradually merged with the silence to become a plaintive melody that reminded me of a Tatar song or those harmonious but elusive rhythms in which the wheels of a moving train abound. Then, forgetting the melody's doleful charm, I would go off to see the archivist and sit with him in the semi-darkness of the basement drinking the vodka that he used to keep behind his cupboard. My wife was always unwell. I would often come in from work and find her lying down with a vinegar compress on her forehead and reading old novels of everyday life, works in which, as she put it, she enjoyed 'their authenticity, reality and truth.' My children, a boy and a girl,—peevish, timid creatures both of them—snivelled and whined at each other so much that I hardly noticed their existence. In the evenings, if it were spring or summer, I would sit on the avenue watching the young clerks throwing pebbles into the river, and think.

When I first asked myself 'What am I? An animal or a man?,' I was filled with horror. The question demanded a straight and unequivocal answer, together with all the conclusions that would flow from it. The thought raged like a mad bull in my mind and I surrendered to its indignant might. I spent a fortnight in the fantastic condition of a chick crawling out of its shell. I thought the whole time—while walking, sleeping, eating, working and out visiting. One fine day, as a result of all this mental tension, I came to the conclusion that I must become a different man and live a different life.

So as to determine precisely and fully just what was beautiful and important to me and what was superfluous and loathsome, I examined opposites or rather contrasts, taking it for granted that everything making up my life at the time was bad. It goes without saying that I had to make a separate appraisal of every aspect of reality, since as a whole, when I tried to picture a new life for myself, my imagination could produce nothing more than the bright curve of a horizon thronged with illusions. The law of contrasts was equally helpful to my mind, my will and the fulfilment of my desires.

So there I was, at the mercy of an irrepressible yearning that lacked direction. I had to find out exactly what I wanted. I looked at my surroundings and, as I said before, set against every aspect of them a contrast that was not only conceivable but also feasible in real terms.

By investigating my spiritual condition in this way, I ascertained the following. My life was passing by amid continual monotony, so I had to make it varied and gay. Moreover, I was engaged in a series of compulsory occupations. The complete absence of *compulsion* or, in the last resort, the presence of work of a casual kind—work that was above all varied—would be much more to my liking. Instead of a dismal life spent with a family I did not love, I wanted either precious solitude or that passionate love which makes remaining alive without one's beloved unthinkable. The social circles in which I moved consisted of people like molluscs—they were inarticulate, faint-hearted, sluggish and grey. I would gladly have exchanged them all for just one man whose words and deeds were out of the ordinary and whose temperament was as different from that of my acquaintances as the north is from the south.

For a long time it had seemed to me that the diversity of earth's forms instead of the monotonous plains of Russia was the rightful patrimony of anyone who chose to regard it as such. I do not like lead-coloured marshes, coniferous forests, fields covered with snow, or rivers running between banks that are as flat as a notched ruler. Nor do I like the grey expanse of distance that conceals endless tedium and poverty beneath its cheerless face. Against what was customary and familiar from the day I was born, I had to set what was completely unknown and foreign to my experience.

Having reflected on all this, I saw that I had solved the first part of the problem by answering the question 'What?' Now the answer to the next question, 'How?,' must lie in the strict accordance of my plans with my ideas of the unusual. The absence of anything that might weaken the impression produced by the final result was a vital necessity. My task was not simply to disentangle the net holding me captive but to tear it apart. If every day the prison governor comes to see a prisoner and says to him over and over again, 'We'll be letting you out soon,' the wretched man is deprived of a good half of the pleasure that awaits him—namely, of running out of his iron cage into the street. So I wanted a liberation that was both swift and sudden.

Now—and this is probably the most important thing of all—I'll tell you why I'm living here. My young son brought a book home from the school library. It was a collection of traveller's tales, written in rather pedestrian but simple language designed to make the young reader's imagination work for itself. My wife was in another room busy removing stains from a woollen jacket, so I was alone. Wearied by the thoughts that troubled me, I sat down at the table where my son had left the book before going to bed, and began to leaf through it, studying the old coloured illustrations as I did so. They were printed rather crudely so that the edges of the colours overlapped in very narrow strips. Soon I was lost in thought over one of them in the way you ponder a phrase which someone utters unthinkingly but which for you is profoundly evocative.

Are you familiar with the charm of old illustrations? The secret of the peculiar impression they make lies in the serene simplicity of lines traced by a firm hand that is devoid of all doubt. The artist was quite sure that what he was drawing was really like that.

Guided only by his dominant visual impressions and filled with the infectious naiveté still characteristic of Japanese painters today, the illustrator had always coloured the leaves of trees green, their trunks brown, the earth yellow, stones grey, and the sky blue. Such a display of creativity by a person who is evidently both ingenuous and placid, has a very persuasive effect. The invincible clarity of line was almost moving in its simplicity, and above all you could see that the work had been done with love.

The picture I was looking at was an illustration for one of the stories that bore the caption 'Shepherds in the Andes.' Moving through a mountain pass that was dark brown on one side and pale yellow on the other, in light blue air under a dark blue sky, along a steep track overgrown with bright green grass, a flock of llamas made its way down to a meadow that was bright green too. Behind them, wearing red cloaks, violet jackets and yellow hats, came a column of men on mules with rifles slung over their shoulders. In the background, painted light blue and white, was a mountain covered with snow, while on a grey outcrop of rock sat a reddish-blue condor.

I lingered over this picture longer than over any of the others, filled with obscure fascination at the sight of the grandiose and unattainable. It was as if the work had flung a bridge across to the vast world of the unknown, giving my thoughts free rein in its inadequate, crude allusiveness. Moreover, the picture contained something that spoke to me with silent words of association. Just as the person who brings his attention to bear on the word 'cuckoo' inevitably imagines in some sequence or other the bird's characteristic call, the stillness of the forest, and the custom of fortune-telling, and then thinks of superstitious feelings and superstitions themselves— so I was mentally transported to a mysterious land. I thought of high slopes covered with lush vegetation, of the sparse population in those regions, of the continual surprises to be found in natural things, and of the everlasting stillness of the mountains. Then I thought of danger and privation, the unfamiliar language of the people, their customs and temperament. Very soon I realised that there was nothing familiar to me here at all and that in my thoughts and associations I was cut off from that land by the sheer impossibility of clearly imagining a thing about it.

Instead, I was in the realm of general words and ideas: mountain, forest, man, river, animal, tree and house. So I had found the unknown in every respect and to the extent that it is possible on earth, within the limits set by the three dimensions. Now I was faced with the task of giving my abstract notions a content that was living, tangible and clear.

I got up and began to walk about the room, continuing to look at the picture in my mind's eye. Soon it vanished: I saw a mountain gorge filled with the cool of evening, the play of light on the rocky slopes, the wide mouth of the valley, the glittering edge of a glacier that resembled a crescent moon, the shadows of huge birds slipping over the earth, and a column of men on mules. They were riding by along a narrow track. I could not see their faces but sensed that they were serene yet stern. The mules walked quietly by, their bells tinkling softly. Distinct in the stillness, the sound was clear and pure. Rattling beneath their hooves, pebbles slipped and fell bouncing into the valley. 'Soon night will fall,' I thought, 'but for a long time yet in the quiet cool of evening the bells will tinkle, the pebbles rattle, and the mules snort.' Then I was filled with inexpressible yearning, as though a supernatural force had snatched me away from those places of grandeur and freedom, and cast me into wretched slavery.

From then on I was in thrall to my desire to go where I longed to be with all my soul and where I had found my second, real native land. There are two of them, but not everyone possesses both. Those who do know that the second must be fought for and won, whereas the first requires only submission and passivity.

III

The Break

Two days later I was sitting on a bench by the gate. It was a warm July evening. Opposite our house was the tall building of the convict prison, and from its barred windows drifted the smell of cabbage soup, buckwheat gruel and cooking oil. In the next street some boys were playing knucklebones. A herd of cows was coming in from the fields, swishing their tails and lowing. Tormented by gadflies, the animals walked slowly by amid clouds of dust, giving off an acrid odour of milk and dung. As each cow went obediently into its own yard, the herd gradually dwindled, but the herdsman kept blowing his horn as he went, pattering nimbly along on his bare feet.

The sun had set but it was still light. The time had come when the people of Kosaya Street came outside and sat on benches at their gates, chewing sunflower seeds in an idyllic mood. Sometimes they would play at 'squeezing the oil,' that is to say those sitting at the ends of the benches squashed their friends in the middle till their bones creaked and they were forced to get up. The pleasant atmosphere created by the mild, warm evening would reach a peak when after roll-call the two hundred prisoners in the corrective institution assembled for prayers. They would sing "Worthy art Thou," "Our Father", and other hymns in their well-practised, powerful voices. In the evening stillness the solemn sound of their singing created a mood of goodwill and peace.

When the convicts had finished their prayers and the loud voices of the warders started to ring out inside the gloomy prison, I returned to my thoughts and began to feel dissatisfied. It seemed to me that I would always live as I was living now, and that I would never dare do anything new, but just then I imagined myself getting up without a moment's delay and going away for ever. I imagined it so vividly that I became alarmed, and was seized by a nervous trembling, that harbinger of decisions. A few more minutes went by while my thoughts continued their semi-conscious work—and then suddenly a blindfold seemed to fall from my eyes: I saw that I was free, not bound by a thing, and completely my own master.

Hesitating no longer, I got up. My wife had gone off with the children to do some 'house-minding'—something that was a custom in our town. It meant that the owners were out visiting and had asked friends to come and stay in their house for a while so as to keep an eye on the servants and children. In our twilit rooms it was quiet and sad. I opened the chest of drawers, took out a hundred roubles, my old gold watch and my identity papers, and went out into the street.

It goes without saying that all this was still only a prelude to action. There was nothing to stop me from going inside again and putting the money back in its place. The path of retreat was not yet cut off. Even from the river landing-stage I could still have turned back. For a time my awareness of this filled me with dejection. I was afraid of a sudden fit of weakness, of faint-heartedness and indecision, but fortunately I realised that I was in the feverish condition of a man on the run who is full of nervous excitement. My first steps were uneasy and slow. Anyone watching me might have thought I was taking a stroll because I had nothing better to do.

Yes, those first hundred yards towards the landing-stage were the most difficult and painful of all. But by then I knew I would not turn back. I was filled with a feeling of isolation immediately as I came out on to the street, but there was something inspiring and nonchalant about it. At the corner I stopped and looked back. Beyond a bird-cherry tree I could see the grey roof of the house I had left behind. Then on I went, quickening my pace so as to catch the evening steamer.

During the next three months I saw and experienced enough to last anyone a lifetime. I managed to cross the frontier all right, though not without hearing bullets whistling from the border guards' rifles. I was very careful with my money but I had so little that soon there was nothing left at all. I remember long days of hunger and privation, nights spent with down-and-outs or under the open sky, and wearisome journeys on foot in scorching heat. I remember being arrested, picking up cigarette-ends on the street, taking odd jobs in vineyards, stealing fruit and begging. But the memory of it all is joyous and dear to me. Then at last I saw the bright lands of the south, with their colourful flowers, the majestic stillness of their dark blue sky, and the glorious expanse of the sea. I heard the throb of a ship's propeller, the song of summer surf, the howl of the mistral and the wail of the ship's siren as white steam jets from her boilers quivering with impatience to get under way.

I found a job as a sailor but left the ship as soon as she cast anchor in the mouth of the greatest river in the world. Rubber workers on a special trading vessel took me far inland, away from the ocean. I worked with the negroes, hacking tree-trunks in the poisonous swamps so as to extract a few drops of the precious sap that hardens quickly in the open air. The rain forests are full of perpetual danger and disease. Pale spurges stand in the sunless gloom, side by side with brilliant, flowering parasites, giant ferns, and other things totally unfamiliar to our European eyes. Growing at a monstrous rate, the bizarre vegetation chokes the earth that is deep in rotting humus.

I fell ill with fever, and lay delirious and exhausted in the negroes' camp. Each day after sunset, in forest clearings that glowed with the light of their fires, my black-skinned friends danced to their ghastly music. Their unfailing gaiety and kindness were truly amazing. In my hours of lucidity I would watch their wild steps carefully, recalling the pretty dance I had once seen performed by rabbits that were as black as soot. But the dim light of day brought delirium and fever once more, and I was pursued by thousands of fiery suns fringed by fat, orange serpents that brushed my fevered face with their agonising chill. I was dying, yet somehow I did not die.

Forgive me, dear—no, not fellow-countryman, but stranger—ten years have gone by since then. But I'll say no more. Do you hear that? There's a loud argument going on inside and everyone's shouting and clapping. It looks as if it's time we got up, doesn't it? Let's see what all the fuss is about!"

IV

We stood up and just then José Chusito came out of the hut and walked unsteadily towards us. With a yawn he looked up at the stars and then, seeing me, said in an unnaturally controlled voice:

"Are you having a walk? I was trying to sleep but I got disturbed—they're asking me to join the party that's looking for a new pass over the mountains. There's been an accident, and it's serious, very serious. The weight of a hundred five-storey houses has collapsed on to the Red Saddle—in other words, sir, the old men can't remember an avalanche like it. The trade route over the pass is destroyed. The mule drivers are desperate and those who have to get to the other side are ranting and raving. So you see, they're choosing a party to find a new way across, and they'll pay well. The rich traders won't grudge their gold. So what d'you think?"

"All right, then," I said with a chuckle. There was no sense in keeping José any longer, and he was evidently tempted by the thought of leaving me and seeking a better fortune than the small sums I had been giving him. He would have made off all the same, pleading a sore throat out of politeness. "I wish you luck," I said.

"What?" he cried sorrowfully. "Don't you need me any more? Anyway," he added hastily, fearing that I might change my mind, "you'll not regret it. I'll give you such a good guide that you'll sing for joy. He's not a man but a treasure. You'll not find another like him anywhere. There's nobody cleverer than he!"

I interrupted his rapturous description of the miraculous fellow and the three of us went up to the counter. Leaning their elbows on it and resting their chins on their palms, stood a large group of people who were discussing the question of the pass. Each kept making remarks, giving advice and describing the most desperate routes over the mountains in enthusiastic terms. First the young men gesticulated and shouted with excitement, while the older ones waited eagerly for the chance to say something. Then they spoke impressively and persuasively of the intense cold at thirteen thousand feet and of the need for warm clothing and wise caution. But I listened to them with only one ear. With his hands thrust in his pockets, my amazing acquaintance, the Russian—but what was I to call him now?—kept looking at a face that was unfamiliar to me, pretending to be lost in thought and glancing at it from time to time in an absent-minded way.

It was that of a woman of about eighteen or twenty, with a slightly turned-up nose, a look of mocking melancholy in her eyes, and a small mouth. Her dark face shone with an obstinacy that seemed capable of turning into hatred. One could not have called her beautiful, though the innate gracefulness of her strong, small body and the unconscious coquetry of her gestures provoked an intent smile in the observer. Like the others, she was listening to the conversation with her tousled head propped on her tiny hands. Her pose and the expression on her face were the picture of gravity. I smiled.

Sensing an intent gaze fixed on her, she looked round.

"Oh, it's you, Diaz," she said in an indifferent tone. "So you've come back, have you?"

"That's all I ever do—come back," said my new acquaintance.

"You'd do better to stay away all the time."

"Now look, Lolita . . ."

With a sigh she drew herself up, and examining Diaz from head to toe, moved to the other end of the counter, where sinking her face into her cupped hands and knitting her brows, she went on listening to what the mule drivers were saying.

José and Diaz mingled with the crowd. Weak with fatigue, I lay down on the blanket spread out for me by the grateful Chusito, and pushing my saddle under my head, began to nod off. New, hitherto unfamiliar ideas and feelings haunted me. I thought of the mysterious power of names that cut across our consciousness and totally transform a person, obliterating race, blood and customary associations. Diaz was Diaz. By no stretch of the imagination could I think of him as a Russian. But perhaps he was not a Russian at all, belonging as he did from birth to that mysterious, majestic race who are capable of anything and whose homeland lies within themselves.

Eventually I fell asleep, dozing fitfully in the way that travellers do. I woke as if someone was shaking me—perhaps an abrupt exclamation was the reason. Through half-open eyes I watched the people crowding round the counter, Lolita and Diaz among them. He went up to her again and said:

"I might go with them."

"Why don't you? You'll make plenty of money. . ."

"I'll go for a long time if I do," he said hesitantly. "And you know why."

"Don't keep on at me," said Lolita. "What are you pacing round for? Sit down! You'd better listen to what they're saying."

"Lolita!"

"Well?"

"Listen. . ."

"I'm listening."

"Haven't you anything to say to me?"

Reluctantly, she shot him a sidelong glance and gave a grunt. Diaz turned despondently in my direction and dazzled by the firelight, screwed up his eyes.

I fell asleep again. It was José who woke me. At the very first glance I could see that he was all ready to set off in search of the new pass. Everything on him was fastened and tied, buttoned up and pulled tight. There was no one left in the hut now apart from us. Bathed in the morning light, the mountains were visible through the open door, gleaming with their woods and ravines, while the sun danced gaily on the earthen floor.

Giving in to José's sympathetic tone (he was looking at me as pitifully as a nanny looks at a child that she is about to leave), I said once again that I was not in the least cross with him, and went out into the yard. Standing in their pens by the hitching rail, the laden mules twitched their ears submissively. Several armed men were checking the harness as they hurriedly finished their meagre breakfast. I went up to Diaz.

"Where are you making for?" he asked.

I told him.

"We'll probably not meet again," he said, "so I'll say good-bye!"

Having pondered the question that had been on the tip of my tongue since the previous evening, I asked:

"How do you feel in this country?"

"Fine, just fine," he answered.

Taking off his hat, he bowed, smiled and walked away. A minute later they began to bring out the mules. Each accompanied by a driver, the animals skirted the building, jingling their bells and snorting. Diaz brought up the rear. The caravan stretched out in single file and the leading mules began to go down through the greenish-black bushes that covered the ravine. All of a sudden the girl I had seen the previous evening came racing up to the rear of the column and drawing level with Diaz, fell into step beside him, laying her hand on his shoulder and telling him something. Then, by way of a parting caress, she thrust her fingers into his hair and began to ruffle it, tossing her gay head submissively. Diaz clearly did not object.

She did not go down into the ravine but stopped on the edge, watching as the mules crossed the gully then climbed the hill-side, walking carefully up the steep path among the limestone rocks. As she came back, she passed me almost without noticing I was there.

I thought about Diaz's story. He had gone now, leaving me filled with quiet joy. People such as he are never alone. Their family, that indomitable and magnanimous gipsy tribe, is scattered all over the world. I recalled the thousands of nameless ones who journey by land and sea—those bands of adventurers who explore uncharted regions, those madmen who fall in love with desert places, those sons of toil who lay the foundations of cities in the forest's heart. Their bones lie strewn in the burning sands of the dark continent, in the primeval deeps of the ocean, and in the snows of the arctic circle. With the triumphant power of passionate love their second, real homeland draws both the lone seeker of adventure and the leader of an expedition who commands a detachment of men. Nothing can stop them, only death. And with their death they enrich life and the joy of struggle everywhere.

The snow-covered mountains surrounded me like huge, white waves. For a long time I gazed at them with a feeling of warmth and friendship, trusting in their silent promise to cleanse my heart and mind.

1913

Mystery On A Moonlit Night

One bright, moonlit night Nikolai Seliverstov, a private in an infantry battalion, was standing at his lonely post on top of a granite rock overlooking a pass into the Carpathian mountains.

His task in this important position was to watch for any encircling movement that the enemy might make, as information had been received that this was a distinct possibility.

The rock was about fifty feet high and dominated the area around it. On the side facing the mountains it fell away to a deep, narrow ravine, while on the other side, facing the plains, it overlooked open country that was bathed in clear moonlight. Far away on the horizon could be seen the misty line of a river and a dark strip of forest. On the opposite side of the ravine was a series of much bigger rocks that were overgrown with shrubs and would have made excellent places for an ambush.

Seliverstov stood on a small rocky platform, well aware that the bright moonlight made him clearly visible to anyone watching from across the ravine. From there the sentry could be seen just as easily as if it were broad daylight.

Any wandering Huzul*—many of whom were still friendly with the enemy—might notice this guard post and report it, or simply shoot the soldier down without further ado. So Seliverstov knew that his position was a very dangerous one and kept thinking about death. He imagined death as a deep well with dark blue water at the bottom of it in which the moon was reflected. Thoughts of death are, of course, perfectly natural in war, especially in such a lonely place as this, but strangely enough, they served to distract him. His mind kept returning to them over and over again, and he found a curious satisfaction in trying to imagine the precise moment of his death and even to anticipate it.

On the rocky platform where he stood lay a large stone shaped like an anvil. The shadow that it cast as the moonlight fell on its pointed top crept gradually from left to right as the moon moved across the sky. Before long it would fall on the edge of the platform itself. Feeling rather tired, Seliverstov sat down on the stone and watched the shadow. Its strange shape reminded him of a sword. Suddenly, from the far side of the ravine came the faint sound of pebbles rolling off a path—the kind of noise made by a man's foot

---

*Ukrainian inhabitant of Carpathian region (translator's note).

slipping on a steep slope. The sentry pricked up his ears and just then a shot rang out from behind the rocks. Plaintive and desolate, the echo rolled out over the wilderness and died away. Seliverstov thought he heard the whine of a bullet.

Then he experienced a very strange sensation. Instead of the feeling that is normal in such situations—if not fear, then at least a certain agitation—he felt apathy and even indifference. It was as though awareness of the danger had merely flashed through his mind, and nothing more. So he went on sitting where he was, not in the least concerned about the shot that had rung out just a moment ago, and watched the shadow that was now almost touching the edge of the rocky platform. Eventually he found himself trying to guess the moment at which it would finally fall on the edge. Then all of a sudden he was filled with mysterious agitation, and realised that he was no longer sitting on the stone but standing at the edge of the platform and gazing into the distance. With immense clarity, just as if he were looking into a mirror, he suddenly saw himself lying face down near the stone. His arms, or rather the arms of his double, were spread wide, and from the bullet-wound in his breast ran a stream of blood that shone black in the moonlight. Then he realised that he had been killed and that he was looking at himself lying dead on the ground. But there was nothing terrible about it at all.

Shaped like a sword, the shadow cast by the stone touched the edge of the platform. Consciousness vanished, and Seliverstov's cold corpse remained lying on the narrow ledge of rock till morning.

1915

Fire And Water

I

In the hope that despite his campaign of opposition to the provincial dictator, a pardon would eventually be granted him, Leon Shtrikh had settled right by the border yet beyond reach of his political opponents. Here he was only twenty miles from the town and the house where his family were living. Meanwhile, influential friends were busy trying to get him permission to return to his native country. This process—a difficult and burdensome one for the many people involved—was moving step by step, or so it was hoped, towards a happy conclusion. Full of infinite love for his family, the impatient Shtrikh would relieve his painful solitude by climbing the Iron Wedge hills on clear days when the surrounding marshes were free of mist, and gazing for hours across the bay at the cluster of hazy sequins that was distant Zurbagan. Fixing in his mind's eye the place where his house stood, he would look into every part of it, and then, after mentally spending time with his wife and children and warming his soul with their company, he would return to his place of refuge—a fisherman's wooden cottage on the outskirts of a village where the Iron Wedge hills came down to the sea.

He had lived here for about a year now, comforted by the thought that he was as near Zurbagan as he possibly could be. His wife and children wrote to him frequently. To make sure that nothing would disturb him, he always drew the curtains before opening their letters, and then read them over and over again until he was tired, trying to guess the thoughts that had run through the writer's mind. Sometimes he would examine individual letters in the words, racking his brains for the reason if they seemed written with either undue haste or care. He did the same with commas and full stops, particularly in letters from his wife. "She couldn't think of anything else to say, she's bored," he thought, and at the sight of a very clear full stop somewhere in the middle of a letter his heart would sink. But on the other hand he rejoiced to receive pages covered in small handwriting with remarks added in the margin and across the text. His wife was twenty-four, his son eight, and his daughter five. He lived only for his family and regretted having to spend time asleep, for he could not think of his loved ones then. Often, at moments of profound abstraction, he could almost see them before him, and in his semi-conscious state would talk to them as though they were sitting beside him. At times he reproached himself for having become involved in politics, and he did so with a fury that probably surpassed that of his opponents.

He spent his time doing absolutely nothing. He simply lived from one day to the next, wandering about for hours on end in the sunshine and wind over the rocks along the shore. He kept out of people's way, and felt painfully jealous of his own feelings whenever he happened to meet anyone, for then he was obliged to enter into their interests and sufferings, their hopes and illusions. The local fishermen began to avoid him. He replied to their questions with reluctance, smiled when they complained of something, pulled a wry face when they told him their good news, frequently said the wrong thing, and then bade them an abrupt farewell.

The owner of the cottage where he lived was a blacksmith, a taciturn fellow who only liked a drink and a smoke in the company of one other man. He was the only person Shtrikh could bear. The smith would appear in the evening. Shtrikh would put a packet of cigarettes and a bottle of wine on the table, and then start talking about his family. He had a little boy and a little girl, he said. Sometimes he was tormented by the feeling that he loved one more than the other, but could never make out which. The boy was called Leon, as he was, but his nickname was "Branda the switch". He had started to read when he was four. Now he was very good at making little boats and simply adored music. The girl, who was called Zella after her mother, was nicknamed "Mumu". When she was very small she used to purse her little lips like a trumpet so that the word "mama" came out as "mumu". Both children had black hair and were very kind, though they were awfully mischievous. They were very beautiful and it was a pity the smith couldn't see them. Mumu rode on the wolf-hound's back and was always laughing. Once she got her finger stuck in an empty medicine bottle and couldn't pull it out (she was three at the time), but she had the sense to break the bottle and what's more managed not to cut herself in the process.

The smith would listen good-naturedly, raising his enormous eyebrows and nodding his head. But he could hardly keep his eyes open. Little by little, without hurrying, he would finish his wine, and then, wiping his mouth on the back of his hand, would thank Shtrikh for the drink and leave, covered in ash from his cigarette. Alone now and excited by the conversation, Shtrikh would pace the room. Drawn with longing, his thin face with its brilliant, intent eyes would flit across the mirror on the wall. Eventually a blue mist would envelop his brain with fatigue and drive him to bed.

Each morning, with his head full of the selfsame thoughts and his heart brimming over with wistful melancholy, he wrote long letters to his wife, continually adorning them with words of affection, intimate turns of phrase, and those little familiarities that in pure hearts are proof not of depravity but of all-pervading, deep adoration. The letter would end with lengthy greetings to the children. Shtrikh wrote about his state of mind, about his plans, hopes and dreams. Sometimes he described his surroundings and his walks, and told of sea-shells, trees, sunsets and squalls out over the bay. He gave a detailed account of his tedious day, offered words of advice, enquired what stage his case had reached, and asked for this or that book to read. Then he would go for his usual walk on the hills overlooking Zurbagan.

Meanwhile friends began to inform him—in increasingly specific terms—that his case was now being regarded in a favourable light. It remained only to pay two or three calls and complete a few formalities (to make a request here and grease a palm there). Shtrikh felt freedom drawing near. He began to sleep less, stayed longer out on the hills, and occasionally even struck up a conversation with the locals, treating them to tobacco as he did so. The immense weight that had oppressed him for so long swayed, and under its far edge he caught a glimmer of light.

II

One Monday sometime after three in the morning Shtrikh suddenly woke, filled with unaccountable alarm. The feeling was so strong that his hands started to shake and it was a long time before he managed to put the match to the wick of the candle. Somehow he pulled on his trousers and vest. Then he caught the sound of hooves splashing through puddles outside (there had been a heavy shower the previous afternoon). The horse came nearer. Then the hooves clattered on the stones under his window and fell silent. Shtrikh waited.

He could hear men's voices outside. One was the smith's who was busy unbolting the door, while the other sounded rather familiar. Three loud knocks coincided with his cry:

"Yes, yes, I'm here. What is it? Come in!"

Gasping for breath, a man appeared in the doorway. It was Mort, a teacher and friend of Shtrikh's. They had not seen each other for over a year now. Mort was pale and covered in mud, and he moved in an odd way. The dreadfully sorrowful look on his face made Shtrikh catch his breath. Mort stayed near the door and gazed at his friend with eyes full of mysterious meaning. Without saying hello, Shtrikh went up to him and clenched his fists in fear, for he saw that the visit was as terrible as destruction itself.

"I got time off work, borrowed a horse and set off as fast as I could," said Mort, hurrying to tell all before Shtrikh's hands clutched at his throat. "Can you sense what's happened? Have you guessed? I asked them, begged them to let you come to Zurbagan immediately, but the swines just refused. . . A telegram would have killed you. I confess I wanted to begin in a roundabout way, but I can see you're horrified, so I'll tell you everything now. Listen, put a blanket between your teeth and bite on it, or knock yourself out with a glass of vodka. Your house has been burnt down, Shtrikh. The fire started on the ground floor and the wood caught straightaway, so the children. . . d'you understand? Your wife's in hospital. She's got about twenty-four hours, that's all. . ."

Even before he had finished, Shtrikh was tearing at the door with all his might, while Mort tried with equally frantic persistence to hold him back. He was shouting something Shtrikh did not understand and did not want to know. Sobbing, he clutched at Shtrikh's hands in the vague hope of finding something reassuring and sensible to say. But there was nothing to be said. With his fists Shtrikh beat Mort's hands off the edge of the door and ran out into the darkness.

He was barefoot and hatless, just as Mort had found him. The heavy, rain-filled gloom hung low over the earth, and from time to time a close, damp wind gusted into his face. Turning the corner of the house, he bounded away with the instinctive sense of direction of a sleep-walker, heading straight for the ruins of his Zurbagan home—just as a pigeon flung out of a balloon plummets through the misty void for an instant and then immediately flies away in the right direction. Unaware of his surroundings, Shtrikh set off across the peninsula. As though in a dream he raced over the extremely rough terrain with its granite outcrops, ravines and copses, its eroded gullies and sandy flats. He kept stumbling and falling then got up again and rushed on once more, feeling and remembering nothing. When it came momentarily to him, the general impression of his headlong flight resembled a frenzied dance inside a tightly-closed carriage. His state of shock—much more profound than we could ever imagine—kept him on the verge of instant death. Driven by immense nervous agitation and heading unerringly in the right direction, he ran on and on, feeling neither the pain of his blood-stained legs, nor the heaviness of his body, nor the rasping of his breath. All he knew was that somehow, after an enormous period of time, he would find himself where he had to be. He would arrive late, but would be able to put things right all the same.

The darkness was pitch-black, but the brilliance of the shapes that accompanied him and floated persistently around him filled his brain with a kind of luminous tension and transformed the gloom into a series of twilit spaces where hideously deformed clouds merged and billowed like the smoke of burning phosphorus. He was surrounded by smoke. He could smell its odour and see the flapping of grey curtains that were shot with the crimson light cast by flickering tongues of fire. In the distance he glimpsed part of a window frame. From time to time he said loudly: "So they were suffocating!. . ."

Both of them, the boy and the girl, moved continuously back and forth in the thick smoke. First they ran towards him, rubbing their eyes with their little fists, then they drifted far away into the mysterious darkness that swallowed up their fading cries, and then, lying on the floor and writhing in convulsions, they butted their heads against the smoke that was swirling everywhere. Or the blazing head of his wife, flung back as though she were in a faint, went rushing by so close that he stretched out his arms and shrieked like a man who has been mortally wounded.

"So," he kept repeating, trying to grasp what he was saying, "they were suffocating. But they didn't choke to death straightaway. No, I couldn't bear that."

Now and then a vivid impression of the horror they had known racked him with agonising pain, and he felt like filling his lungs with all the air on earth and bursting out in a horrendous scream. But instead he just moaned softly and biting his lips, ran on even faster still.

Meanwhile dawn was breaking, and losing its power over the earth, the darkness grew feeble and faded. The rain suddenly stopped. Through the thin mist hanging close to the ground Shtrikh looked over the top of a distant, slender tree, and saw the pale edge of the sun. Its light banished the apparitions floating around him. Then beneath his feet he noticed a strange-looking plain. Its colour—exactly the same everywhere as far as the eye could see—was a dull green, transparent like smoky glass and iridescent with light. Then a gentle gust of wind sent the mist swirling away before him, driving it up towards the sun, and in the airy space left behind it Shtrikh noticed the greenish colour below him change first to light and then to dark blue, and the further away he looked the darker it became. Now that he could see again, he had regained that part of human consciousness which observes and evaluates our surroundings.

Quivering, the greenness swayed to and fro beneath him and shimmered with countless ripples. Following each other in rhythmic waves, the wrinkles and furrows resembled the surface of choppy water.

"It's an earthquake," said Shtrikh, hoping desperately that the ground would open wide and spare him his agony by swallowing him up. With the ease that comes only in dreams, he glided swiftly along, moving like mist towards the coast that was now only a short distance away. Suddenly a gust of warm wind, prolonged and even, dispersed the mist, and resplendent in the morning light, the bay shone before his inflamed eyes in all its quiet beauty. Beneath his feet there was water swaying gently to and fro, but he was neither amazed nor afraid.

"Now I know I'm asleep," he said, but his certainty did not extend to what had happened in Zurbagan. Each thing existed in its own right, and he did not think it odd that reality should be combined with what he considered a dream.

After the darkness of night, the bright radiance of the sky resurrected the fire in all its savage cruelty. Shtrikh looked to one side. There, about a hundred yards away, enormous and gay, was a ship in full sail. The business-like sturdiness of her heavily-laden hull was crowned by the gleaming whiteness of her sails. Their delicate shapes rose from her deck to her topmasts like a flock of white birds. The ringing voices of her crew reached Shtrikh's ears, and clasping his breast in his agony, he flung them a curse. He could not bear to see this embodiment of brisk, purposeful toil sailing joyously towards her distant goal now that he himself had lost everything. Then, without realising how it came about, he suddenly found himself in a forest and surrounded by butterflies and flowers. The wet grass was steaming in the slanting sunlight. All of a sudden a blurred, pale shape rose before him. It was a border guard. But the soldier did not try to stop him, did not cry out or open fire—he simply saw him hurtling by, and that was enough to root him to the spot with fear.

Beyond a copse was a wide plain with a high road running across it, and on a steep cliff above the river lay the curving sweep of Zurbagan.

Shtrikh raced down the road...

III

At eight o'clock in the morning a man was led into one of the wards of the municipal hospital. Blood-stained, half-naked and covered with mud, he tried to break free from the staff restraining him. Reeling with exhaustion, he went up to one of the beds. There was a woman lying on it. Her body was wrapped in sheets and her head completely swathed in bandages. Between the strips of gauze only her swollen eyes without their lashes were visible. Dimming, the last sparks of life still glittered in them. She was groaning softly.

Shtrikh stared at her in silence, his look wild and gay.

"Zella!" he said.

There was a barely noticeable flicker in the woman's eyes. Was it awareness of what was happening or a moment of delirium before she died? No one could say for certain.

"I always used to be able to wake up in time if I had a bad dream," said Shtrikh, turning to the anxious doctor. "Some dreams can be very vivid, you know. Of course, this isn't my wife. Besides, the children would be here if it were. Well, I feel better now. I think I'll wake up soon."

But he woke only a year and a half later, in a nursing-home for people such as he who are not convinced of the reality of what has happened. Death came as the result of a heart attack.

Afterwards Mort maintained that because of the curving shape of the peninsula—it resembled a sickle with its free end pointing towards the mainland—Shtrikh could not have reached the town on foot by eight in the morning, having made the journey in only four hours. The roads in that area are so unreliable and bad that he himself had taken five and a half hours to cover the distance—and on horseback at that. But the doctor (and others) insisted that it was exactly eight o'clock in the morning when Shtrikh came in. Then Mort said that their watches were wrong. However, as many people affirm, the watchmakers of Zurbagan enjoy no mean reputation. In our opinion there is truth in every argument, but it does not lie with those who do the arguing, otherwise they would not get so hot under the collar about it.

1916

Ships In Liss

I

Some people remind you of an old-fashioned snuff-box. Picking up such a thing, you gaze at it in profound reverie, for it represents an entire generation that is completely strange to you. A snuff-box gets put with other knick-knacks and is sometimes shown to guests, but its owner very rarely uses it as an everyday object. Why is this? Does he feel awkward about making regular use of something so old? Or are the forms of a bygone age—deceptively like contemporary ones in the geometrical sense—really so different that to come into contact with them all the time means to live unwittingly in the past? Or are we perhaps dimly aware of the complex incongruities between old-fashioned things and the present day? It is hard to say. As we said before, though, some people remind you of an antique object, for in the spiritual sense they are just as alien to the way of life around them as an old snuff-box is to a petty thief. Once and for all, perhaps in childhood or at one of those turning-points in life when human character resembles a saturated mineral solution—shake it gently and its crystals instantly set forever—at a crucial moment like this, because of a chance impression or for some other reason, the soul assumes its lasting shape. From then on its needs may well be poetic and ingenuous. It requires completeness, wholeness, and the charm of accustomed routine, in which dreams are so vivid and fluent when unhampered by distractions. A person with a soul like this will prefer horses to a railway carriage; a candle to an electric light bulb; fluffy plaits to some intricate coiffure that smells of curling-irons and musk; a rose to a chrysanthemum; a ponderous sailing ship with her lofty mass of white canvas—the whole vessel resembling a face with a heavy jaw and a smooth brow above dark blue eyes—to a toy-like, pretty steamship. The inner life of such a person is necessarily withdrawn, while his outer life consists in mutual opposition between himself and his surroundings.

II

Just as there are people like this, so there are families and homes, even towns and harbours that resemble a person who has his own poetic spiritual life.

There is no port more disarrayed and wonderful than Liss—

except, of course, Zurbagan. The international, polyglot town is distinctly reminiscent of a vagrant who has finally decided to plunge into the thickets of a settled life. The houses are set at random amidst vague allusions to streets, but there could be no streets in the true sense of the word here, for the town sprang up on fragments of rocks and hills, linked by bridges, steps and spiralling, narrow paths. All this is enveloped in dense, tropical greenery, amid whose leafy gloom flash the child-like, fiery eyes of women. Everywhere you look are yellow stones, blue shadows and picturesque fissures in the old walls. Somewhere in a knoll-shaped yard you glimpse an enormous boat being repaired by a barefoot, silent fellow smoking a pipe. You hear the sound of singing far off and its echo in the ravine. You see a market on piles, under huge umbrellas and awnings. You catch the glint of a weapon and the flash of bright clothing, and smell flowers so fragrant that they evoke an obscure, dream-like yearning for assignations and romance. The harbour is as grubby as a young chimney-sweep. At night the furled sails are all asleep, but then the winged morning comes, with its green water, black rocks, and the ocean's expanse. And in the evening you are surrounded by the magnetic fire of brilliant stars and boats full of laughing voices. This, then, is Liss.

There are two taverns here, the "Prickly Pillow" and the "Heaven Help You." Naturally, the sailors crowd more tightly into the nearer one. Which of them was nearer to begin with, though, is hard to say, but these respectable establishments soon began to compete with each other and raced down towards the harbour at top speed. They changed sites, took over fresh quarters and even built new premises for themselves. But the "Heaven Help You" finally emerged victorious: it played a very clever trick, thanks to which the "Prickly Pillow" was left rooted to the spot amid miserable ravines far from the centre of town. So it was that after a ten-year struggle, its triumphant rival took pride of place right by the harbour, destroying three eating-houses in the process.

The population of Liss consists of adventurers, smugglers and sailors. The women of the town are either angels or shrews. The angels, of course, are young and ravishingly beautiful, while the shrews are old. But even shrews, it should be remembered, can lead useful lives. For example, it has been known for a shrew to attend a happy wedding, repent of her devilish intrigues, and turn over a new leaf.

We shall not analyse the reasons why Liss always was and still is a port of call exclusively for sailing ships. These reasons are of a geographic and hydrographic kind. All in all, everything in this town produces exactly the impression of independence and poetic ease that we have endeavoured to elucidate by describing the kind of person who has distinct spiritual needs.

III

At the moment our tale begins, four men were sitting upstairs in the "Heaven Help You" tavern at a table by a window which had a picturesque view of the harbour. They were: Captain Duke, an extremely large and effusive character; Captain Robert Estamp; Captain Renior; and a man who was better known by the nickname "I know you", precisely because he greeted everyone, even strangers, with these words if they displayed any intention of going on the spree. But his real name was Captain Chinchar.

It goes without saying that such a distinguished, even aristocratic company could hardly sit at an empty table. It was covered with various festive bottles of the kind brought out by the landlord on special occasions such as this, when the captains—generally speaking, men who for reasons of professional vanity have no particular liking for each other—gathered together to do some hard drinking.

Estamp was a middle-aged, taciturn man with grey eyes and ginger eyebrows that stood out on his pale face. Renior, with his long black hair and bulging eyes, looked like a monk in disguise; while Chinchar, an agile old man with black teeth and one sad blue eye (he had lost the other), was noted for his malicious tongue.

The tavern was full. There was a lot of shouting and singing, and now and then someone who was very drunk indeed staggered towards the door, knocking over chairs as he went. Plates and glasses clattered constantly, and twice amid all the hubbub Duke caught the name "Bitt-Boy". Somebody was evidently talking about the famous man. His name was very much to the point, too, as the captains were discussing an extremely difficult problem.

"Now if I'd got Bitt-Boy with me," exclaimed Duke, "I wouldn't be afraid of an entire enemy squadron! But he's not here. It's terrible to say so, my friends, but I'm carrying explosives, you know. Not me, the *Marianna*, I mean. But the *Marianna*'s me and I'm the *Marianna*, so it's me that's carrying them really. What an irony—me loaded with gunpowder and shot! Lord knows, though," he went on darkly, "after the ferocious refreshment they treated me to at the commissariat, I'd even carry soda water!"

"That pirate ship appeared again the day before yesterday," Estamp put in.

"I can't understand what she's looking for in these waters," replied Chinchar, "but I'm afraid to weigh anchor all the same."

"What are you worried about now then?" asked Renior.

"Nothing at all, my friend. I'm only carrying tin-ware and perfume, but I've been promised a bonus!"

Chinchar was lying, though. He was not worried about the tin-ware but about his insurance policy, because he was looking for a convenient place and time to scuttle his *Anchorite* in return for a large sum. Such abominable frauds are not uncommon, though they require great caution. Chinchar was seriously concerned about the privateer now, because he had heard that his insurance company was about to go bankrupt. So he had to be quick if his little scheme were to succeed.

"I know what the pirate ship's after!" declared Duke. "Have you seen the brig that's anchored right by the harbour mouth? The *Felizzata*? They say she's carrying gold."

"I don't know the vessel," said Renior. "But I've seen her, of course. Who's her captain?"

Nobody knew. Nobody had even seen him. He hadn't paid anyone a visit or called at the inn. Once just three sailors from the ship—sedate-looking, middle-aged fellows they were—had come into Liss followed by dozens of inquisitive eyes, bought some tobacco and hadn't appeared again.

"He's some greenhorn or other," muttered Estamp. "Go on then, you lout, stay in your cabin," he cried angrily, turning to the window, "then perhaps your whiskers'll grow a bit!"

The captains burst out laughing. When the laughter had died away, Renior said: "Whichever way you look at it, we're well and truly trapped. I'd give up my cargo with pleasure—after all, what good are other people's lemons to me? But as for giving up the *President*..."

"Or the *Marianna*," said Duke, interrupting him. "What if she blows up?" He turned pale and downed a double measure. "Don't say things like that, Renior!"

"You've bored me to death with all your talk about the *Marianna*," Renior shouted, "so there's nothing I'd like better than for her to blow up!"

"Then your *President* will sink too!"

"Wha-at?"

"Don't argue now," said Estamp.

"I know you!" cried Chinchar to an astonished customer. "Come over here and stand an old man a drink!"

But the customer turned his back. The captains were deep in thought now. Each of them had his own reasons for wanting to leave Liss as soon as possible. A distant prison awaited Duke if he did not set sail soon, and Chinchar was in a hurry to act out his swindler's comedy. Renior longed to see his family after two years away, while Estamp was afraid that his crew, a motley assortment of men, might desert. A couple of them had already run away and now sat bragging in the "Prickly Pillow" about their fantastic adventures in New Guinea.

Various vessels—the *Marianna*, the *President*, Chinchar's *Anchorite* and Estamp's *Aramea*—had taken refuge in Liss from the privateer. The fast *Marianna* had come racing in first and the *Anchorite* had crept in the following day, while the *Aramea* and the *President* had hurriedly dropped anchor forty-eight hours later. In all, together with the mysterious *Felizzata*, there were five ships in Liss, not counting the many barges and small coasters.

"So what I'm saying is that I want Bitt-Boy," began Duke who was rather drunk now. "I'll tell you a story about him. You all know that silly fool Beppo Malastino, don't you? Well there he was, sitting in Zurbagan drinking 'my God'* with chubby little Butuzka on his knee. Bitt-Boy comes in and says: 'Malastino, weigh anchor and I'll take your ship through the Kasset strait. You'll be in Akhuan-Skap before anyone else this season'. And what do you think happened? Well I've sailed through Kasset many times with a full cargo, and it was obviously to Malastino's advantage to do just what Bitt-Boy said. But the fool took two days to make up his mind. 'Oh dear, it's a rough stretch of water. . .,' he says, 'and all the buoys have been swept away!'. . . But the buoys aren't the point, my friends. Ali, a Turk who used to be Beppo's bosun, made a hole in his brig right by the mizzen and plugged it with pitch. The water should have washed it out in no time. Well, eventually, sick with fear, Beppo sailed through the strait with Bitt-Boy. He was late, of course, the silly fool, so the money of Akhuan-Skap went into other people's pockets instead of his, but. . . d'you know Bitt-Boy's luck? In the Kasset strait they got thrown on the reefs. . . A few barrels of honey standing near the hole in the ship's side must have started fermenting before she left Zurbagan. They'd burst open and about four tons of the stuff had covered the hole with such a thick layer that the planking didn't even give way. Beppo went cold with fright when they unloaded in Akhuan-Skap and he saw what had happened. Hey, Chinchar! Give me a drop out of that bottle!"

"Bitt-Boy. . . I'd get him to come with me all right!" said Estamp. "They're bound to hang you some day, Duke, for carrying gunpowder, but I've got children."

"I'll tell you about Bitt-Boy," began Chinchar. "It was. . ."

---

*A murderous drink: pure alcohol mixed with Cayenne pepper together with a small amount of honey. (*Author's note*)

But the old rogue was interrupted by a tremendous cry of joy. Everybody turned to the door and many started waving their caps, while several others rushed to meet the newcomer. Like a wind the chorus of roaring voices swept through the spacious room, and now and then above the rapturous noise could be heard isolated shouts of "Bitt-Boy! Bitt-Boy, the bringer of luck!"

IV

The man whom they welcomed with this significant and delightful name stopped in the doorway, blushed deeply and laughed. Then he said hello to everyone and went over to the captains' table. No more than thirty and of medium height, he was well-built and had a pleasant, kindly face that expressed both strength and gentleness. There was a calm yet vivacious look in his eyes, and his features and movements possessed the dignity that is a reflection of inner tranquillity rather than a habitual trait of character. His voice was extremely clear yet soft at the same time. He was wearing a pilot's cap, a brown knitted jersey, a light blue belt, and a pair of heavy boots. Over his arm he was carrying a waterproof cape.

He shook dozens, no, scores of hands. . . Smiling, he glanced around the circle of friendly faces that grinned with pleasure to see him. The spiralling smoke of pipes, the gleam of white teeth in weathered faces, and the shine of many-coloured eyes surrounded him for several minutes in cheering, warm welcome. Eventually, he managed to break away and fell into Duke's arms. At this even Chinchar's sad eye grew more cheerful and the set of his malicious jaw softened, while the ox-like Renior mellowed a little and the hard, proud Estamp smiled faintly, rather like a child. Bitt-Boy was everyone's favourite.

"You're the drummer boy of fortune!" cried Duke. "The cat's whisker! Weren't you Jonah himself? Where on earth have you been all this time? What news have you got? Choose which of us you want—the whole drunken fleet's right here! But we're caught like rats in a trap, you know. Save the *Marianna* for me!"

"Is it the pirate ship you're talking about?" asked Bitt-Boy. "Well I've seen her, so let's get straight to the point, shall we? Listen to this. Yesterday I got hold of a skiff in Zurbagan and came to Liss. It was a dark night. I'd heard about the pirate ship earlier, so I made my way along the shore, staying among the rocks where the cliffs are overgrown with moss and keeping under cover all the time. Twice the privateer's searchlight just missed me, and the third time something told me to lower the sail. I was just in time. . . the skiff was lit up just as if it were broad daylight. But there are plenty of rocks and shadows along the shore, so they couldn't see me, but if I hadn't got my sail down, then... Anyway, here I am, safe and sound with you. Renior, do you remember that firm called Haven & Co.? The one that sells tight boots with nails sticking through the soles? Well, I bought a pair yesterday and now my heels are all covered with blood."

"Yes, I do," said Renior, "but you're a brave man, Bitt-Boy. Take the *President* out of Liss for me! If you were married..."

"No, take the *Anchorite* out instead," declared Chinchar. "After all, I know you, Bitt-Boy, and I'm rich now, don't forget."

"But why not take the *Aramea*?" asked Estamp sternly. "I'd fight for the right to have you with me, Bitt-Boy, because it's quite safe with you."

The young pilot was about to say something else, but suddenly looked serious and sad. Propping his chin on his little hand, he glanced at the captains, and a quiet smile flickered in his eyes. Then, sparing other people's feelings as usual, he controlled himself. Draining his glass, he tossed it in the air and caught it, then lit a cigarette and said:

"Thank you, thank you for your kind words and for your faith in my good luck... It's not something I look for. But I can't say anything to you at the moment—anything definite, that is. It all depends on *certain circumstances*.

I've already spent all the money I earned in the spring, but still... Anyway, how can I choose between you? Should I take you, Duke?... Oh, dear old man! Only people who are short-sighted fail to see your tears when you look at the open sea! And I don't mind telling you all about it either—so there you are! You're part of the sea like I am, Duke, and I love you for it. And what about you, Estamp? Who was it hid me from those stupid sepoys when I rescued the rajah's pearls in Bombay? I love Estamp too, because he's got a warm corner in his heart. As for you, Renior, you lived with me for two months and your wife fed me for six when I broke my leg. And you, Chinchar, 'I know you', you inveterate sinner! How you wept in church when you met that old woman...! There were twenty years between you and you'd only got a chance tie of blood in common. But I've had too much to drink, my friends, and I'm rambling now. Anyway, I love you all. That pirate ship probably means business, though, but how on earth am I to choose between you? I can't even imagine it!"

"Let's draw lots," said Estamp.

"Yes! Yes!" they all cried. Bitt-Boy looked round. People who had pulled up their chairs a long time ago were following the conversation now. There were many elbows resting on the captains' table, whilst at others nearby men stood listening. Then Bitt-Boy's glance shifted to the window. Through it he could see the harbour shining quietly as the smoky haze of evening descended on the water. When his eyes had asked the mysterious *Felizzata* something that only he knew, he said:

"That's a graceful brig, Estamp. Who's her master?"

"A lout and a boor! But nobody's seen him yet."

"And what's she carrying?"

"Gold, gold," muttered Chinchar, "sweet gold. . . ."

And around him several voices affirmed:

"So they say."

"A ship *was* supposed to pass through here carrying gold. She's probably the one."

"Her crew keep a very strict watch."

"They don't let anyone aboard."

"Everything's quiet on her. . ."

"My friends," Bitt-Boy began, "I'm rather ashamed of my strange reputation, and really and truly, the hopes people pin on me are embarrassing. Listen: let's forget the usual way of drawing lots—there's no need to roll up little bits of paper. In a lively affair like this something special's bound to show up. I'll go with whoever turns out to be the lucky one, as long as *certain circumstances* don't change."

"You tell 'em, Bitt-Boy, tell 'em the plain truth!" shouted someone who was only just waking up in a far corner of the room.

Bitt-Boy laughed. He would have liked to be far away from Liss at that moment. But all the noise and jokes distracted him, and it was for the same reason that he had devised his own special way of drawing lots—so as to spin out the time and gather as many people around him as possible, trying to forget himself amid the dense crowd of busy sailors with all their noisy talk. But he would keep his word just the same, provided the "certain circumstances" did not change. At the moment, however, while he gazed at the *Felizzata*, those circumstances were still much too obscure even to himself, and he had mentioned them only at the prompting of his amazing instinct. So it is that an impressionable man reads or works while waiting for a friend, then suddenly gets up and walks straight to the door to open it: his friend is coming, but the man opening the door has already cast his distractedness aside without realising it, and is astonished at the timeliness of his movement.

"To hell with your circumstances!" said Duke. "What are we going to do then? Play guessing games? But what were you saying, Bitt-Boy?"

"Evening's coming," the pilot went on, "so the person who gets me to go with him hasn't long to wait. Whoever it turns out to be, I'll send a boy to his ship at midnight to tell him what to do. But remember that I may simply refuse to go. In the meantime, though, play the game just the same."

They all turned to the window. Bitt-Boy was gazing through it into the distance, evidently looking for a natural sign or chance token. Lying quietly at anchor, all the ships were clearly visible: the graceful *Marianna*; the long *President* with her high bowsprit; the *Anchorite* with the figurehead of a monk at her bow, bulldog-like and sullen; the ethereal, tall *Aramea*; and the elegant, aristocratic-looking *Felizzata* with her well-proportioned, sturdy hull, neat as a yacht with her jute rigging and elongated stern—the same *Felizzata* that they were all talking about, wondering whether she was carrying gold or not.

How sad summer evenings are! The steady twilight descends upon the hushed earth, slowly enveloping the weary sun; sounds gradually die away, their echo long drawn-out and lingeringly sorrowful; and the expanse of distance grows dim amid the silent melancholy of fading light. To the eye everything around you still seems cheerful and full of life, but the rhythm of an elegy already oppresses your saddened heart. For whom do you feel pity? For yourself? Or is it the groaning of the earth, inaudible earlier, that you can hear now? Is it the dead who throng round us at this pensive hour? Or is it our memory, unconsciously striving to express itself in the solitary soul. . .? Whatever it is, you feel pity, pity for someone who seems lost in the wilderness. . . And many minutes of decision pass silently by during these disquieting evenings.

"Look," said Bitt-Boy, "there goes a cormorant. He's going to settle on the water in a minute. Let's see which ship he settles nearest to. Is that all right, captains? Now," he went on after they had all agreed, "let's decide things like this. The one he settles nearest to I'll take out tonight, provided. . . as I said before. Come on then, you fat thing!"

At that the four captains exchanged such fierce glances that even the devil himself, the father of fire and brimstone, could not have kept his seat where their eyes met without being burnt to a cinder. But in order to understand them at this moment, one must be familiar with the superstitious nature of sailors. Meanwhile, completely unaware of all this, the cormorant described a few ponderous figures of eight among the ships and then settled right between the *President* and the *Marianna*, so near the middle of the gap that Bitt-Boy and all the rest gave a wry smile.

"Our feathered friend's taking them both in tow," said Duke. "Well, Renior? Shall we both shout together, or what?"

"Wait!" cried Chinchar. "The cormorant's swimming, you

know! Where will he swim to, that's what matters!"

"All right! The one he swims to wins," agreed Estamp.

Duke covered his face with his hand, almost as if he were nodding off, but he watched the cormorant through his fingers with eyes full of vigilant hatred. Out in front of the other ships and closer to the *Felizzata* was the *Aramea*. It was towards her, keeping a little closer to the brig, that the bird began to swim, diving as it went. Estamp drew himself up, his eyes flashing with pride.

"That's it!" he declared. "Did you all see that?"

"Yes, yes, we did!"

"I'm off," said Bitt-Boy, "so good-bye for now—someone's waiting for me. The cormorant's a stupid bird, but I swear that if I could have divided myself into four parts for you all, then I would have done. Well, Estamp, it's you who'll be hearing from me tonight. We'll either sail together or. . . part for good."

He uttered these last words under his breath, and so the others either did not hear them properly or only half-understood them. The three unlucky captains were sunk in gloom and Estamp was busy picking up his pipe from the floor, so no one managed to bid the pilot farewell. Getting to his feet, he waved his cap and went quickly towards the door.

"Bitt-Boy!" came the cry as he walked away.

He did not turn round, though, and hurried off down the stairs.

V

Now it is time for us to explain why this man played the role of a living talisman for people whose profession amounted to what might be called a calculated risk.

In defiance of logical minds which have a niggardly attitude towards life—minds which fly their miserable little grey flag over the majestic vastness of the earth with its countless unsolved mysteries, in the ludicrous hope that all profoundly disturbed people will bend their steps towards this flag—in defiance of such minds there are people who, as it were, have set themselves the task of making others examine the mysterious whisperings of the unexplored. *Some people move in the sombre realm of baneful coincidence. Their presence evokes melancholy, their words ring with foreboding, and their proximity brings misfortune.** But on the other hand there are colloquial expressions in everyday use that define a very different kind of person. "An *easy-going* man," "a *lucky* man," we say. Although we should not draw

---

* Grin's italics (translator's note).

hasty conclusions or debate the accuracy of our own conjectures, it is a fact that in the company of *lucky* people the general atmosphere is more relaxed. It is a fact, too, that such people alter the course of our lives in an amazing way by a seemingly trivial remark or gesture, and that the initiative they show in our affairs really does bring success in its wake. Sometimes these people are happy-go-lucky and absent-minded, but more often than not they are vigorous and earnest. They always have one characteristic in common: unaffected laughter. They laugh simply because something is funny and nothing more, and their laughter does not express any attitude towards people around them.

Such was the pilot Bitt-Boy, a man with inexplicable and unerring powers. Everything that he undertook for others invariably ended in success, however unfavourable the circumstances, and sometimes it even brought an unexpected bonus. No vessel had ever been wrecked after he had piloted her out of port, and the incident involving Beppo of which Duke had spoken was no fiction. Never did a ship which Bitt-Boy had personally guided out to sea suffer epidemics, piracy or other misfortunes; nobody on her ever fell overboard or committed any crime. Bitt-Boy had an excellent knowledge of Zurbagan, Kasset, Liss and all the coast of the peninsula, but he never lost his way in minor channels either. He had occasionally piloted ships in dangerous stretches of distant seas where he only happened to be by chance, yet in his hands the helm invariably took the right direction, just as if he could see the whole sea bed with his own eyes. People trusted him blindly, just as he trusted himself. Whether we call his gift keen instinct or not makes no difference... "Bitt-Boy, the bringer of luck" he was called—and by that name he was known wherever he had shown his skill.

The pilot crossed a series of ravines, turned the corner of the "Prickly Pillow" tavern, and made his way along a little path that wound amid stupendous gardens towards a short, stony street. Deep in thought, he walked with his head bowed the whole way, turning pale occasionally when something painful occurred to him. Reaching a small house with windows that looked on to a shady courtyard, he stopped and took a deep breath. Then he drew himself up and went through a gate in the low stone wall.

He was expected, or so it seemed. No sooner had he entered the garden, his feet rustling in the grass, and peered through the windows at the lamp flickering in their twilit depths, than a young girl appeared, her shoulder stirring the curtain at the window. The visitor's familiar figure had not deceived her. She was about to rush to the door, but after hurriedly considering the distances involved, leapt through the window and ran towards Bitt-Boy. She was about eighteen, with two dark plaits that emerged from under her yellow and purple scarf to grace her slender neck and then to follow the line of her body, the whole of it so svelte that as it moved it seemed like a restless ray of light. Her mobile, child-like face with its shy yet proud eyes was delightfully feminine.

"Rezhi, Queen of the Eyelashes!" exclaimed Bitt-Boy amid her kisses, "as long as you don't smother me, I'll have something to remember this evening of ours by!"

"Yes, darling, it's our evening, all ours, my inseparable one!" she replied. "I didn't go to bed because after what you said in your letter, I thought you'd be arriving any moment."

"Girls like you should eat and sleep a lot," he said absently. But then he shook off his momentary feeling of depression and asked: "Did I kiss both your eyes?"

"No, you didn't even kiss one, you old skinflint!"

"But I think I kissed the left one. . . That means the right one's offended. Give it to me then. . ." And she did, together with all its radiance.

But the essence of such conversations does not lie in our inadequate rendering of them, and we are well aware of it. Just try listening to one of them, and you will feel sadness and pity, for you can see two hearts struggling to convey to each other their own peculiar feelings. But sitting on a small bench in the garden, Rezhi and Bitt-Boy talked and talked until it grew dark.

Then, as often happens at times like these, a silence fell. It comes when hearts are full and is the prelude to decisions, if they are pressing. Bitt-Boy thought the moment had come to mention what he had to say, without putting it off any longer.

Unwittingly the girl helped him:

"Let's get married then, Bitt-Boy—I'm going to have a little one."

The pilot roared with laughter, but then the sudden awareness of his position cut his laughter short with a brief sigh.

"Now look," he said in a changed voice, "don't interrupt me, Rezhi." Sensing her alarm, he began to speak quickly, "I've made enquiries, been everywhere. . . and there's no doubt about it. . . So I can't marry you, darling. Oh, don't cry! Wait, and listen to me! Can't we just be friends? Rezhi. . . you silly thing, you're the best girl in all the world! How on earth could I make you unhappy? I've only come to say good-bye for a little while, you know! I love you so much my heart feels as if it's going to break. . . But it's already dead, Rezhi, dead! Besides, am I really the only man in the world? Are there so few good people around you? No, Rezhi, listen, then you'll understand and agree with me. . . What else can we possibly do?"

He went on talking like this for a long time, clenching his teeth to suppress his agonising tears, but the emotion filling his heart finally threw his thoughts into confusion.

Broken in body and spirit, he fell silent, and then pulling her little palms from her eyes, kissed them gently.

"Bitt-Boy...," she said through her sobs, "Bitt-Boy, you're just a silly chatterbox! You still don't know me properly. I won't give you up to either trouble or fear. Now you see," she went on, becoming more and more impassioned, "you're all upset. But I'll make you feel better... there then, there!" She took hold of his head and pressed it to her breast. "You just lie there quietly, my little one. Listen! If things are going to be bad for you, then I want them to be bad for me as well. And if they're good for you, then they'll be good for me too. Let's divide everything that's painful in half, and give me the bigger share. You'll always be like precious china to me... What else can I do to convince you? Kill myself, perhaps?"

She drew herself up and slipped a hand into her bodice where, in accordance with local custom, girls usually carry a stiletto or small dagger.

Bitt-Boy restrained her. He was silent, amazed by this unfamiliar side of someone who was so dear to him. But his mind was made up, and in his resolve he had already found a way out of the situation.

"Bitt-Boy," she went on, carried away by her own words and deceived by his downcast look, "you're very good to keep quiet and listen to me." Nestling up against his shoulder, she went on: "Everything'll be all right, believe me. That's what I think sometimes when I'm dreaming or feeling cross about your being away. We'll have a horse called 'Bitt-Boy', a dog called 'clever fellow' and a cat called 'Rezhi'. You'll not really need to leave Liss any more then, and you'll buy us a whole new set of copper pans for the kitchen. I'll smile at you everywhere, just everywhere: in front of friends, enemies and all our visitors—let everyone see just how much I love you. We'll play at bride and groom—how could you think of slipping out of it, you old good-for-nothing?—and I shan't cry any more either. And then when you've got your own brig, we'll sail round the world thirty-three times..."

Her voice sounded unsteady and drowsy, and her eyes kept opening and closing all the time. For a few minutes she described the imagined voyage in a confused way, and then tucking up her legs and settling herself comfortably, she gave a gentle yawn that sounded more like a sigh. Now she was dreaming that they were sailing through a starlit garden over brilliant underwater flowers.

"...And there's lots of seals there, Bitt-Boy. People say they're very kind, and they've got eyes just like ours, you know. No, please don't move—it's more comfortable like this. You won't drown me, will you, Bitt-Boy, because of some... little Turkish girl you happen to meet? You said I was Queen of the Eyelashes... so take them, darling, take everything, everything..."

Bitt-Boy's ear caught the even breathing of sleep. The moon was shining. He looked at Rezhi sideways and saw her soft eyelashes lying on her pale cheeks. He smiled awkwardly, and then, trying his utmost to move as gently as possible, got up from the bench and laid her head on the oil-cloth cushion. He was barely alive. But time was passing and the moon had risen higher... He softly kissed her feet and with a cry wringing his soul, walked out on to the street.

On his way down to the harbour he dropped in at the "Prickly Pillow" for a few minutes.

VI

It was about ten o'clock in the evening when a rowing boat came up to the *Felizzata* and bumped gently against her side. There was only one man in it.

"Ahoy there on the brig!" came a restrained cry.

The sailor on watch walked to the rail.

"Ahoy there," he answered sleepily, peering into the darkness. "What do you want?"

"Judging by the voice, that's you, Reksen, isn't it? It's Bitt-Boy here."

"Bitt-Boy! Really?.." The sailor shone his lantern on the boat. "What a surprise! Have you been in Liss long?"

"We'll talk later, Reksen. Who's your captain?"

"I don't think you know him, Bitt-Boy. He's called Esquiros and he comes from Colombia."

"No, I don't."

While the sailor quickly began to lower the ladder, Bitt-Boy stood in the middle of the boat deep in thought.

"So you're roaming about loaded with gold, are you?" he asked.

The sailor laughed.

"Oh no, we're only carrying some provisions for ourselves and a small cargo for the island of Sandy."

He let down the ladder.

"But all the same, you're probably carrying gold too... as I understand it," muttered Bitt-Boy as he climbed up on deck.

"No, we've thought of something else, pilot."

"And do you agree with it?"

"Yes, I think it's a splendid idea."

"Excellent. Is the captain asleep?"

"No."

"Well take me to him then, would you?"

Through a chink in the captain's door they could see a light showing in the cabin. Bitt-Boy knocked and went in with swift, purposeful strides.

He was dead drunk and as white-faced as a man before his execution, but he was in full control of himself and behaved with amazing poise. Getting up from his charts, Esquiros came towards the stranger, screwing up his eyes as he peered at him. The captain was a middle-aged man with a weary air and a slight stoop. His face had a rather unhealthy look, but it was amiable and pleasant all the same.

"Who are you and what brings you here?" he asked without raising his voice.

"My name's Bitt-Boy, captain," began the pilot, "you may have heard of me. I'm here. . ."

"You? Bitt-Boy, 'the bringer of luck'? People turn round when they hear that name! I know all about you. Sit down, my friend! Have a glass of wine and a cigar. Let me shake your hand and thank you for coming!"

Bitt-Boy sat down, forgetting for a moment what he wanted to say. But gradually his thoughts came back to him. He took a sip of wine, lit his cigar and gave a forced laugh.

"Where's the *Felizzata* bound for?" he asked. "What's the plan of her course? Tell me that, captain."

Esquiros was not surprised by the direct question. Aims—or rather intentions—such as his sometimes inspire frankness. But before beginning to speak, he walked up and down for a few moments so as to collect his thoughts.

"Well now. . . let's talk," he began. "The sea sometimes produces strange characters, my dear pilot, and I expect my own character will seem strange to you. In the past I've known much misfortune. It's not broken me, though, and because of it I've discovered new desires. My outlook has become broader and the world has grown more accessible. It draws me, the whole of it, and I long to visit every corner of it. I'm single, I've done every kind of shipboard work, and I've been a good sailor. But what's behind me is familiar ground. Besides, I have—and I've always had—a great need to move from place to place. So what I've thought up now is a voyage of my very own. We've got thirty barrels of someone's salt beef to unload on Rocky Sandy, and then attentively and lovingly we'll sail the seas without any specific plan. To look at the way others live, to seek meaningful encounters, to travel without haste, occasionally to rescue victims of a shipwreck or shelter a fugitive; to lie moored in the luxuriant estuaries of vast rivers; perhaps to put down roots for a while in some foreign land and allow the anchor to become encrusted with salt; and then, filled with yearning to be away again, to break free and let the sails catch the wind once more—is that not good, Bitt-Boy?"

"Go on," said the pilot.

"My crew are all new, and I wasn't in any hurry to choose them either. After paying off the last one, I sought promising meetings and talked to many people, and one by one I found men who were suitable. They're a crew of dreamers! But the pirate vessel is keeping us in Liss now. I managed to give her the slip the other day, though only because this harbour was so close. Stay with us, Bitt-Boy, and I'll give the order to weigh anchor right away! Did you say you knew Reksen?"

"Yes, I know him from the *Radius*," replied Bitt-Boy, surprised at the captain's question, "but I've not said so yet. I. . . was just thinking about it."

Esquiros did not press the point, thinking that the pilot's slight mistake was just the result of forgetfulness.

"So you trust me, do you, captain?" asked Bitt-Boy.

"Perhaps I was expecting you all along, but without realising it," Esquiros replied.

There was a silence.

"Good luck to you then," said the pilot suddenly in a bright, cheerful voice. "Send the ship's boy over to the *Aramea* with a note for Estamp, would you?"

After writing the note, he handed it to Esquiros. It said:

"My dear Estamp, I am as stupid as that cormorant. The 'circumstances' I spoke of have come about. Farewell to you all—you, Duke, and you, Renior and Chinchar. These shores will never set eyes on me again."

After sending off the note, Esquiros shook Bitt-Boy's hand.

"Let's weigh anchor!" he cried in a ringing voice, and his manner suddenly became brisk and authoritative. They went up on deck.

The soul of each was filled with a wind that sang its own song: in the captain's case it was the song of restless movement, in the pilot's that of a desolate graveyard. Esquiros summoned the bosun with a whistle, and within ten minutes the deck was covered with men silhouetted against the lanterns hanging on the stays. The vessel was waking in the darkness, and as her sails flapped and gathered the wind, fewer and fewer stars could be seen flickering among the yards. Creaking, the windlass turned, and pulling on the ship, the cable slowly dragged the anchor from the sea bed.

Taking the helm, Bitt-Boy turned to look for the last time at the shore where Rezhi was fast asleep.

*   *   *   *

The *Felizzata* sailed without lights. All was silent and still aboard her. Taking the ship out through the narrow harbour entrance, Bitt-Boy swung the wheel hard to port and steered in that direction for about a mile. After that he turned almost at right-angles and headed due east, before obeying his instinct and swinging to starboard again. Then, seeing no sign of the pirate ship anywhere in the vicinity, he steered due east once more.

Just at that moment something odd happened: a kind of soundless cry rang out behind him. He looked round, and Esquiros who was standing by the compass did the same. Behind them a huge beam of pale blue light rose from the coal-black turrets of the privateer and fell on the rocks of Liss.

"You're looking in the wrong place," said Bitt-Boy. "But put on more sail, Esquiros."

The wind had stiffened now, and running at twenty knots with extra canvas, the brig soon covered about five miles. Within a short time she had rounded the cape.

Bitt-Boy gave the helm to the sailor on watch and went down to the captain's cabin, where Esquiros opened a bottle. For their part, the men on deck had already toasted the ship's successful escape, and the gay sound of their singing could be heard below. It was the song of "Dicky John":

> Don't murmur, ocean, don't affright us,
> Earth's scared us a long, long time.
> To a much warmer clime,
> A southern paradise,
> We'll come sailing sure enough.
>
> *Refrain:*
>
> Let's clink our glasses, dear old girl,
> Now that we've quaffed a-plenty,
> Or Dicky John, make no mistake,
> Will drain our tankards empty!

Oh earth, dry land, you're a desert for me now;
My heart is grieved... I'm turning grey... Adieu!
That's the mark, you know,
You've left on me...
So farewell and let us go!

Refrain:

Let's clink our glasses, dear old girl,
Now that we've quaffed a-plenty,
Or Dicky John, make no mistake,
Will drain our tankards empty!

The Southern Cross shines high above,
With night's first wind the compass will awake.
Oh Lord! Save Thou
Our gallant ships,
And have mercy on us sailors!

When for some reason the ship's boy who had taken the note across to Estamp came in, Bitt-Boy asked him:

"Did he go on at you for a long time, young fellow?"

"I wouldn't tell him where you were, sir. He shouted and stamped and threatened to hang me from the yard-arm, but I ran off."

Esquiros was jovial and gay now.

"Bitt-Boy!" he said, "I've been thinking how fortunate you must be if bringing other people luck is so easy for you."

Sometimes words can kill. Slowly the pilot turned pale, and his face looked wretched as the shadow of an inner spasm passed across it. Putting his glass down on the table, he pulled his jersey up to his chin and unbuttoned his shirt.

Esquiros winced. On the whitened flesh above the left nipple was a hideous, ulcerous swelling.

"Cancer...?" he asked, feeling instantly sober.

Bitt-Boy nodded, and turning away, began to straighten his clothing. His hands were shaking.

Up on deck the men were still singing the same song, but it was for the last time now. A gust of wind scattered its final verse, and all that could be heard down below was:

"The Southern Cross shines high above. . ." There was a faint echo, and then through the cabin door which had closed with the ship's rolling, came the words:

". . . And have mercy on us sailors!"

These were the words that Bitt-Boy, "the bringer of luck," heard most clearly of all.

1922

The Heart Of The Wilderness

I

The discovery of diamonds at Cordon-Brun brought with it a liking for civilised things. What most concerns us here, though, is the splendid "Congo" café that was opened there. Among its customers we would like to point out three men of artistic temperament whose inveterate scepticism had turned them into three lost souls. There was no doubt that they were talented, but they had ceased to perceive the *kernel* of things, and in their various ways had come to see only the *shell*.

This outlook had led them to engage in the mischievous deception of others, a pursuit which had become their calling. Deception was in fact their religion now, and in their own way they had achieved perfection in it. Thus, for instance, the legend about the diamond of eighteen hundred carats—devised with subtle malice over a glass of champagne while they listened to the aria from "Jocelyn"*—had produced an amazing effect, sending thousands of dubious characters off to the waterfall of Alpetri where, so the trio said, the monstrous gem could be seen glittering in the rocks above the water. And so on and so forth. Thanks to them, Stella Dijon became convinced that Harry Evans, who was hopelessly in love with her (this was not true), had married O'Neill's daughter out of despair. The shameful outcome of all this did no one any credit: Evans got Stella on the brain and shot himself.

Hart, Weber and Conseil liked to amuse themselves. The visions that they saw in the smoke rising from their strong cigars determined the pattern of their carefree lives. One morning they were sitting in their comfortable rocking-chairs in the café, smiling silently like soothsayers. Pale despite the heat, their expressions affable yet pensive, they were men without souls and without futures.

Their yacht was still anchored at Cordon-Rouge, and they were reluctant to leave, savouring their impressions of the diamond fever with all its filth and the greed that glittered in men's eyes.

It was no longer early, and in the shade of the banana trees the morning heat was becoming more bearable. Through the open

---

*An opera by the French romantic composer Benjamin Louis Paul Godard (1849-1895), first produced in 1888 and based on Lamartine's poem *Jocelyn* (1836). By aria Grin may have meant the "Berceuse," a piece for which the opera is well-known (translator's note).

doors of the café dusty mounds of earth could be seen across the narrow street, and every now and then a pick would fly into the air above them. Cork helmets flashed white among the diggings and straw hats gleamed in the sun. A cart was going past, pulled by buffaloes.

The café was one of the few wooden buildings in Cordon-Brun. It had mirrors, a piano, and a mahogany bar in it.

Hart, Weber and Conseil were drinking. Then Emmanuel Steel came in.

II

The man who had just appeared was very different from the three snobs: powerfully built and handsome, he possessed a childlike belief that no one would ever wish to do him any harm—a conviction which always shone in his grave eyes. He had big, heavy hands, the physique of a soldier, and the face of an innocent. He was wearing an inexpensive cotton suit and very good shoes, and the butt of a revolver could be seen bulging under his shirt. His hat had a white kerchief sewn to its brim at the nape of his neck, and it looked like a tent big enough to hold a giant. He never said much and would nod in a charming way as though inclining his head in agreement with the whole world. In short, when Steel came into the room, people always felt like standing aside.

Gently swinging one leg, Conseil glanced at Hart's withered-looking face with its evasive smile, while Hart looked at Conseil's white forehead and pale blue eyes. Then they both winked at the truculent, peevish Weber, who in his turn shot them the sharpest of glances from behind his spectacles. After that all three began to talk.

A few days earlier Steel had sat drinking with them, and they had realised what kind of man he was. Although quite serious, the conversation had been full of concealed, arid laughter on their part, except for odd moments when Steel had said something unusual and riveted their attention. But he had not even suspected that they were making fun of him.

"It's him," said Conseil.

"A man out of the fog," put in Hart.

"In a fog, you mean," said Weber, correcting him.

"Searching for the secret angle."

"Or the fourth dimension."

"No, he's a seeker of rarities," replied Hart.

"What was he saying the other day about the jungle?" asked Weber.

Mimicking Steel, Conseil said in a rapid patter:

"This vast forest that stretches for thousands of miles into the heart of the continent must conceal the mines of King Solomon, the mysteries of Scheherazade, and hundreds of other things simply waiting to be discovered."

"Let's suppose," said Hart, dousing with brandy a fly that was already lying drunk in a pool of wine spilt on the table, "let's suppose he hadn't put it quite like that. He was thinking aloud at the time and what he said was rather vague. But the essence of it was this: in these boundless forests there must be a place, not yet discovered, that would produce the most enormous, the most staggering effect upon whoever saw it, an astonishing Himalaya among Himalayas, a place where impressive sights are scattered in abundance. And if he knew how to find it, he'd go there."

"He's got an odd temperament for Cordon-Brun all right," remarked Conseil, "and he's good material for a bit of fun. Let's try him."

"How?"

"I've worked out a little plan in the way we've done many times before, and I think I can explain it in a fairly credible fashion. All you've got to do is say 'yes' every time he gives you an inquiring look."

"Right," said Weber and Hart.

"Hey!" shouted Conseil without a moment's delay. "Steel! Come and join us."

Steel was talking to the barman, but he turned round and made his way over to the group. They gave him a chair.

III

To begin with, the conversation was of an ordinary kind, but after a while it turned to rather more interesting things.

"You're a lazy fellow, Steel!" said Conseil. "You've salted a few thousand pounds away and now you're kicking your heels! Have you sold all your diamonds?"

"Yes, a long time ago," replied Steel quietly, "but I've no wish to undertake anything else of that kind. I liked the diggings because they were a novelty, that's all."

"But what will you do now?"

"I'm new to this country, and I find it beautiful and terrifying at the same time. I'm waiting till I feel an inner urge to start something else."

"I noticed the peculiar nature of your temperament during our last conversation," said Conseil. "By the way, the day after that I happened to talk to Pelegrin, the hunter. He'd collected a lot of ivory about five hundred miles from here on the other side of the river, in those forests that so captivate your soul. He told me of a curious phenomenon: deep in the jungle there's a small plateau with a delightful settlement on it. You come upon it quite unexpectedly, because in the twilit forest you suddenly find yourself looking at high walls made out of logs. These are the rear of buildings that face on to an inner garden full of flowers. (Pelegrin came upon the little colony as evening fell and spent a day there.) He was walking along and all of a sudden thought he caught the sound of a guitar playing among the trees. He was absolutely amazed because only forest and nothing but forest stretched in every direction, and there wasn't even a native village nearer than two weeks' journey away. But he made his way towards the sound and was received with warm hospitality. There were seven families living in the colony, all closely linked by similar tastes and by love for the luxuriant remoteness of their surroundings. And it's true, you know, it's hard to imagine anywhere more remote than that village in the wilderness. The way the inhabitants made a living contrasted strangely with the completely civilised fashion in which their dwellings were run. They lived solely by hunting, sending their catch off by boat to the trading post at Tankos and exchanging it for all the supplies they needed, right down to electric light bulbs.

How had they been chosen, how had they got there, and how had they established themselves? Pelegrin never found out. He only spent a day there—it was no more than the flash of a magnesium flare above a wreck—just enough to grasp and perhaps to forget what was essential about the place. But what the settlers had accomplished was tremendous. He saw beautiful, carved balconies; flowers entwined around windows hung with blue and purple awnings; the skin of a lion; a piano with a rifle propped up beside it; suntanned, carefree children with the fearless eyes of heroes out of a fairy-tale; beautiful, slim girls with revolvers in their pockets and books by their beds; hunters with the sharp eyes of an eagle—what more could anyone want? It was as if these people had come together to sing a melodious song in wonderful unison. And Pelegrin remembered his first impression of the place particularly vividly. It was rather like an obscure drawing, he said: there was a narrow passage between timbered walls, a little hand waving from a balcony to his left, and before him a sunlit garden that looked like paradise.

I expect you've stayed the night with an unfamiliar family, haven't you? Their life goes on around you, a fragment as full of fascination as a page torn out of an unknown book. You glimpse the face of an old woman or a young girl, and never see it again for the rest of the evening; you hear a snatch of conversation about something private, and can't grasp its meaning; you surrender yourself to events and things of which all you know is that these people have given you shelter; you haven't entered into their lives, and so they remain pervaded by strange poetry. Well that's how it was with Pelegrin too."

Steel listened attentively, looking Conseil straight in the eye.

"I can see it all," he said simply. "It's tremendous, isn't it?"

"Yes," said Weber, "it is."

"Yes," affirmed Hart.

"Words can't express what I feel," Steel went on pensively, filled with emotion, "but how right I was! Where does Pelegrin live?"

"Oh, he left with a caravan for Ogo some time ago."

Slowly at first then more quickly, Steel drew his finger across the table in a straight line, as though brushing something away.

"What was this place called?" he asked. "And how did Pelegrin find it?"

"It was called the Heart of the Wilderness," Conseil replied, "and he came upon it somewhere between Cordon-Brun and Lake Ban. That's right, Hart, isn't it?"

"Oh yes."

"There's another detail," said Weber, sucking his lips. "Pelegrin mentioned a short cut, a steep forested slope running northwards that cut diagonally across his path. He was searching for his family who thought he was dead, (in actual fact he'd only been stunned by a falling tree) and he'd been walking southwards all the time instead."

"Does the slope run up to the plateau?" asked Steel, turning his whole body towards Weber as he spoke.

Then Weber gave several topographical details which were so precise that Conseil shot him a warning glance and whistled 'Where are you hurrying to, my pretty one, for the sun has not yet risen...'* But Steel did not notice anything.

He listened to all that Weber said and nodded several times in his warm way. Then he got quickly to his feet, and as he bid the three men farewell, the look on his face resembled that of someone who has only just woken up. He did not see their sharp eyes carefully watching his every movement. It was hard to tell what he was thinking, though, for he was a man of complex emotions.

"Weber," asked Conseil when Steel had gone out, "how do you know so much about the region? Where did you get all that

---

*The origin of these words is very obscure, but they would appear to derive from some Russian folk song popular around 1900 (translator's note).

information about the unknown?"

"From the account of Penn's expedition. . . and my own imagination."

"I see. Well then, what now?"

"That's his business," replied Weber with a laugh, "but if I know Steel. . . Anyway, we're sailing at the end of the week."

A shadow fell across the sunlit doorway. It was Steel.

"I've come back again but I won't come in," he said quickly. "I've seen the name of your yacht's home port on her stern, Conseil. Melbourne, it says, but go on. . ."

"Two, Flag Street," replied Conseil. "And. . ."

"That's all, thanks."

Steel disappeared.

"This could turn out badly, you know," remarked Hart coolly when the silence had said meaningful things to them all, "and he'll track you down."

"What?"

"Men like him never forgive."

"Bah!" Conseil retorted, tossing his head. "Life's short and the world's a big place."

IV

Two years went by, and in the course of them Conseil visited many more places on the globe, observing the variety of life and continually attempting in his mocking way to interfere in its giddy progress. But eventually he grew weary of this too. Then he returned to the bitter solitude of home, and though he did not suffer the aesthetic convulsions of des Esseintes,* he was filled with a chill emptiness that he found impossible to understand.

Meanwhile hearts went on being broken and mended, and the world thundered on its way. Then one day, amid life's tumult, came the sound of measured footsteps. They stopped outside the entrance to Conseil's apartment. A few minutes later he received a small visiting-card that reminded him of Cordon-Brun.

"I'll see him," he said after a short silence, feeling a burning curiosity despite the extreme unpleasantness of his position. "Show him in."

The two men faced each other at a distance of twenty yards across the vast hall. Its translucent, silvery light enveloped the figure

---

*The decadent aristocratic hero of the novel *A Rebours* (1884) by the French novelist J. K. Huysmans (translator's note).

of Steel as he appeared in the doorway. He stood there for a time, watching Conseil's impassive face, and at that moment both men felt that their meeting was inevitable. Then they walked quickly towards each other.

"Cordon-Brun," said Conseil amiably. "You disappeared and I left without giving you the engraving by Morad as I'd intended. I think you'll like it—the fantastic landscape of Saturn that it portrays evokes the mystery of the universe."

"Yes," replied Steel with a smile. "As you can see, I remembered your address—I made a note of it. I've come to say that I visited the Heart of the Wilderness and saw what Pelegrin did. But I saw much more, because I live there now."

"I'm to blame," said Conseil drily, "but my words are my business and I'll answer for them. I'm at your service, Steel."

With a laugh, Steel took Conseil's limp hand, and lifting it, clapped it with his own.

"No!" he cried, "that's not the point! You don't understand! I've *made* the Heart of the Wilderness. Yes I have! I couldn't find it because of course it didn't exist, and I soon realised you were joking. But the joke was a splendid one. There was a time when I used to dream about things like that too. Yes, I've always loved discoveries which touch the heart like a beautiful song. People call me a crank, but so what? I admit I was terribly envious of Pelegrin, so I set off to try and see what he did. Yes, a month's journey showed me what the jungle's like. Hunger. . . and thirst. . . I was completely alone. Then came ten days of fever. I had no tent. The flames of my camp-fire looked multi-coloured, just like a rainbow. White horses kept coming out of the forest, and my dead brother appeared and sat watching me. He used to whisper all the time, calling me to follow him. I kept taking quinine and drinking. All this delayed me, of course. Then a snake bit me on the arm. Oh, how it exasperated me, the prospect of death! But I pulled myself together and listened to what my body was trying to say. Then, like a dog, I felt drawn to a particular kind of grass, ate some of it, and was saved. After that I was utterly exhausted and slept for days. I was lucky, I suppose. Everything was like a dream: wild animals, fatigue, hunger and stillness, and I had to keep killing the wild animals too. There was nothing at all in the place you and your friends spoke of—I explored the whole plateau. It descends to a small tributary where the forested slope widens out. Of course, everything became clear to me then. But the whole region's so incredibly beautiful that you just can't describe it. There are things words simply can't convey. . . like hail on a window pane. . . it only makes a faint, tapping sound. . ."

"Go on," said Conseil softly.

"It just *had* to be there," Steel went on quietly, "so I built a raft and sailed downriver to the fort, where I hired all the men and materials I needed from the agent. Then I made everything exactly as it was in your story, just as I wanted it. Seven houses—that took a year. After that I travelled about and searched high and low, looking for the right kind of people. I considered thousands of them, delving deep into their souls. Of course, I was bound to find them in the end, given the sort of person I am—that's clear. So let's go and have a look at the place, shall we? You've evidently got an artistic imagination, and I'd like to know whether you visualised it as it is."

He said all this with the terrifying simplicity of a little boy talking about a great historical event.

Conseil's face had turned pink. Long-forgotten music resounded in his soul, and in an effort to control his emotion he paced back and forth across the hall. Then he halted, as if rooted to the spot.

"You're a tornado," he said in a choking voice, "you are, you know, a real tornado! And that's not an insult."

"When you can see something clearly. . ." Steel began.

"I've been asleep for a long time," said Conseil gravely, interrupting him. "So. . . But it's all just like a dream! Perhaps I ought to live again, eh?"

"Yes, I should," replied Steel.

"But the place didn't exist, it just didn't exist!"

"Yes it did!" said Steel, raising his head without wishing to produce any effect, but the gesture sent his words rolling away and they thundered in every corner of the room. "It did exist, because I carried it deep in my heart."

This meeting produced a conclusion which closely resembled the fantasies devised by Conseil's subtle imagination back in Cordon-Brun. With their heads still full of the vast expanse of forest left behind them, the two men gazed at the timbered walls screened by foliage. The sun was setting, and as the shadows lengthened, from a balcony overlooking the luxuriant garden came the soft sound of a woman singing.

Steel smiled, and Conseil realised why.

1923

Voice And Eye

I

The blind man lay with his arms folded on his chest and smiled. But he smiled without being aware of it. He had been lying like this for three days now, with a bandage over his eyes, and had been told to move only if it were absolutely necessary. Despite his fixed expression though, his spiritual condition was that of a condemned prisoner who hopes for clemency. From time to time the possibility that he might begin to see again—dependent as it was upon the mysterious workings of his pupils in the bright void around him—struck him with such thrilling clarity that his whole body twitched as if he were dreaming.

Wishing to spare Rabid's nerves, the professor had not told him that the operation had been a success and that he would almost certainly see again. A chance in ten thousand that something might go wrong could easily result in tragedy. So each day, as he said goodbye to Rabid, the professor would add: "Don't worry—we've done all we can for you, and the rest will take care of itself."

Amid the anguish of wondering and waiting, Rabid heard footsteps coming up to him. It was Daisy Haran, a girl who worked in the clinic. Often at moments of distress he would ask her to put her hand on his brow and this time too he gladly awaited the soft pressure of her palm, for he felt stupefied by the long hours of immobility. She did exactly as he had expected.

When she took her hand away, he—who had looked deep into himself for so long and had learnt to understand the feelings of his heart—realised once again that what he had feared most during the last few days was that he might never see her. Even when they had first brought him into the clinic and he had heard a woman's business-like voice dealing with arrangements for the new patient, he had been filled with the joyous feeling that she was a graceful, gentle creature, a feeling evoked by the soft sound of her voice. It had the heart-warming ring of youthful life about it, and was rich in melodious inflections that were as clear as a spring morning.

Gradually a distinct image of her arose within him, one that was fanciful like all our notions of things we cannot see, but one that was vitally necessary to him. After three weeks spent talking only to her, three weeks in which he had submitted to her gentle but firm care, Rabid knew he had loved her from the very beginning. Now he was determined to get better—for her sake.

He thought she felt profound sympathy for him—something that augured well for the future. But because he was blind, he did not consider he had the right to ask her about such things, and so put them off until Daisy and he could look into each other's eyes. But he was completely unaware that this girl, whose voice made him so happy, thought of his probable recovery with fear and sadness. The reason was that she was extremely plain. Her feelings for him stemmed from her loneliness, from her awareness that she had an influence over him, and from her sense of security. After all, he was blind, and she could look calmly at herself through his notion of her, as it were, a notion that he expressed not so much in words but in the whole way he treated her. And she knew he loved her.

Before his operation they talked a great deal and touched on many things. Rabid told her about his former wanderings, while she spoke of events taking place in the world at large. What she said was as charming and gentle as the sound of her voice. When it was time for her to leave, they both tried to think of something to say. Her last words were: "Good-bye for now." "For now..." he replied, and it seemed to him that in those two words there was hope.

Tall and dark-haired, he was young and gay. He should—if everything turned out well—have a pair of shining black eyes and a bright, steady gaze. Imagining what he might look like, Daisy would walk fearfully away from the mirror, and her pale, unattractive face would blush softly. "What's going to happen?" she wondered. "Well, it may mean the end of a marvellous month together, but all the same I beg you, Professor Rebald, please make him see again!"

II

When the time for the test came and the light had been adjusted so that Rabid's weak eyes could cope with it, the professor and his assistant, together with several people from scientific circles, gathered round the patient's bed. "Daisy..." said Rabid, thinking she was there and hoping to see her first. She was not there though, because at that moment she had insufficient strength to witness and share the emotion of a man whose fate was to be decided by the removal of his bandage. As though bewitched, she stood in the middle of the room, listening to the footsteps and voices around her. By one of those strange tricks that the imagination plays on us at moments of painful apprehension, she suddenly saw herself as a different person in another world—the kind of person she would like his new-born eyes to see. Then she sighed and submitted to fate.

Meanwhile the bandage had been removed. Continuing to

sense its pressure while aware that it had gone, Rabid lay there filled with agonising yet blissful doubt. His pulse became weaker. "It's done," said the professor, his voice shaking with emotion. "Open your eyes and look!"

Rabid raised his eyelids, still thinking that Daisy was there but reluctant to call her again. Right in front of his face hung the folds of a curtain. "Move that material," he said, "it's in the way." And having said it, he realised that he could see again, and that the material which seemed to be hanging over his face was the window-curtain at the far end of the room.

His chest began to heave as sobs shook his wasted body, but almost unaware of it, he began to look around him, just like a person sitting up in bed with a book. Illumined by the radiance of his ecstasy, object after object passed before his eyes, and then, seeing the door, he instantly fell in love with it because he realised it was the one that Daisy always came in through. With a happy smile he took a glass from the bedside table, and though his hand was shaking, managed to put it back almost exactly in its place.

Now he waited impatiently for all the people who had restored his sight to leave the room, so that he could call Daisy again. Feeling that he was able to face life once more, he wanted to tell her all the important things he had to say. But several minutes of learned, quiet conversation went by, during which he was obliged to describe what he could see and how he felt.

Because of his immense excitement and the fleeting thoughts that filled his head, the details of these minutes were lost, and he found it hard to decide when he was finally alone. But eventually the longed-for moment came. He rang the bell and telling the ward orderly that he wanted to see Daisy straightaway, began to look blissfully at the door.

III

After hearing that the operation had been a brilliant success, Daisy went back to the neat solitude of her room. With tears in her eyes, she summoned up her courage before this encounter that would cancel out all those before it. Putting on a pretty summer dress, she arranged her thick hair in a simple way (she could not have done anything better with it, that dark wave with its smooth lustre) and holding her head naturally, came out with a smile on her face and a death-sentence in her heart—out towards the door beyond which everything was now so extraordinarily changed. She even began to feel that it was not Rabid lying there any more but someone completely different. Swiftly recalling in these last seconds many details of their conversations together, she realised that he loved her.

Touching the door, she lingered a moment before opening it, almost wishing that everything could remain as it had been before. Rabid lay with his head turned towards the door, his alert eyes seeking her. She went into the room and stopped.

"Who are you?" he asked with an enquiring smile.

"I'm a new person for you really, aren't I?" she said, the sound of her voice instantly reminding him of all the time they had spent together, short though it was.

In his black eyes she saw brimming joy, and suddenly her suffering was no more. Though there had been no miracle, all her inner self—her love, her fear, her pride, her thoughts—all the emotion of this crucial moment was expressed in such a radiant smile on her blushing face that to Rabid she seemed like a melodious string garlanded with flowers. She was beautiful in the light of love.

"Now, and only now," he said, "do I realise why your voice is so gentle that I loved to hear it in my dreams. Even if you went blind yourself this very minute, I would make you see again just by loving you. Forgive me—I'm a little crazy because I've risen from the dead, so you mustn't mind what I say."

At that moment his precise notion of her—a notion born of the darkness—was one she had never expected, not even in her wildest dreams.

1923

Gatt, Witt and Redott

I

Wishing to make their fortune so that they could possess their own houses, gardens and cars, three men set off for Africa. At that time the diamond-fields situated on the Vivera River (it is so small that you will not find it on any map), were producing from one thousand to three thousand carats of gems a month. And so the steamer which sailed to that part of the African coast from Zanzibar every four weeks would regularly disembark hundreds of people eager to try their luck.

The three men were: a postman, a cabby, and a baker. The first was called Gatt, the second Witt, and the third Redott. After saving up for the journey, they set off for the land of monkeys, lions and snakes intending to dig the sands there.

As soon as they arrived unfortunate things began to happen. First Redott fell ill with fever, then Witt, and finally Gatt. While they were lying in their tent sipping coconut beer and quinine, some negroes stole their money, horses and tools. When they recovered from the shock, they found themselves a claim which they reckoned ought to have diamonds on it. Then they borrowed three spades and started work.

After a month's strenuous digging they had only found one single diamond, and even that was as dull as a piece of dirty glass. True, it was as big as a nut, but it was worth practically nothing, and the broker only gave them three pounds for it.

Meanwhile, their energy was starting to dwindle. They tried changing claims but could not find a thing anywhere else either. Apart from that, the intense heat was having a bad effect on their health: they were growing thin, drinking a lot of water, and could hardly sleep at all, for their anxiety gave them no rest.

One evening they were sitting silently by the camp-fire.

"So we haven't got a thing," said the pensive Redott after a while, "and we haven't even got the strength to chop any wood for the fire. We're living almost entirely on vegetables, and if we go on like this we'll soon be dead."

"I don't want to die," replied the gluttonous Gatt who was weaker than the others. "You see, I want plenty of steaks, wine and money. I'd just like to enjoy life to the full, damn it!"

"Enjoy it then," said the irritable Witt mockingly. "I'd just like to get a bit of strength back, that's all. Then I'd go and see that Dutchman Van Klops. He'd lend me some ammunition and a gun, and I'd go off and join the ivory hunters. But alas, I'd have to eat good meat many times to be able to do that."

"Yes, it would be good to be strong," answered Redott. "What use am I?" He rolled up his sleeves and looked at his thin arms. "If I was a bit stronger than Samson, for example, I could make myself a real pile by digging here, couldn't I?"

"I'd catch elephants just as easily as if they were mice," said Witt. "I'd tear out their tusks with my bare hands and pile them up like cigarettes. And then I'd catch a couple of dozen lions—any zoo would buy them from me. Do you know what a decent lion fetches? A thousand pounds, they say, so just you add that up."

"About twenty thousand," said Gatt. "With the kind of strength you're talking about I'd simply spit in the river from where I stood and kill as many fish as everyone here needs. Fresh fish! Roll up, folks, and cash down!"

II

"So where's the problem?" someone asked, and the words rang out above their heads.

The flickering camp-fire cast its ruddy light into the darkness, and the bronzed figure of a Hindu appeared out of the gloom. His turban shone with rich embroidery and a gem-encrusted dagger flashed in his belt. His shining eagle's eyes expressed dignity and pride. He had arrived at the Vivera River not long ago together with a large number of servants and horses, but he did not intend to stay there long. People said he was making for the heart of Africa.

"Your grace..." mumbled Gatt, getting to his feet. "Do us the honour of taking a seat with us."

"Sit down," muttered Witt sullenly.

Redott stood up and answering the Hindu's gesture of greeting with a bow, said:

"Sahib Shakh-Duran, please light your pipe at our fire. We have nothing more to offer you."

"But you will have," said the Hindu. "I was walking past and overheard your conversation." He sat down. "So I repeat, where's the problem?" he went on. "If you wish to be strong, I can fulfil your wish."

"You're joking!" cried Redott.

"In India we do not joke about such things," said the Hindu.

"Tales of the Arabian nights," snorted the jocular Gatt, and Witt answered him in a whisper:

"It looks like Shakh's been down to the mission and had a drop of liquor."

The Hindu's keen ear caught what they were saying.

"I do not drink liquor," he replied, and though not annoyed, he said it so impressively that Witt and Gatt were lost for words. "And as for your tales of the Arabian nights, it would be better if I got down to business straightaway. Do you want to be strong or not?"

"Oh!" said Witt.

"Aha!" answered Gatt.

"Yes!" replied Redott.

Shakh-Duran unbuttoned his cloak and took three grains of wheat out of a tiny pouch.

"These grains," he said, "were taken from the sarcophagus of the Egyptian pharoah Rameses I, who lived thousands of years ago. They contain the force of life. For five thousand years it has been growing greater and greater inside them, and now whoever eats one of them will be stronger than a whole herd of buffalo."

"Allow me to ask you," said Gatt, "why it is that these particular grains possess such strength while the ones we bake our flat cakes with only give us indigestion?"

"You haven't the patience to cook your cakes properly. As for these grains, I'll explain why they contain such colossal strength. In a good harvest Egyptian wheat yields two hundred times its own weight. Consequently, from one grain—provided it germinates—you get two hundred grains."

"He's not been drinking," Gatt whispered to Witt as softly as he could. "One times two hundred is two hundred, that I can guarantee."

"No, I have not been drinking," Shakh-Duran affirmed in a melancholy voice while Gatt tried to look all innocent, "and to prove it I'll do the following calculation for you. The Nile floods twice a year, and twice a year her flat banks yield their harvest... So one grain of wheat with its two hundred offspring produces forty thousand grains a year. The following year the forty thousand produce eighty million descendants. In the fifth year—just in the fifth year, mark you—the number of grains increases to one hundred and two centillions, four hundred sextillions, that is..."

The Hindu picked up a stick and drawing the figure 1024 on the sand, added twenty-three noughts to it.

"There," he said, "that's how many grains there'll be in five years from one grain alone."

"Higher mathematics!" whispered Gatt reverently.

"And what if one speaks of five thousand years?" asked Shakh-Duran with a chuckle. "Then there'll be so many noughts that you'll get tired of writing them."

"I'll go crazy," said Witt.

"Or. . ." put in Gatt.

Redott said nothing.

"Now an ear of corn weighs one zolotnik,*" the Hindu went on. "The number I have written down will equal the weight of the number of ears in it, that is to say sixty-four quintillion poods† of grain. This is the strength we are dealing with. And what would it be like after five thousand years?"

"But this *strength*," replied Witt acidly, "can easily be tossed about on your palm, and it's multiplied three times, what's more."

"Yes," said Shakh-Duran. "All the generative power of one grain accumulated over five thousand years will be given to whoever swallows it. How and why this is, though, I cannot tell you. Now—do you wish to possess such strength?"

Dulled as the three prospectors' minds were by fatigue and want, they all understood what was being offered to them—and they turned cold with horror. But Redott soon mastered his fear, and with a smile stretched out his hand.

"Will you take it?" asked Shakh-Duran.

"Yes."

Placing the dark grain on his palm, Redott took a needle and scratched the seed with it. As he did so, a minute speck of dust flew off the grain and he licked the place on his hand where it must have fallen.

The Hindu gave a kindly smile.

"You are very careful," he said, "and I think you are wise to be so. But even with such a meagre portion as that you could easily smash a stone house down with your fist. Throw that grain away, it's no good any more. Let it go down into the earth and quietly set its strength free there. Well then," he said, turning to the others, "what do you say?"

"So many sextillions can't come from one little seed," thought Gatt flippantly, and taking his grain, chewed it and swallowed it.

"That's that," he said, and leaning back good-humouredly against a rock, fell to the ground.

There was an ear-splitting roar.

Rearing up when Gatt's elbow knocked against it, the ten-ton rock streaked into the sky and climbed to an immense height. Then, glowing red-hot with the friction of the air, it blazed like a meteor

---

* zolotnik: old Russian measure of weight, equivalent to 1/96 of Russian pound (409.5 grammes) or approximately 4.25 grammes (translator's note).

† pood: old Russian measure of weight, equivalent to 16.38 kg. or approximately 36 lb. avoirdupois (translator's note).

and disintegrated in a shower of brilliant dust.

"Half a grain!" cried Witt, sobered by the spectacle. "Give me half a grain, just a tiny piece! Or else the strength will blow me to smithereens!"

The Hindu took out a penknife and cut off half a grain for him. Filling a cup with water, Witt washed the seed down with a big mouthful.

"That's so it can dissolve a bit," he explained, slapping his belly. Shakh-Duran stood up.

"Good-bye," he said, and with a bow disappeared into the darkness.

Holding their breath, the three friends watched his white turban melt away in the gloom, then carefully sat down and closed their eyes.

III

What they felt was staggering. It seemed to Gatt that railway trains were hurtling through his veins and hooting as they went; Witt could hear the strength flooding into him with the roar of a waterfall; and Redott picked thoughtfully at a huge tree-stump with his nail, breaking off chunks of wood that weighed hundreds of pounds.

But their astonishment at what was happening to them soon passed, because their bodies had already forgotten what it meant to be weak. Gatt was the first to leap up, and shouted with all his might:

"With strength like mine you shouldn't play the fool! Oh, where can I show it?... What can I use it for rightaway?... There's nothing suitable round here!"

He spun round and round, waving his arms and stamping his feet as he looked for something to pick up. Then, knocking Witt off balance with a jolt that rendered him senseless, he rushed towards a thousand year-old baobab tree, pulled it out of the ground as easily as we might pick up a match from the floor, and hurled it down over the Vivera River.

It was a mighty blow. Smashing through the water, the tree plunged two hundred metres into the river-bed and shattered into fragments. Carried away by his own strength, Gatt instantly vanished amid the furious maelstrom of water and mud, and there was nothing left of him. The Vivera overflowed her banks and the ground shuddered for three hundred miles around, waking up the natives and sending them running for their lives in the belief that there was an earthquake.

"Did you see that?" Redott asked Witt when Witt had come round after the jolt Gatt had given him. "He did eat the whole grain, it's true, but you had a fair-sized piece too, so watch you don't make a mistake!"

"I'll go elephant-hunting," said Witt, "I don't need a gun now."

So the two friends began to live their separate lives. Witt went off into the jungle with an axe to look for elephants, and was gone three weeks. First let us tell what he did, then we will come back to Redott. Witt's technique was extremely simple. His first encounter with an elephant went like this: the animal rushed at him with its trunk lifted high in the air; Witt wound the trunk round his wrist, and bending the startled creature's head to the ground, ripped out its tusks; after that the beast took to its heels. Then Witt thrust the tusks into the earth and continued on his way. First one, then another, and then a whole herd of elephants crossed his path, and pulling them by the legs or knocking them over with his fist, he tore out their tusks just as easily and coolly as a dentist pulls a tooth.

Before very long he had collected one thousand two hundred poods of ivory. "This is a bit better than diamonds," he said to himself when he had made a raft of thousand year-old trees and loaded it with his booty. The raft lay moored by the river-bank while Witt sat by his camp-fire smoking and enjoying himself. It was very easy for him to find food now. He only had to clap his palm against the trunk of a coconut or mango tree for all the fruit to shake off and scatter on the ground around him. And if he happened to hit a herd of antelope with a boulder, then at least one of them was sure to be torn to shreds.

And because he had grown so incredibly strong and was killing animals every day, he became very cruel. It gave him great pleasure to tear a lion's jaws apart, to crush a panther or lynx with his fingers, or to tie all his victims together by the tail—rhinos, giraffes, elephants, crocodiles and buffaloes—and to watch the whole group trample and savage each other in mad frenzy. He would roar with laughter and then, gathering up enormous, heavy rocks, would hurl them at the captive beasts till they were no more than a heap of steaming flesh.

Then one day, when he was sitting by the fire looking at his raft and wondering whether to load it with more ivory still, a little coral snake fell from a tree above his head, and before he had time to crush it, sank its fangs into his knee. Then Witt broke out in a cold sweat, and writhing in agony, turned black and died. And the hyenas dined off his corpse.

IV

Meanwhile Redott—who felt so strong that he could have stirred the earth with his hand as easily as we stir porridge with a spoon—thought for a long time about what he should do. He was well aware that it was dangerous to reveal the full extent of his strength because people would be envious or afraid of him, and he would make enemies. If a foe were to shoot him on a dark night, no amount of strength could staunch the blood pouring from a bullet-wound in his heart.

"Well, I must do some work all the same," he said to himself, "but it'll be very easy for me now, nothing but child's play."

He got a job at the mine digging earth. To begin with he found it very amusing to pick at the ground with his spade, occasionally pretending to be tired. But he could not keep this up for long, and arousing immense astonishment, began to dig as much earth in a day as the biggest negro could dig in three.

"There's a strong fellow for you!" people would say, but because such enormous strength does nevertheless exist, however rarely, nobody suspected that Redott could smash down a stone house with one blow of his fist.

He did a great deal of work and earned a lot of money because he was paid five times more than anyone else. After a while he happened to become friendly with a Belgian workman, and having had a drop too much to drink one day, revealed his secret to him.

The Belgian burst out laughing.

"I never thought," he said to the frowning Redott, "that a sensible fellow like you could tell such a stupid lie!"

Redott looked at him calmly and then got up.

"Come with me!" he said sternly.

They went out of the tent and walked over to some rails piled up beside the railway line.

"D'you see this heap of rails?" asked Redott. "Now watch and judge for yourself."

He picked up a rail and plunged it into the ground to a depth of about three arshins* so that its end stuck out level with his face. The Belgian stepped back in amazement, but then Redott slapped the end of the rail with his palm and drove it out of sight into the earth.

"In that case," said the Belgian—he had fallen over with fright but was back on his feet now and wiping his hands on his trousers— "we must set about conquering Africa tomorrow. I'll be your minister. You're surely not going to hang on to your superhuman

---

*arshin: old Russian measure of length, equivalent to 28 inches (translator's note).

strength without doing something useful with it, are you?!"

"I don't know," said Redott. "I'll see. Perhaps the day will come when I need all my strength, so I'd better save it."

And he made his friend promise to keep quiet.

"I swear by Belgium!" said the frightened workman.

"All right, I believe you," replied Redott.

V

It was night when Redott was woken by a terrible rumbling sound. He leapt up and ran to the mine. Many people were already running in the same direction, shouting "cave-in, cave-in!," and it was not long before everyone realised that deep in the earth where hundreds of men were digging for diamonds, there had been a dreadful accident.

Various reasons were suggested for it, but it soon became clear that some boxes of dynamite had blown up. The blast was so strong that all the upper galleries had collapsed, making it impossible to get underground any more.

Seeing a line of lanterns, Redott made his way towards them. The mine engineers had gathered together and were arguing heatedly about how to save the men buried by the cave-in, many of whom were perhaps still alive but would soon die for lack of air. Here too, weeping wretchedly, huddled the women whose husbands were working underground. All of them had already flung themselves on their knees before the engineers, imploring them to save their dear ones, but the men only spread their hands in a gesture of helplessness. After reckoning up the approximate number of days needed to open the shaft, they said it would take ten. Only after ten days, they said, would it be possible to go down and bring out the living and the dead,—if the living had not died by then of starvation and lack of air.

To the right of the shaft, the mountainside ended in a sheer wall of rock that was at least two hundred feet high. It was to this that Redott turned his attention as he listened with one ear to what the engineers were saying. Finally he hesitated no longer, and knocking out his pipe, went up to the men who were deep in discussion. He no longer made any attempt to hide his strength because he was in a hurry now. Making his way through the crowd, he simply spread his arms wide as though he were wading through water, and at these movements—gentle enough for him—the people scattered like peas. But it was all put down to the confusion and crush, and so no one was surprised by it. They just shouted at him:

"What are you pushing for?"

"Mr. Witson," said Redott to the chief engineer, "there's a way of saving all the men or nearly all of them. Let me do it."

The engineers fell silent. The foreman miner who was a friend of Redott's, said in annoyance:

"Go away and sleep it off, Redott! This is a bad day to be drunk!"

"Have a smell!" said Redott, and taking hold of the miner by the head, pulled him close and breathed straight into his face. "Does that smell of vodka?"

"No, it doesn't," said the foreman, "but you can't be quite right in the head all the same. Go away and don't interfere!"

"Witson," said Redott, turning to the chief engineer, "listen, I'm telling the truth: I'll save them all. And right now."

"Explain clearly what you want."

"I want you and everybody else here to get ready to see a small exercise in gymnastics. The task's not easy, I'll tell you straight. Oh, and order the people to move further away from the shaft so there are no more accidents."

They were all distraught, talking nineteen to the dozen and interrupting each other all the time, and Redott could see that nobody believed him. Then the Belgian came up as white as a sheet and stood beside him. He was looking at Redott and trembling with expectation.

"He'll do it," he said, "he *can* do it, trust him, I swear by Belgium!"

Not knowing what to say, Witson gave in to the workers' demands that Redott be allowed to do what he could, and ordered everyone back as far as possible from the shaft. Barely had his order been carried out when Redott walked steadily away to the rock face at the foot of the mountain and disappeared from view. In the darkness they could not see what he was doing. With bated breath the crowd waited.

And then there took place a tremendous event that will be remembered forever in the annals of the Vivera diamond-fields. Setting his right shoulder against the rock and crossing his arms, Redott summoned up all his strength and moved the whole mountain-side away. (Beneath where he stood ran the galleries of the mine.) He simply raked the mountain away as easily as a locomotive flings a snowdrift off the rails, and by so doing immediately opened up several passages. In the same way a small boy knocks the top off an ant-hill and exposes its inner galleries.

The rumbling of the rocks that Redott tore away sounded like the terrible roar of a tropical storm. It was followed by the cries of men who had been buried by the cave-in. They came scrambling out into the open, carrying their unconscious comrades whom they had dug out alive. To save the rest would take only hours now, instead of days.

They found Redott's body lying by the rock which he had overturned and pushed far to one side. Because of the excessive effort, the skin on his arms and legs had split, and the blood vessels in his neck and chest had burst. Among the people who followed his coffin was the Belgian, saying to anyone who would listen:

"He really did wring that mountain's neck, you know, I swear it by Belgium!"

1924

Augustus Esborn's Marriage

*I dedicate this tale to
Nina Nikolaevna Grin.*

I

In London in the year 1903, Augustus Esborn, a handsome and wealthy man of twenty-nine (he was a shareholder in a shipbuilding firm), married the young Alice Besant, an orphan who was nine years his junior. He did not pay court to her for very long: her dependent position as a governess and his ability to please soon produced the desired response.

When the young couple returned from church and entered Esborn's apartment, it was clear to all the guests that they were witnessing the start of one of the happiest journeys through life together which a man and woman had ever undertaken. Esborn's sumptuous apartment was radiant with flowers and blazing fires, the table sparkled with its magnificent silver service, and a group of musicians greeted bride and groom with a deafening flourish. Everything was surrounded by an aura of that ingenuously egoistic warmth characteristic of happy people. The expression on the faces of Alice Esborn and her husband dictated the general mood, for everyone could see two pairs of blissful eyes radiant with the irrepressible smile of inner peace.

Nevertheless, they all noticed that after the first toast, proposed by Colonel Rips, Esborn bent his head to the flower in his buttonhole and seemed lost in thought. When he looked up there was a decidedly distracted look in his eyes, but it soon passed and he began to joke just as before.

When the banquet was over and all the guests had left, Esborn went up to his wife and kissing her hand, said he was going out for about ten minutes to get rid of his slight headache in the fresh air. Feeling giddy after a day filled with excitement, and succumbing to the fatigue brought by intense happiness, Alice kissed her husband's bowed head awkwardly and went to her room to await his return.

Deep in thought, she sat before the mirror, tidying her loose hair and gazing with wide-open eyes into the depths of the glass. And then there occurred in her mind that lucid interplay of ideas which, when you recall it later, resembles reality itself. It seemed to her that Esborn was standing behind her chair, but for some reason he was not reflected in the mirror. After a while this feeling made her anxious, and tossing her shining black hair, she turned round, though she knew perfectly well that there was no one there. Just then the clock on the mantelpiece struck midnight. That meant it was an hour since Esborn had gone out—an hour which had raced by amid confused, tense feelings that a change in her destiny was imminent.

Not knowing what to think, she called a servant and asked him to check the neighbouring streets and nearest public garden. By the time the man returned after a fruitless search, another half-hour had passed. Now Alice was beside herself with anxiety, and felt as if all the doors and windows of the comfortable apartment had been flung open on a winter's day, letting in the cold and damp. At about five in the morning, when she could hardly stand up any longer, she rang the police. At the station they took down particulars of Esborn and in a brisk, business-like tone promised to do "everything they could."

On that terrible night Alice Esborn buried her dreams, her husband and the freshly expectant warmth of her happy soul. Her mind suffered a severe shock. She waited for Esborn for another two days, but on the morning of the third the last stone seemed to break loose within her and hurtle down from a fearful height—the stone to which she had been clinging as she hung over the sudden abyss that now yawned in her life.

She fell ill, and in accordance with her wishes was moved back to her room in the house where she had been a governess. Her previous employers showed exceptional concern for her fate. When she recovered, there was nothing left of her wedding night but fear—fear of a ring on the bell or a knock at the door. She kept thinking that Esborn would walk in at any moment, already inconceivable and even unwanted now. . . Whatever had happened to him, she could never forgive him for deserting her in those first minutes of her trust for him, even if he had meant to do so only for a moment.

A year passed, then another. She met a man who was moved by her story, fell in love with her and became her husband.

II

When Augustus Esborn went out into the street, it was at the merry bidding of the imp who revels in innocent mystification. He was filled with happiness and drank in the air avidly, for it too seemed steeped in joy. In actual fact he had no headache at all and had gone out simply because during the colonel's speech—in which the latter had wished the newlyweds "a life spent hand in hand, never parting asunder,"—he had visualised with the vivid imagination characteristic of him the immense joy of seeing his bride again after a brief separation. He was not a hard-hearted or cruel man, but at times was seized by a force which he could not resist, and for that reason he would explain it away as a whim. He had always possessed an unconscious craving for suffering and repentance, and recalled how as a small boy he loved to hide in a dark cupboard and jump out only when alarm in the house had reached a peak and the servants were at their wits' end trying to find him. Filled with joy and yet with torment too, he would dash sobbing to his mother, as though he had a foreboding of the sorrow he was fated to know later in life.

As he walked off towards the public garden nearby, Esborn thought how glad Alice would be when he returned. He intended to wander about for an hour or so, but quickly thinking everything over and walking rapidly at the same time, he was astonished to hear a clock strike one and to see fewer and fewer people on the streets. He turned and wanted to go back immediately, but suddenly met with an obscure resistance deep in his soul. It was the kind of feeling of which women, doing themselves obvious harm by refusing to yield to the arguments of reason, say wearily: "Oh, I don't understand a thing, not a thing!" whereas men realise that their behaviour is very strange and detect in it the workings of fate. Esborn was confused and frightened by his state of mind, and it occurred to him that it would be much better to return home next morning and so avoid the inevitable upset of the rest of that night—especially since in the morning he intended to explain everything to his wife as an absurd escapade that had only been prolonged by accident. At first, such a decision seemed preposterous, but there was no other way out. He went to a hotel, and giving a false name, entered his cold, gloomy room just as he was—in evening dress with a white tie and a flower in his buttonhole.

The hotel staff thought he was a customer from a restaurant. Tormented by thoughts of home and the position in which he found himself, Esborn knocked back a bottle of whisky and began to doze, plagued by horrifying nightmares. All the time there was an agonising feeling of resistance present within him—a relentless black needle pointing at his heart that longed to go home. Eventually he fell asleep and did not wake until eleven the next morning. Then he was faced by the question "What should I do now?"

III

He realised that everything was lost or about to be lost, and saw that if he were to do anything at all, then he must do it immediately. His plan of the previous evening to return home the next day seemed virtually impossible to carry out now. Alice would have spent the night in tears, haunted by fear and shame, and even if by a supreme effort of selflessness she did understand him, she could not possibly equate his behaviour with love and respect for her. With his thoughts in utter confusion, he felt exasperated both by himself and by her, yet all the while kept obeying the mysterious centrifugal force that had now reached an acutely painful pitch within him and was continually making him put off any normal decision. He tried to write a letter but could not find the right words, and at the first serious effort of thought was overcome by immense lassitude. Augustus Esborn was now like burnt-out slag, for he had lived through so much during the past few hours.

He drew his hand over his eyes. Then, suddenly remembering that people must be thinking about him, he sent for a newspaper. Opening it, he took malicious pleasure in finding an announcement about the mysterious disappearance of A. Esborn in circumstances of which he himself was fully aware. As he read, though, he began to doubt that he was in fact Esborn, reading about himself.

The harm was done, irreparable harm, for with his loving hand he had dealt his bride a terrible blow. He could not go home now, because Alice would be forever fearful of his soul, a soul of which he himself knew so very little. Moreover, he did not feel capable of lying in a way that would turn untruth into the flesh and blood of everyday life.

But however strange it may seem, his thoughts about the impossibility of returning home brought him some relief. Although he was suffering more than anyone could imagine, he still had the courage to look his destiny in the face. Gradually his thoughts became more ordered, acquiring about as much equilibrium as a battered body lying semi-conscious in the middle of a dark road at night.

He changed his name and swearing a friend to secrecy, told him what had happened. Then he took his money out of the bank by promissory notes made out to the friend at an earlier date. After that he moved to a distant part of the city and started another business which soon proved a success. So it was that Augustus Esborn became a person who was "missing, presumed dead." John Turner, the man who took his place, assumed his station in life and lived like anyone else. As a reminder of what had happened, he was left with prematurely grey hair and constant, fanciful thoughts of Alice—now Alice Rengold.

IV

He could not think of her as a stranger, and from time to time made enquiries about her, finding out the necessary information through a private detective. He learnt of her nervous shock, her illness and her marriage. In Esborn-Turner's queer head kept appearing the notion that he was constantly with her, in the person of her husband, a business employee. In his own mind he was still her real husband, though at a distance now, invisible and perhaps even non-existent as far as she was concerned. On the basis of the information supplied by the detective, he created a picture of her daily life, her hopes and cares. He learnt of the birth of her children, was excited and glad when things went smoothly in the Rengold household, and felt distressed and anxious if the children fell ill or the couple found themselves in financial difficulties. He either dreamt of what his own life could and should have been like, or constantly imagined himself beside her. Sometimes he wondered what would happen if he turned up and said: "Here I am," but to do that seemed just as impossible as to become the real John Turner.

So over a decade went by. Twelve years after his "disappearance" Esborn heard that Rengold had gone to India for six months, and despite the fact that he had always forbidden himself to do it, he felt a growing desire to see Alice. And so one day, a day of stifling, breathless heat, he set off to the house where she lived, feeling like a man going to his execution.

As his car whirled the wretched Esborn towards this inconceivable, staggering encounter, he felt as if he were hurtling into the depths of bygone years and that time was nothing but a torment. The wheel of life had come full circle, and his soul trembled before the past that was returning now in all its newness. The painful play of his feelings hampered his thoughts, and grown suddenly very weak, he climbed the steps to the door and pressed the bell.

He was drifting from one dream to another, his body shuddering and burning hot. In his anguish he was oblivious of how he was led to the open door of the lighted drawing-room. Stepping over the threshold on to the carpet, he saw a woman in a blue-grey dress coming towards him. Although no longer young, she was still beautiful. He did not recognise her at first, but then he did, as if he had seen her only the day before.

She turned pale and gave a cry that told all. Reeling, he fell to his knees, and reaching out to her, grasped her cold hand.

"Forgive me!" he said, horrified at his own words.

"I'm glad you're alive, Esborn," said Alice eventually from a long way off, in a voice that was agonisingly familiar to him. "Thank you for coming. All these years. . ." and falling into an armchair, she broke into violent sobs. "All these years I've thought the worst," she went on, "but not now. Go away and write to me. Oh! It's so painful for me, Augustus."

"I'll go," said Esborn. "It's all in my diary. . . I used to write in it every day. . . Perhaps you'll understand. . ."

His heart was unable to bear the agony of this terrible moment, and with a cry he clasped the feet of his bride and died. But his soul had died long ago.

1926

The Snake

"Ned Garlan's heirs", as their friends jokingly nicknamed them, were a group of seven students who jointly owned a motor boat given to them by Garlan before he died in Switzerland of tuberculosis.

In the middle of July the young people had their first outing when they set off for Lake Snark to "get away from it all."

An eighth person was invited to go along too. It was Colbert, whose unhappy love for Joy Tavis, one of the three girls in the party, had been common knowledge in the university the year before, and had become a frequent topic of conversation.

From the age of sixteen onwards Joy had inflicted wound after wound upon men, and although she was either unwilling or unable to heal them, the wounds mended quite quickly by themselves. But Colbert was hurt more seriously than anyone else and did not hide it.

He had proposed to Joy three times. On the first occasion she had simply laughed, and on the second she had said that they should remain "just good friends", but on the third she had been rather annoyed. She did not like him. She was afraid of tall, serious men who gazed longingly at her and were lovesick and miserable. The mere thought that a man of such enormous self-restraint could become her husband filled her with angry resentment and made her resist anything which might force her to submit to him.

Colbert did not persist though, so she made no attempt to avoid him. All she did was to ask for his word that he would not propose to her again. He gave it, and then began to behave as though he had never troubled her with the simple question: "Will you marry me?"

On the third day of the holiday, Joy felt an urge to go into the forest. Vaguely hoping that Colbert's firm promise not to propose again might meet with grounds to dispel it, she invited him to accompany her. For three months now no one had spoken to her of love, so she longed for a harmless, minor flirtation that would arouse the light-hearted mood reminiscent of genuine romance. As Colbert followed her, she felt as if there were a great wall advancing behind her that threatened to collapse at any minute. She only had to guess the right moment to step aside, and the wall would crash down and miss her altogether.

On they went through the forest. The short, dark-haired girl walked in front, her beautiful though rather lazy-looking face wearing a faintly sly smile. Behind her, swinging his shoulders awkwardly and frowning, came her tall companion, keeping a careful eye on the path and thoughtfully warning her of every obstacle.

Anyone watching them would have thought that Colbert was utterly bored, but in actual fact he was over the moon and could have gone on walking like this for a thousand years. He could see Joy and she was close by. For him that was quite enough.

They came to a grassy clearing littered with boulders and sat down, each thinking his own thoughts. Colbert said that when they had rested for a while, it would be time to go back.

"Are you glad things between us are easier now?" she asked after a silence.

"I think that question's already been settled," he replied warily, not without reason suspecting a trap. "I've given you my word. But if. . ."

"No," she interrupted, "I've already forbidden you to talk about it any more, and you said you wouldn't. You surely don't want to break your promise, do you?"

"I'd rather die than do that," he answered gravely, "so you needn't worry."

Annoyed, she glanced at him. He sat there smiling so submissively and sadly that her annoyance turned to indignation. Her little scheme had failed.

If she went any further, she would make herself look ridiculous. For a while she kept hoping that he would not be able to bear it and would say something after all, but he just rolled a piece of grass thoughtfully between his palms. Suddenly she felt that by his whole bearing, by his firmness and quiet devotion, he was teaching her a lesson, and she was filled with such hostility towards him that she could not help saying in a cutting tone: "I think you gave me your word out of cowardice. It's easier to sit and keep quiet, isn't it?"

"Joy," he said, feeling alarmed now, "the heat's having an effect on you. Let's go back and you can sit in the shade!"

The girl stood up. She suddenly wanted to seize hold of his thick chestnut hair and shake his heavy head that did not seem to understand the meaning of this game. Colbert just would not respond to her playful mood. Agitated and offended, she bit her lip and stared at the ground.

Then something flashed in the grass and caught her eye. "Look, a lizard!" she cried.

Colbert nearly knocked her over, and she staggered as she tried to keep her balance. Waving his arms, he was stamping on something in the grass. Then he squatted down and taking hold of it by its middle, carefully picked up a small snake. It hung limply from his fingers.

"D'you see this?" he asked in alarm, looking into her angry face. "I'm sorry I pushed you so hard, but it's a bronze snake! One of the most dangerous there are! Women nearly always take them for lizards. If you're bitten by one of these, you've only got three minutes!"

She came nearer.

"Is it dead?"

"Yes," he replied, flinging the snake down and then picking it up again.

Joy thought it was awfully brave to pick up a dead snake and she did not want to be outdone by Colbert. Taking it from him, she wound it round her left wrist so that it made a sort of bracelet. Crushed in several places by Colbert's heel, the snake lay on her dark skin, gleaming like burnished gold.

"Drop it, drop it!" he shouted.

He had no time to say that a barely perceptible tremor had passed over the lifeless body. For an instant the snake had revived and, feeling the alien warmth of human flesh, had opened its mouth and bitten Joy on the arm. Quickly grasping it by the head, Colbert crushed it and tore it to pieces. Then, as he flung its remains from her wrist, he saw two drops of blood. The meaning of them was as clear as though someone had shouted it at the top of their voice.

"Don't lose your head!" he cried. "Just remember this can kill you!"

His body shuddered as he did his best to stop himself trembling. Joy looked helplessly at her arm. Though the pain was awful, she did not think as fast as he did, and the staggering realisation that her end was near had not yet come home to her. But Colbert's abruptness put her in full possession of her independence, for she saw it was now severely threatened by the great service he was about to render her.

"Let go," she said, breathing rapidly. "I'll do it myself. Give me the knife!"

At moments like this, time is more precious than life itself. Opening the knife, he tried to push her to the ground so as to get on with his task. At the same time he quickly ran his tongue over his palate and gums to check whether he had any scratches in his mouth.

"I've got to suck the poison out!" he cried. "There's nothing else for it, so don't argue, Joy!"

Silently, clenching her teeth, she wrestled with him, preferring to die rather than receive life from his hands. She knew perfectly well what that would mean. Colbert now had the chance of becoming her husband, and instinctively realising it, she struggled desperately in his arms. Beside himself with alarm, he dragged her to a tree that had a fork in its trunk. Forcing her arm through the gap and tearing the skin as he did so, he went round the other side and grasped her by the hand. Now her arm was gripped in a vice.

Squeezing it so hard at the elbow that her nails turned blue, he made a deep cut by the bite, and pressing his lips to the wound, filled his mouth with blood. He spat it out and did it again. Then, pausing for breath, he sucked the blood of his beloved for the third time. After jerking her arm once or twice, Joy stood still and leant quietly against the tree. Despite all her fear, she was weeping with anger and humiliation, and kept saying:

"Colbert, it doesn't make any difference—I still won't marry you! Let me go!"

He did not reply. Then, releasing her hand, he finally took stock of what she was saying and answered:

"You'll marry someone though, that's what matters. And you can't do that without being alive!"

His moustache and chin were covered with blood, and after he had wiped them, his hand was smeared with blood too.

Stretching out her arm, Joy pressed a handkerchief to the wound. Both Colbert and she were breathing heavily, as though they had run a long way. Finally she tore the handkerchief and bandaged her arm. Colbert was looking at his watch.

"That's five minutes gone—I feel better now."

Standing with her back towards him, Joy did not reply. When she turned round, he was no longer in the clearing.

Astonished, she called his name. Without forgiving him for what he had done and still filled with the inner resistance over which he had triumphed, she followed the track of trampled grass. Then she glanced into the bushes and was rooted to the spot.

Colbert was lying on his back, his face black and distended. He looked completely different now. His eyes were swollen and his bloodstained moustache and mouth testified to the suffering that he had spared his beloved. Bloated with poison, his appalling face filled her with terror, for she saw her own end—averted now—in all its unforgettable horror. She broke into a run, shouting: "Help, I'm dying!"

But it was too late for that, since she was already saved.

1926

The Voice Of The Siren

I

Emilon Detervy's family were crossing open country near Angudor, with fighting going on around them. They were making their way to an area free from hostilities, but in an attempt to shorten their journey they took a wrong turning and suddenly came under fire. Bursting against the blue sky, a stray shell flung out a hail of shrapnel, and a piece hit Detervy's son, Arthur, in the back.

What happened to the injured boy's nervous system and quite how it was affected—we do not know. Shortly afterwards, though, he began to feel a heaviness and numbness in the lower part of his back. Then he found it hard to walk and finally lost the use of his legs altogether.

The Detervy family were well-to-do, but despite the handsome fees which they paid, a succession of doctors and clinics could only say that Arthur was incurable. In every medical establishment that he visited the patient would find a warm welcome but very little hope. Eventually, on the advice of Professor A. Renold, the boy was moved to a large port in the south of the country. On the outskirts of town was a nursing home with mud-baths, and renting a comfortable dacha nearby, Detervy installed his sick son in the best of conditions. Arthur's room opened on to the verandah and, lying there in the afternoon, he could see both the coast and the open sea and, running away into the purple distance—part of the harbour. He was always surrounded by flowers—on the window-sills and the table, and in the garden too. The doctor used to call once a week, and in addition, two nurses would take it in turns every twenty-four hours to care for him with exemplary patience and skill.

Once Arthur's father had arranged everything, he devoted himself to the task of playing the stock market, and so was seldom at home. The boy's seventeen year-old sister, Beatrice, was feverishly busy enjoying herself, turning from horse-riding to rowing with the tirelessness of a young animal eager for life. Two aunts—sisters of Arthur's father—were absorbed in their work at the biological institute, and in dilettante fashion would sit for hours on end over their microscopes. Shortly after her arrival, Arthur's mother went off to the other side of the bay to stay with relatives. And so, hardly able to move, the sick boy was nearly always alone.

Aged a little over eighteen, he had a nervous, restless temperament, and being forced to spend his days sitting in an armchair or lying on his bed would drive him to a frenzy. In the dacha high on the cliffs overlooking the luxuriant coast, he felt as if he were in a perpetual prison. He was not allowed to read books which might agitate him, and so in annoyance would often cast aside the flaccid, verbose works he had to be content with—works which would have been enough to send even a healthy person to sleep. His favourite pastime was to gaze at the sea and the port. At the foot of the cliffs far below, the white tracery of surf washed endlessly to and fro, while the smoke of steamers and the white sails of schooners drifted slowly over the horizon. Filled with the smell of wind and salt, the world lay before him in all its vastness. From the distant harbour came a continual hum that sounded like the rejoicing of grasshoppers in summer. Amid sunlight and smoke, he could see the slanting outlines of cranes, pointed masts and, canted slightly backwards, giant funnels with their coloured stripes. Between the jetties the water gleamed in the sun. Clouds of smoke and steam billowed in the air, and sails flapped and gathered the wind, while like great black wedges, ocean liners sailed out into the roads. Occasionally the avid chorus of ringing voices issuing from the port would isolate a melody of whistles which coincided in such a way that, beginning with the shrill piping of launches and ending with the bass wailing of sirens—a cry that seems to lift mammoth weights in the depths of one's being—all the voices of the various ships fused in a whirlwind of harmonious sound. Then, amid the wistful reverie in Arthur's soul, an incomprehensible feeling of pride and tenderness would well up like tears in his throat. Pale with yearning and gladness, he would bend forward in his chair and gaze out at the distant port, as though longing to be close to the towering sides of the graceful ships come from afar.

When the moment of emotion had passed, he would lean back wearily on his pillows and, picking up a book, would look beyond it into the distance.

II

Early one morning—so early that everything seemed watery and drowsy in the pale light—Arthur woke up and, unable to fall asleep again, lay looking at the line of the horizon showing above the window-sill. To his left there was another window from which the harbour was visible. Glancing out of it, he noticed a slender jet of white steam spurting up beyond the window frame, a jet so small at this distance that you could have taken it for a wisp of smoke rising from someone's pipe. Climbing steeply into the air, it seethed. Then he heard the window-panes trembling slightly, and after a few moments they filled the room with a noise that reminded him of the humming of bees on glass. A low, groaning sound—like that made by someone lifting an immense weight, a distant, mighty 'o-o-o-o-o' which wrung the ear as it drew closer in great, enveloping waves—made Arthur lift his head. There could be no doubt about it: it was the siren of the transatlantic liner *Ecuador*, a sound that rooted you to the spot and compelled you to listen. Of all the roars and booms of the port, it was this—a cry as terrible as fate itself—that agitated the sick boy most of all.

It was neither roar nor howl, but howl and roar together. Eventually the jet of steam died down. Fading away, the sound slid to the lowest possible note and, as if destroying itself with this leap into the abyss, disappeared in the distance like a bird on the wing.

As Arthur listened, the awesome sound dispelled his drowsiness, making the blood race in his heart and head. Then something very strange happened: he felt a slight twitching in the muscles of his right leg—so slight that it was like the mere thought of it—and almost with horror he thought he had moved it. But he hadn't.

For a few minutes more he lay with his hands pressed to his temples, listening to the thoughts surging within him. Finally a profound yearning that was born of mad hope filled him with inspiration. Raising himself a little, he crawled to the chair, climbed on to it and looked out of the window into the garden.

The sun was already licking the grass with fire. Just then the gardener and his five workmen came walking by.

"Listen, my friends," said Arthur, "you all know I've got something wrong with my legs, so do me a favour, would you? While everyone's still asleep, carry me down to the *Ecuador* and back again—I'll pay you well."

He had to repeat his request several times, though, and put it in various ways before the men felt sure that they were not being asked to do anything wrong.

Giving them the money in advance, Arthur dressed and then, settling himself in the armchair, sailed off down the path on four pairs of strong hands.

III

As he went down towards the harbour, talking with the men about things that concerned them, as well as about his illness, Arthur felt peace gradually filling his soul. At last he was drawing near to the world of tireless activity that he had dreamed of for the past three years. He breathed in the odour of sea water and coal, and caught the strangely alluring smell of sailing ships tempered by sun and wind. Moored side by side with their sterns looking like the backs of a rank of soldiers' heads, they crowded along the jetty but slightly below it, revealing all the disarray of their decks to anyone who passed. Further on to the right the harbour stretched away into the bay, its waters crowded with smoking funnels and granite quays. In the distance, obscure amid haze and dust, great piles of chests and casks rose towards the sky, as if trying to climb one above the other. At first the eye did not see the crane's rope holding them, and so it looked as if all these things were moving of their own accord. Along the overhead railway ran lines of open goods trucks loaded with cotton. It seemed to Arthur that all this mass of ships, screening each other with their funnels and masts so that whole streets of rigging stretched along the quay, was belching smoke from its stacks with impatience to be off and sail to lands far away.

He sat in his armchair with his legs wrapped in a rug. Once on the road, the chair rolled along quite easily on its castors, so two of the men pushed it while another two walked behind, changing places with their fellows from time to time. Passers-by kept looking at Arthur and he answered them with a glance that seemed to say "No, I can't walk." Women raised their eyebrows in sympathy and whispered among themselves. A couple of small boys followed for a while but then got left behind.

Meanwhile morning had come with its smile of flame that sent a bright glitter dancing over the water. Suddenly, at a bend in the road, Arthur caught sight of the *Ecuador*.

It was then that he remembered Gulliver and the Lilliputians. The ship—so big that the eye could only take her in at a distance—rose behind the warehouses and stood like a wall between him and the harbour. Towering high above the quay and, it seemed, stretching as far as the buildings around the docks, she looked big enough to hold an entire small steamer. By the gangway that led steeply upwards, the little procession stopped. Here, in the dense crowd bustling amid mountains of baggage, Arthur felt lost. Feeling tired now, he looked up.

High among the funnels wreathed a slender jet of white steam. Steadying, it streamed upwards and then swelled to become a long, white cloud that billowed up to burst far above the harbour. Then the siren began to sing, and with its song, everything grew dim, quiet and small. For a while, just as in a silent film, there was no sound at all except the waves of triumphant booming that rent the air asunder. Thoughts and breath became feeble, and colours and objects grew dim as the awesome roar thundered deep in the hearts of everyone around.

Beside himself with ecstasy at hearing the force that filled him to overflowing, Arthur felt his whole being reverberate with sound. Then he got up from his chair. To begin with he felt nothing at all, just as if he were spinning round and round on the spot, but then shivers started to run through his numbed joints like icy needles. He took a step, swayed, and caught hold of the chair.

"Let's go back now," he said to the men, "my legs are still weak. Oh, how that siren roars! It goes right through me!"

"Yes, it'd be better if you didn't walk," replied one of his companions who saw nothing unusual in what Arthur had done and thought that he could stand. "My, what a noise that steamer makes!" he added, "it really hurts your ears!"

1927

The Legend Of Ferguson

This story is an accurate account of how Eberhard Ferguson went down in people's estimation because of the eye-witness testimony of a man who was given a cookie by him as a child. What follows will convince the reader that the child was an ungrateful creature, and will show that Ferguson's reputation found an unexpected champion in a girl who till then had never distinguished herself in any way whatsoever.

All of us—at least, those who have visited the valley of the Singing Trees—have heard that Ferguson was renowned for his exceptional strength and that single-handed he defeated a gang of forty-eight bandits by toppling a huge three hundred-ton rock down on their camp from the summit of Taulok mountain.

You can still see the rock today. After smashing the hut belonging to Utlemann, the leader of the gang, it rolled down the hillside into the forest and coming to rest, gradually became overgrown with bushes.

About five years ago the low-lying coast between Swampy Ford and Poket was flooded by torrential rain. An unusually high tide caused by a hurricane made matters worse by washing away the railway embankment. The train travelling from Gel-Giu to Docher had to set its passengers down at the station of Lim, and then everybody began to wait for the teams of workmen to arrive.

Some of the travellers went back to Gel-Giu, while others stayed in Lim and put up at the wooden "Kingfisher" hotel. Among them were: the brothers Cecil and John Mastakar, who were agents for a celluloid firm; the doctor Faurfdol who had accepted a post in Docher but was in no hurry to get anywhere; a tipsy gentleman with a nervous-looking face and frightened eyes; an independent-minded, haughty spinster with a shapeless figure who had very definite views on everything; and the engineer Mannenheim who was accompanied by his sixteen year-old daughter, a quiet girl with big eyes called Roy.

Lim is the kind of place where you can stand in the middle of town looking out in every direction and see nothing beyond the houses but brown fields and a forest on the horizon, while further away still you can just make out distant blue mountains which seem to float in the air. That's why by the third day of enforced inactivity the travellers were irritable and gloomy.

They could hear the tipsy gentleman walking about his room upstairs and humming: "I'm awfully fond of dancing..." The doctor was sitting on the terrace examining some of the local leeches, and the Mastakar brothers were playing sixty-six in the shade of a cork tree by the hotel entrance. The engineer had made his way to the kitchen where he was patiently teaching the hotel cat to shake hands, while his daughter was leaning against the garden wall chewing the nuts that always filled her dress pockets. "What would happen if I closed my eyes then suddenly opened them again?" she wondered. "Perhaps I'd find myself in Africa!"

No one suspected that coming towards the hotel was a restless, greedy character who already considered the stranded travellers fair game. It was none other than Bitter Syrup, whose real name had been lost without trace long ago.

The Mastakar brothers were the first to see his long, pimply nose and cantankerous look. He tugged at the peak of his cap and asked:

"Do the gentlemen wish to amuse themselves? If so, they can see the local sights."

John Mastakar counted "fifty-one" and added: "Go away," but Bitter Syrup came nearer.

"First," he said, "there's the pole that three negroes were lynched on in 1909."

The tipsy gentleman appeared at his window. He was really drunk now and kept laughing all the time.

"Second," the hobo went on, "there's the sign painted in oils that hangs over O'Connell's bakery. If you look at it carefully, among all the loaves and biscuits you can clearly make out the figure of that famous commander, Napoleon."

"Ha ha!" said the tipsy gentleman. "If you have enough to drink, you can even see green elephants!"

Just then the engineer came out with his daughter. She was quietly chewing nuts as usual.

When he saw her, Bitter Syrup was transformed.

"Third," he said in a very loud voice, "in a tree near the railway sheds a swallow has built its nest in a shoe belonging to the travelling actress Molly Flanagan, who threw it there after drinking a bottle of champagne out of it."

A second window opened and the upper half of the middle-aged spinster appeared. She was cross now.

"You ought to get a job, Dachezhin!" she said in a very definite tone. "People should work instead of sponging off others!"

The doctor came listlessly down from the terrace.

"Isn't there anything else?" he asked with a yawn.

"Last but by no means least, there's the rock weighing three hundred tons that Ferguson threw down," replied Bitter Syrup with dignity. "The rock he sent crashing down on Utlemann's camp! It's two miles from here. The marks of Ferguson's mighty hands remain on the stone to this day. You can even see where his fingers gripped it."

"Daddy, I want to see the rock," declared Roy.

"You have expressed a very sensible desire, Miss," said the hobo. "After all, it's an absolutely unforgettable sight!"

The engineer did not object to his daughter's request. She wanted to see the rock, and that was enough for him.

The weather was perfect. The Mastakar brothers and the doctor were persuaded to go too, while the tipsy gentleman came without being asked. But the independent spinster turned sharply away from her window and did not appear again. The hotel proprietor supplied a roomy old car in which everyone managed to find a seat. Then, keeping his knees together so as not to bump anyone and perhaps reduce his fee, Bitter Syrup said with his hand on his heart:

"Ferguson was a noble but mysterious character. He was seven feet tall and very handsome, with eyes that seemed to scorch anyone who came near. He had a voice like a trumpet, a black moustache and beard as smooth as silk, and a face as white as marble. He lived in the forest beyond the Taulok mountain, but nobody knew what he did there. People said he was unhappy because of his unrequited love for the daughter of... er... an engineer. Every day he used to go to the mountain and push the rock to and fro, trying to soothe his inconsolable sorrow with its furious swaying. And then he heard that Utlemann was going to rob and kill the settlers. So one night, when the bandits were asleep in their camp, he climbed the mountain and set the seal of everlasting silence on them all. A hundred and twenty were killed, while five others went mad and were caught."

The doctor gave a lazy smile and the engineer laughed, while the Mastakar brothers wondered whether their company might put Ferguson and his rock on the combs they made.

Eventually the party reached the place where the rock was, and everybody got out of the car. Going a little further on foot, they saw a huge stone shaped like an irregular rhombus. It lay among the trees looking rather like a grey house without doors or windows.

"It wouldn't do you much good being hit by that," said John Mastakar.

"Show us the marks made by his fingers!" demanded Roy.

"They're underneath, so you can't see them," replied the hobo.

The doctor contemplated the rock idly, wondering how many amputations he could perform on a hundred and twenty patients. Just then a little old man came up to them. Though he looked very decrepit, his eyes were piercing and bright.

"Are you talking about Ferguson?" he asked, addressing the group. "I bet Syrup's telling you a pack of lies! The fact is, I knew Ferguson myself, though for the life of me that doesn't make any difference. Actually it's nothing but a nuisance. I met him when I was eleven. But if. . ."

"Tell us about him then. . ." drawled the tipsy gentleman.

"I was standing by the village shop," the old man went on, "when he came out and asked: 'D'you want a cookie?' I said: 'Yes,' and I took the cookie and ate it. Well, he lived near the swamp, this Ferguson fellow, and he used to make a living by petitioning for plots of land. There were bandits in these parts, it's true, but they were further away, over near Kotomakha. Ferguson had a stammer, and he was rather short and puny. He took quite a liking to me and I used to go along with him on his walks. We'd often come and push this stone together. But it wasn't any harder to rock than a big rowing boat. Then one day he says to me: 'I'm sick of this stupid stone!' That same night a storm toppled it over—the wind got hold of its upper edge, I suppose, then the base slipped and that was that. Over it went, of course, and crushed two cows standing quietly down below—you know the way they just. . . stand and chew. Now it really makes me laugh to hear how people have changed the whole story."

Two days later, Roy Mannenheim arrived in Docher and chewing nuts as usual, began telling her aunt about the journey. Studying the white kernel of a nut with her big, thoughtful eyes, she suddenly said:

"What's more, daddy and I saw a rock weighing five hundred tons that Ferguson threw down on a bandits' camp. From a terrible height too!"

After thinking for a while she pulled a fresh handful of nuts from her pocket and chewing them busily, went on:

"He was very handsome, with a black beard, and he was strong and brave. An old man told us all about him, you see. And when he talked it sounded just as if he was singing. Everybody was frightened of him but he wasn't afraid of anyone. And after he'd thrown the big rock down on the robbers, he gave a little boy a cookie because he was a very kind and simple man. . . He was in love with a girl and they got married."

Then she thought a little longer and added:

"They got married before he threw the rock down."

1928

The Port Commandant

I

It was dark when Tils the Commandant came up the brightly-lit ladder of the freighter *Record*. An erect but frail little man of seventy-two, he was an extremely popular figure in the harbour. His clean-shaven face was as wrinkled as a dried pear, his small, grey side-whiskers stuck out like the fins of a fish, and from under his bushy grey eyebrows his little blue eyes sparkled with a friendly smile. In the bright light cast by the electric lamp his peaked sailor's cap, brown jacket, white trousers, blue necktie and cheap walking-stick were visible in all their wretchedness, a condition from which no amount of painstaking repair could ever rescue them. His yellow boots had split dozens of times and had been reinforced just as often with small pieces of wire or mended with thread. In the breast pocket of his jacket was a scrap of coloured silk, sewn firmly in place.

Fingering his little collar thoughtfully and shrugging his shoulders because his braces were too tight, the old man stopped in front of the sailor on watch and, cocking his head on one side, suddenly flung out his arms with joy.

"It's Tom Laston!" he cried in a trembling voice. "I knew I'd see you again soon on this fine ship dreaming of your dear Betsy so... far away. Thunder and lightning! The voyage is going well, I hope?"

"Coothay!" shouted Laston into the darkness. "The Commandant's come! What shall I do with him?"

"Send him away!" came the firm reply.

The old man's face expressed bewilderment, playfulness and entreaty all at the same time. His little stick rose and fell like the tail of a dog trying to guess its master's mood.

"Well, then, be off with you this minute!" Laston echoed, clapping Tils on the shoulder in a friendly way and bending him almost double as he did so. "But Coothay, you'll want to say hello to him, won't you?," he shouted, then added softly: "Don't worry, Commandant, he's only joking."

"What d'you mean, joking?" asked Coothay as he came up. He was the chief stoker, a broad-shouldered, bony fellow. "Whenever we call at Gerton, the Commandant's sure to turn up. We've got sick of seeing him! It's time you went home to bed, old man!"

"I've just come from the *Abraham Repp*," said Tils, breaking into his usual prattle and pretending not to hear the stoker's words. "All's well there and they've had a good voyage. She sails again at dawn. I had some coffee and a game of draughts with Tolby, the bosun. He's a remarkable man, you know. Well, how are you, Coothay? Everything all right, I hope? And your dear family?"

"Have a smoke," said Coothay, thrusting a cheap cigarette at the old man. "Hold tight to it or you'll drop it!"

"Ah, and here's the Captain himself!" cried the Commandant, quickly straightening his jacket and bustling up to Captain Henry Halton who was on his way to the theatre with his wife. "Good evening, Captain, sir! Good evening, much esteemed and... h'm... ma'am... It's such a fine evening it makes you want to stroll down the esplanade listening to wonderful music, doesn't it? How are you? All's well, I trust? You've had no storms? Are you... in the very best of health?"

"Oh... it's you, Tils!" exclaimed the Captain, pausing on his way ashore. He was a tall man of about thirty-five with a big, weather-beaten face. "So you're still up and about, are you? That's good! Glad to see you! But we're in a hurry, I'm afraid, so take this dollar and off you go to see Butler down in the galley. You'll be able to have a chat with him there, so all the very best to you. By the way, Mary, this is the Commandant."

"So that's who you are!" said the young woman with a smile. " 'The Port Commandant' ? I've heard all about you!"

"Everybody knows me!" chuckled Tils in his old man's voice, holding his cigarette in one hand and the dollar and his stick in the other. "Sailors are great people, and our tastes, I hope, are mutual. I should tell you I worship sailors. I feel drawn to the deck of a ship... like... like..."

Without waiting to hear him finish, the Captain and his wife went ashore. Raising his cap politely as they left, Tils said to Laston:

"Your Captain's a fine fellow! A real gale-force chap, from head to foot!"

At this point we should explain that the Commandant (that was his nickname) was known to everybody in the harbour without exception, from employees in the excise building to customers in the last tavern. Tils had worked all his life as a clerk in the warehouse of a large company but had eventually been retired because of his venerable age. Since then he had been kept by his childless, widowed sister, the fifty year-old Rebecca Bartels with whom he now lived.

He had been unable to go to sea because he suffered from epilepsy, and although his attacks had ceased as he grew older, he had remained a sailor only in his imagination. Each morning his sister would put a big sandwich into his jacket pocket and give him ten cents to cover any expenses he might incur. Then with a wave of his stick the Commandant would begin his rounds of the port. But his purpose was not in the least mercenary. He had been attracted to sailors and ships ever since his childhood, ever since the day when as an infant in his mother's arms he had stretched out his little hands towards the spectacle of white sails floating across the blue wall of the sea.

Lighting his cigarette with a trembling hand, the Commandant made his way with neat little steps down to the galley, where the cook burst into laughter at the sight of his bushy side-whiskers and eyebrows.

"I knew you'd come, Tils!" he said, pulling up a stool and pouring out a mug of coffee for the old man. "Where've you been? I don't suppose you've noticed the *Stella*, have you? She's berthed beyond the oil jetty, opposite the factory, and they're playing cards and drinking aboard her right now."

"I'm not going there just at the moment, my dear Peter Butler," answered Tils with a sigh, and pulling his stool up to the table, sat down with his hands resting on the crook of his stick. "And how is your esteemed health? Did you have a good voyage? Your highly respected spouse patiently awaits your return, I trust? H'm... I've already been aboard the *Stella*. They hadn't started playing then, you see, because they'd only just sent the second mate ashore to buy a pack of cards. But I soon left, you know, because there were two men there who always treat me... well... in a rather unfriendly way. They called me a troublesome old goat and said that... Naturally, I was a bit upset and couldn't tell them about my love for... gallant sailors... and their ships... But it's always like that with me, you know..."

Feeling sad, Tils gave a sob, at which Butler reached into a cupboard and banged a bottle of pineapple liqueur down on the table.

"An old salt like you ought to have a drink," he said. "Right? So let's have a drop and forget those scoundrels. Here's to your health and to mine! Cheers! Hup!"

Tossing half a glass of liquor into his fleshy mouth, Butler wiped his lower lip with his thumb and stared at Tils, who after sipping his drink was moving his lips as if trying to say "am". Then, having shed a few tears, he blew his nose and began to pull on his cigarette which by this time had gone out.

"A drop more?"

"No thank you—later perhaps. Thunder and lightning! The *Stella*'s a very fine ship, very fine indeed," said Tils, and with every word his head shook slightly. "She was launched in 1901. Cherley isn't on the *Howler* any more, you know,—I saw him yesterday at Marley's hotel. 'I'm going to have a rest,' he says, 'I'm on bad terms with the company, you see, because they didn't pay me all my bonus.' I was at the 'Black Bull' today—I just called in to ask how everyone was getting on and see how things were. Everybody's fine. Rumper's moved his bar to the opposite corner of the street because the building he used to have has been sold for a shop. And Watson just can't get his pension, you know, it's a real shame! He's drinking, strike me dead if he isn't, and drinking plenty too, knocking it back like a fish! It's good to watch him, though. He'll pick up a tankard and look at it, and then he'll say: 'In the Philippines,' he says, 'oh yes! There were some pretty fine goings-on there! And in Jamaica,' he says, 'it's really grand!' The *Royal Star*'s gone down, you know, they say she got caught in a cyclone. Cannon and shot! Did you know Simon Lakray? The pirate? He treated me once after. . . a certain little affair of his. Like this, he says: 'They couldn't have sunk the *Notch*,' he says, 'if the devil himself hadn't helped 'em.' And then he started cursing so hard that he set everybody thinking. He was a handsome fellow, make no mistake! Thunder and lightning! Then I says to him: 'I'll tell you what, Lakray, take me with you! Let me come aboard! Hip, hip, hurrah! For death or glory!' But he was busy doing something, so he didn't listen to me. If he had, the *Notch* would've been all right, I know she would. With me aboard the devil himself. . ."

"Of course, Commandant," said Laston, appearing in the galley door, "you'd have taken good care of 'em all, wouldn't you?"

"Of course I would," Tils affirmed, "I certainly would."

After another glass the old man grew rather excited. He was evidently not ready to leave yet, and began to enumerate all the people he had met, confusing actual encounters with what he had seen and heard during his long life. He was not drunk, only garrulous, and felt like a healthy young man ready to sail to the ends of the earth. But twice now he had called Butler "Senor Rivera," (taking him for the chief engineer on the steamer *Grenelle*), and Laston "Herr Baumann", (confusing him with the bosun on the schooner *Bolivia*), so the cook thought it was high time to send him home. Although there was only one way of persuading him to leave, both sailors knew that he would fall for it without fail. Giving the cook a wink, Laston said:

"Well now, Commandant, come over and help us make fast to the *Pilgrim*—we're going to berth alongside her in a few minutes."

Tils flinched and shooting Laston a glance from under his brows, adjusted his collar nervously.

"I know the *Pilgrim*," he began to babble in a pitiful voice, "and she's a very fine ship, but in 1914 she smashed two holes in her hull on the reefs near Cape Famine. . . she'll do twelve knots. . . Yes, of course."

"Off you go, Tils, and give our lads a hand," said the cook, pretending to be serious.

Slowly the Commandant pulled his cap down on his head and tearing himself away from the stool, got to his feet. The thought of the *Record*'s massive mooring ropes had driven the flickering drunkenness out of his old man's head, and he suddenly felt cold and tired.

"I'd better be off," he said with a quick smile at Butler and Laston who sat importantly before him with their arms folded on their chests and their eyes half-closed. "Yes, I must go, because I promised not to stay any later than eight. Make fast, then, lads! Get this old tub alongside the *Pilgrim*! Ha-ha! Enjoy yourselves! I'm off..."

"Now what's all this?" exclaimed Butler. "Are you going already? Look, Commandant, the bosun and the lads'll be back any minute, so just you stay and lend us a hand!"

"No, no! I must go," replied Tils hastily, "I promised to get home a bit earlier tonight, you see."

"And which way are you going from here?" asked a young sailor as he came in. It was Shenk.

"Hello, young man! Did you have a good voyage? How is your dear..."

"...My mother, you mean—so you don't get it wrong—yes, she's very well indeed, thanks. But that's not the point. Call in at the Sailors' Club, would you? There's a girl works behind the bar there—Peggy Scotter."

"Peggy Scotter?" mumbled Tils, cheering up a little and no longer dismayed by thoughts of the *Record*'s thick ropes. "Of course I know her! She's a splendid girl, I swear it by a shot in the bull's eye! Oh, I know her all right!"

"Then tell her that her friend Willy Brant died from plague in Eno a month ago. The *Cock's Comb*'s just put in and one of her crew was aboard the *Eureka* with some of our lads. It was he who gave us the news. Who's going to tell her about it, though? Nobody wants to do it—they're all too frightened. Anyway, how can you possibly tell her? She'll just start crying. But *you*'ll do it, Tils, you're a strong fellow and as old as the hills too, so you'll do it, won't you?"

"Right," said Laston firmly, shifting one foot.

"Right," agreed Butler after a silence.

"But just make sure you come out with it straightaway. Don't torment her, and don't be frightened to say it," Shenk instructed him.

"Yes, it's much worse to drag it out," affirmed Butler. "Get it said—and then away with you."

Pursing his lips, the old man bowed his head. Only the deep breathing of the sailors could be heard, as though they were all hard at work.

"The point is," Shenk went on, "that coming from you it'll only sound like... the rustling of a tree or the ticking of a clock: 'Brant / has / died / from / plague / in / Eno.' It'll be easier that way. But if I go in, then, you know, I won't be able to do it properly. I've got to be drunk to do a thing like that."

"Yes, I'll do it rightaway!" cried Tils in a hoarse voice and stamped his little feet. "Courageously and with fortitude. That girl's heart is as tough as steel, it's made of real sea shell! I promise you all I'll do it rightaway!"

II

Peggy Scotter was in charge of the buffet in the lower hall of the Sailors' Club, to the right of the lobby. She was a slim but well-built girl with a turned-up nose and freckles. Her grey eyes had a look of grave enquiry in them, and her auburn hair, fastened at the nape of her neck with a dozen strong pins, shone like polished bronze.

When for the umpteenth time the girl who was helping her paused to admire the cut of her superior's lace-trimmed sleeves, Peggy caught sight of Tils. He was walking up to the bar by a roundabout way, bowing politely to people he knew and halting frequently as he came.

"Look, Melly, the Commandant's arrived," said Peggy as she arranged some pastries on a big earthenware dish, "and he's heading this way. Come on then, get your little legs moving, you funny old windbag!"

Greeting Peggy from a distance, Tils came right up to the bar. With a glance she inquired about his health and the day's cares, and then smiled at his solemn expression.

"Hello, my dear lady, blooming as always, are you?..." he began, but then started to blink and said softly: "You've had a good voyage, I trust... Forgive me, I've got it wrong... A wonderful evening, isn't it? How are you?"

"D'you want one, Commandant?" asked Peggy, holding out a biscuit to him. "Eat to William Brant's health—you were asking about him not long ago. He's coming back soon—that's what he wrote just a fortnight ago anyway—and when he arrives I'll put a decanter of beautiful rum on that little table for you... neat, I mean,—and I'll have a drop of it myself. But be off with you for the time being, there's a good fellow, because when those waiters come running up with their trays you'll get jostled."

"Thank you," said Tils, slowly putting the biscuit into his

pocket. "Yes. . . When Brant comes. . . Peggy! Oh, Peggy!" he blurted out.

But he said no more, and though his wrinkled cheeks only quivered, his eyes were confused and moist.

Peggy was surprised because the Commandant had never allowed himself to be so familiar with her before. She stared at him and then leant towards him over the counter.

But Tils could not bring himself to go on, for this cheerful bar with its beautiful crockery and gay flowers was no place for a woman's grief-crazed shriek to ring out and fill the room. Nervously he gulped back the words which, had he uttered them, would have struck Peggy down, and then he shuffled apprehensively away, bowing to and fro like a spinning top as he went.

Peggy was not talking to Melly about the cut of her sleeves any more, for Tils's words had filled her with a strange feeling of anxiety. After thinking about Brant for a whole hour, she became as gloomy as a dimmed lamp, and finally banged the marble top of the bar in annoyance.

"What a fool I am for letting him go!" she muttered. "He's started me worrying about something now."

"You surely realised he was a bit tipsy, didn't you?" asked Melly. "He smelt of drink—I could tell."

At that Peggy cheered up a little but from then on there was a black cloud hanging over her, and when a few days later she received written news of Brant's death from Tils's sister, the black cloud helped to soften the painful blow.

"Well, here I am, my girl," said Tils, arriving home to find his sister sitting at her sewing-machine in a corner of the room. "I'm very tired, but everything's all right, it seems, and everybody's in splendid health. They've all had a good voyage too. I've been aboard the *Traviata*, the *Stella*, the *Abraham Repp* and the *Record*. I met Captain Halton as well. 'Hello,' he says, 'hello, Tils,' he says, 'you're a fine fellow! You can still do a few knots, can't you? He invited me to the theatre, but I always feel shy in a crowd of noisy people, so we had a drink instead and he gave me a biscuit, a dollar and this. . . No, I'm wrong, it was Peggy Scotter who gave me the biscuit. Her fiancé's died, you know. It was an unpleasant task, but I carried it out with fortitude. What tears there were, . . . then she gave a shriek. . . and I came away."

"You didn't say anything to Peggy at all," Rebecca answered, "I know just what you're like. If you're hungry, there's a bowl with some chops in it on the shelf, but if not, then off you go to bed."

*   *   *   *

A year passed and the *Record* called at Gerton again. But the Commandant did not come—he had died after choking over some soup. He had coughed and gasped for so long that a blood-vessel had burst in his feeble throat. Then he had grown weak and taken to his bed. Two days later he was dead.

"Something's missing," said Laston to Butler as evening fell. "Who'll tell us all the bits of news now?"

Scarcely had he spoken these words when a strange-looking, barefoot fellow appeared on deck and hurried down into the crew's quarters. He was tall and brash, and had a red face.

"Hello there!" he shouted, waving his peculiar hat. "How was the trip, sailor lads? Did you have a good voyage? And are your families all well? Come on then! Treat me to a drop of something!"

"Who are you?" asked Butler.

"The Port Commandant! Tils has given up the ghost, so... I've come instead."

Laston gave a wry grin, got silently to his feet, and just as silently took the fellow's elbow and led him off the ship down on to the quay.

"Good-bye!" he said, "and don't come back."

"What's all this?" cried the newcomer when he was a safe distance away. "If somebody steals your boots, then you buy a new pair, don't you? I just wanted to do you a good turn, that's all, you lousy swindlers, you filthy scum!"

"No, no," replied Laston good-humouredly from up on deck, "the imitation's much too obvious. And anyway, your face doesn't look right, so you'll never ask 'Have you had a good voyage?' like the Commandant did."

1929

The Green Lamp

I

In London one winter's evening in 1920 two well-dressed, middle-aged men stopped on the corner of Piccadilly and a side-street. They had just left an expensive restaurant where they had dined and joked with actresses from the Drury Lane theatre.

Now their attention was drawn by the sight of a poorly-dressed man of about twenty-five lying motionless on the ground with a crowd starting to gather round him.

"Stilton!" said the stouter of the two to his tall companion, seeing him bend down and peer into the man's face. "Honestly, why bother with that down-and-out? He's either drunk or dead!"

"I'm alive... and starving," mumbled the wretched man, lifting his head to look at Stilton who seemed to be deep in thought. "I fainted."

"Rymer!" said Stilton. "Here's a chance to have a bit of fun. I've just had an interesting idea. I'm sick and tired of our usual amusements, you know. When all's said and done, there's only one way of playing a trick properly and that's to play with people."

He said this quietly so that the man who was now propped up against a fence could not hear him.

But Rymer was not interested, and shrugging his shoulders, said good-bye and went off to spend the rest of the evening at his club. Meanwhile, as the crowd looked on approvingly, Stilton got the man into a cab with the help of a policeman. Then the cab set off, heading for one of the inns on High Street.

The down-and-out's name was John Eve. He was an orphan who had been brought up by an Irish forester and had come to London in search of work. Apart from primary school he had received no education whatsoever. When Eve was fifteen the forester had died and all his grown-up children had left home. One had gone to America, a second to Europe, and a third to South Wales, while Eve had taken a job on a farm. After that he had worked as a miner, a sailor and a waiter in an inn. At twenty-two he had fallen ill with inflammation of the lungs, and after leaving hospital had decided to try his luck in London. But the fierce competition for jobs and the high unemployment there soon proved to him that finding work wasn't so easy after all. He had spent the night in parks and on wharves, gone without food, grown thin, and then, as we have just seen, had been picked up by Stilton, who owned several warehouses in the city.

At forty Stilton had experienced everything that money could buy for a bachelor who never had to worry about food or shelter. He possessed a fortune of twenty million pounds. What he had thought of doing with Eve was a mere trifle, but he was very proud of his idea for he considered himself a person of enormous ingenuity.

When Eve had eaten his fill, finished his wine and told his story, Stilton said:

"I want to make you a proposition that will fill you with joy. I'll give you ten pounds on condition that first thing in the morning you rent a room on one of the city's main thoroughfares. It must be on the second floor with a window overlooking the street.

Every evening, between five and twelve midnight, you must have a lamp with a green shade burning on your window-sill. While the lamp is lit, you must not go out of the house, receive visitors or talk to anyone. In short, the job's not difficult, and if you agree to do as I ask then I'll send you ten pounds every month. But I can't tell you who I am."

"Provided you're not joking," replied Eve, absolutely astounded by the proposition, "then I'll even agree to forget my name. Tell me though, how long will this prosperity of mine last?"

"Who knows? Perhaps a year, or perhaps all your life."

"That's better still. But may I ask what the green lamp's for?"

"That's a secret!" replied Stilton. "A tremendous secret! The lamp will serve as a signal for people and things that you'll never know anything about."

"I see... or rather I don't... All right then! Give me the money and rest assured that tomorrow there'll be a lamp burning in my window!"

So it was that the strange bargain was struck, and the millionaire and the down-and-out went their separate ways, well satisfied with each other.

As he bid Eve farewell, Stilton said:

"Make a note of this poste restante number: 3-33-6. And don't forget that one day, next month perhaps or next year, you will suddenly be visited by people who will make you rich. How and why this will come about, I cannot tell you. But I assure you it will happen..."

"Well I'll be damned!" muttered Eve, fingering the ten-pound note thoughtfully as he watched Stilton's cab drive away. "Either that man's out of his mind, or I'm incredibly lucky! Fancy promising so much money just for burning a pint of paraffin a day!"

The following evening a window on the first floor of 52, River Street shone with a soft, green light. The lamp had been put right up against the window-frame.

For a while the two passers-by looked up at the window from the opposite side of the street. Then Stilton said:

"So you see, my dear Rymer, when you're bored you can come here and smile. In that room sits a fool—a fool bought cheaply on instalments for many years to come. He'll either turn to drink from boredom or go out of his mind, but he'll wait and wait without knowing what for. And there he is!"

He was right. Pressing its forehead against the window-pane, a dark figure peered down into the twilit street as if asking "Who's there? What am I waiting for? Who'll come?"

"But you're a fool too, my dear fellow," said Rymer, taking his friend by the arm and leading him away to their car. "What's so funny about this little joke of yours, eh?"

"A game played with a living person," replied Stilton, "is the most delightful game of all!"

II

One evening in 1928 a hospital for the poor situated on the outskirts of London echoed with the wild cries of an old man who had just been brought in suffering terrible pain. He was a poorly-dressed, dirty fellow with a very thin face and had broken his right leg when he fell down the back stairs of some dark haunt.

He was carried into the surgical department. The injury turned out to be serious as the compound fracture of the bone had ruptured several blood-vessels.

From the inflammation that was already apparent, the surgeon who examined him concluded that an amputation was necessary. The operation was performed immediately, and after it the man was put to bed where he soon fell asleep. When he woke he saw the surgeon sitting before him.

"Fancy our meeting like this!" said the doctor, a tall, grave man with a sad look in his eyes. "Do you recognise me, Mr. Stilton? I'm John Eve, the person you told to keep watch every night with a green lamp. I recognised you straightaway."

"What the devil!" muttered Stilton, peering at him. "Is it possible?"

"Yes. But tell me what's changed your way of life so abruptly?"

"A few heavy losses. . . panic on the stock-exchange. . . and I went bankrupt. . . I've been destitute for three years now. But what about you?"

"I lit the lamp for a while," said Eve with a smile, "and to begin with out of boredom and then out of interest I began to read everything I could find. One day I opened an old book on anatomy that was lying on the bookcase in my room, and I was astounded. Before me lay revealed the fascinating mysteries of the human organism. Like a drunk I sat up over the book all night, and in the morning went to the library and asked: 'What should one study to be a doctor?' The answer was derisive: 'Mathematics, geometry, botany, zoology, morphology, biology, pharmacology, Latin and so on'. But I kept asking questions and wrote everything down so as not to forget it.

By that time I'd already been lighting the lamp for two years, and one day as I came home in the evening (I didn't consider it necessary any longer to stay inside for the whole seven hours), I saw a man in a top-hat gazing up at my window with a look of annoyance and contempt.

'Eve's a classic fool!' he muttered, without noticing me. 'He's waiting for all the wonderful things he's been promised... yes, he's got hopes at least, while... I'm almost ruined!' It was you. Then you added: 'What a stupid joke! It certainly wasn't worth throwing all that money away!'

I'd bought enough books to study to my heart's content, whatever happened. When I heard what you said, I felt like hitting you but then I remembered that thanks to your strange generosity I could be an educated man..."

"And what then?" asked Stilton quietly.

"What then? All right. If you want something very much, then fulfilment's never long in coming. There was a student living in the same rooms as I. He took an interest in me, and about a year and a half later he helped me take the exams to enter medical school. As you can see, I turned out to have ability..."

There was a silence.

"I've not been to look at your window for a long time now," said Stilton, astonished by Eve's story, "a very long time. But I think the green lamp's still burning... and lighting up the darkness of night... Forgive me."

Eve took out his watch.

"It's ten o'clock—time for you to sleep," he said. "You'll probably be able to leave hospital in about three weeks. When you do, call me and I might be able to find you work in our out-patients department taking the names of people who come in for treatment. And next time you go downstairs in the dark... do at least light a match!"

1930